STARBORNE

STARBORNE

ROBERT SILVERBERG

Bantam Books
New York   Toronto   London   Sydney   Auckland

STARBORNE

A Bantam Spectra Book / June 1996

SPECTRA and the portrayal of a boxed "s" are trademarks of Bantam Books, a division of Bantam Doubleday Dell Publishing Group, Inc.

Library of Congress Cataloging-in-Publication Data

Silverberg, Robert.
Starborne / Robert Silverberg.
p.   cm.
ISBN 0-553-10264-8
I. Title.
PS3569.I472S76   1996
813'.54—dc20   95-44862
                                        CIP

Published simultaneously in the United States and Canada

Bantam Books are published by Bantam Books, a division of Bantam Doubleday Dell Publishing Group, Inc. Its trademark, consisting of the words "Bantam Books" and the portrayal of a rooster, is Registered in U.S. Patent and Trademark Office and in other countries. Marca Registrada. Bantam Books, 1540 Broadway, New York, New York 10036.

PRINTED IN THE UNITED STATES OF AMERICA
BVG   10 9 8 7 6 5 4 3 2 1

FOR

DAVE AND NANCY DEROCHE

Friends, take heart, banish all fear.
One day—who knows?—we will
look back even on these
things and laugh.

—THE AENEID
BOOK ONE

STARBORNE

Sixteen light-years from Earth today, in the fifth month of the voyage, and the silken force of nospace acceleration continues to drive the starship's velocity ever higher. Three games of *Go* are in progress in the *Wotan*'s lounge. The year-captain stands at the entrance to the brightly lit room, casually watching the players: Roy and Sylvia, Leon and Chang, Heinz and Elliot.

Go has been a craze aboard ship for weeks. The players—some eighteen or twenty members of the expedition have caught the addiction by this time, more than a third of the entire complement—sit hour after hour, contemplating strategies, devising variations, grasping the smooth black or white stones between forefinger and second finger, putting the stones down against the wooden board with the proper smart sharp clacking sound. The year-captain himself does not play, though the game once interested him to the point of obsession, long ago, in what was almost another life; his shipboard responsibilities require so intense an exercise of his energies that he can find little amusement in simulated territorial conquest.

But he comes here sometimes to watch, remaining five or ten minutes, then going on about his duties.

The best of the players is Roy, the mathematician, a large, heavy man with a soft, sleepy face. He sits with his eyes closed, awaiting in tranquillity his turn to play. "I am purging myself of the need to win," he told the year-captain yesterday when asked what occupied his mind while he waited to put down his next piece. Purged or not, Roy continues to win more than half of his games, even though he gives most of his opponents a handicap of four or five stones.

He gives Sylvia a handicap of only two. She is a delicate woman, fine-boned and shy. Genetic surgery is her specialty. Sylvia plays the game well, although slowly. She makes her move. At the sound of it Roy opens his eyes. He studies the board the merest fraction of a second, points, and says, "Atari," the conventional way of calling to his opponent's attention the fact that her move will enable him to capture several of her stones. Sylvia laughs lightly and retracts her move. After a moment she moves again. Roy nods and picks up a white stone, which he holds for nearly a minute, hefting it between the two playing fingers as though testing its weight, before he places it. Which is not at all typical of him: ordinarily he makes his moves with intimidating speed. Perhaps he is tired this morning. Or perhaps he is simply being kind.

The year-captain would like to speak to Sylvia about the anaerobic gene-cluster experiment, but evidently the game is barely under way; he supposes that she and Roy will be occupied with it for another hour or more. His questions can wait. No one hurries aboard the *Wotan*. They have plenty of time for everything: a lifetime, maybe, if no habitable planet can be found. All the universe is theirs to search, yes. But it may well be the case that nothing useful will be found, and this ship's walls will mark the full boundary of their universe, forever and a day. No one knows, yet. They are the first to venture out this far. At this point there are only questions, no answers. The only thing that is reasonably certain is that they are bound on a voyage from which there is no expectation of returning.

All is quiet for a time in the lounge. Then Heinz, at the far side of the room, loudly places a stone. Elliot acknowledges it with a little chuckle. Chang, at the board next to them, glances over to look; Sylvia and Roy pay no attention. The year-captain scans the board of Roy and Sylvia's game, trying to anticipate Sylvia's next move. His eyesight is sharp: even at this distance he can clearly make out the patterns on the board. Indeed, everything about the year-captain is sharp. He is a man of crisp boundaries, of taut edges carefully drawn together.

Soft footsteps sound behind him.

The year-captain turns. Noelle, the mission communicator, is approaching the lounge. She is a slim sightless woman with long gleaming blue-black hair and elegantly chiseled features. Her tapering face is a perfect counterpart of the year-captain's own lean, austere one, though she is dusky, and he is fair-haired and so pale of skin that he seems to have been bleached. She customarily walks the corridors unaided. No sensors for Noelle, not even a cane. Occasionally she will stumble, but usually her balance is excellent and her sense of the location of obstacles is eerily accurate. It is a kind of arrogance for the blind to shun assistance, perhaps. But also it is a kind of desperate poetry.

He watches in silence as she comes up to him. "Good morning, year-captain," she says.

Noelle is infallible in making such identifications. She

claims to be able to distinguish each of the members of the expedition by the tiny characteristic sounds they make: their patterns of breathing, the timbre of their coughs, the rustling of their clothing. Among the others there is a certain skepticism about this. Many aboard the starship believe that Noelle is simply reading their minds. She does not deny that she possesses the power of telepathy; but she insists that the only mind to which she has direct access is that of her sister Yvonne, her identical twin, far away on Earth.

He turns to her. His eyes meet hers: an automatic act, a habit. Her eyes, dark and clear and almost always open, stare disconcertingly through his forehead. Plainly they are the eyes of a blind person but they seem weirdly penetrating all the same. The year-captain says, "I'll have a report for you to transmit in about two hours."

"I'm ready whenever you need me." Noelle smiles faintly. She listens a moment, head turned slightly to the left, to the clacking of the *Go* stones. "Three games being played?" she asks. Her voice is soft but musical and clear, and perfectly focused, every syllable always audible.

"Yes."

What extraordinary hearing she must have, if she can perceive the sounds of stones being placed so acutely that she knows the number of game-boards that are in use.

"It seems strange that the game hasn't begun to lose its hold on them by now."

"*Go* can have an extremely powerful grip," the year-captain says.

"It must. How good it is to be able to surrender yourself so completely to a game."

"I wonder. Playing *Go* consumes an enormous amount of valuable time."

"Time?" Noelle laughs. The silvery sound is like a cascade of little chimes. "What is there to do with time, except to consume it?" Then after a moment she says, "Is it a difficult game?"

"The rules are actually quite simple. The application of the rules is another matter entirely. It's a deeper and more subtle game than chess, I think."

Her glossy blank gaze wanders across his face and suddenly her eyes lock into his. How is she able to do that? "Do you think it would take very long for me to learn how to play?" she asks.

"You?"

"Why not? I also need amusement, year-captain."

"The board is a grid with hundreds of intersections. Moves may be made at any of them. The patterns that are formed as the players place their stones are complex and constantly changing. Someone who—isn't—able—to see—"

"My memory is excellent," Noelle says. "I can visualize the board and make the necessary corrections as play proceeds. You would only have to tell me where you are putting down your stones. And guide my hand, I suppose, when I make my moves."

"I doubt that it'll work, Noelle."

"Will you teach me anyway?"

I have not yet ceased to wonder at the fact that we are here, aboard this ship, carrying out this voyage, acting out this destiny that the universe has chosen for us. How many times have I made this entry in my journal, after all? Five? Ten? I keep returning to this one slender point, worrying it, prodding at it, marveling that this is happening and that it is happening to us. Not to me, particularly—what good would all my training on the island have been if I were still the center of my own world, like a child?—but to us, this larger entity, this group of individual and disparate and oddly assorted people who have come together willingly, even joyously, in this curious endeavor.

How odd it all is, still! Traveling through endless night to some unknown destination, some virgin world that awaits our finding. There has been nothing like it in all of human history. But this is the proper time, evidently, for it to be happening. It is our fate that we fifty people live at just this moment of time, this present epoch, when it has been made possible to journey between the stars, and so here we are, making that journey, seeking a new Earth for mankind. Someone had to do it; and we are the ones who have stepped forward to be selected, Leon and

The year-captain leaves the lounge and walks a few meters down the main transit corridor to the dropchute that will take him to the lower levels, where Zed Hesper's planetary-scan operation has its headquarters. He stops off there at least once a day, if only to watch the shifting patterns of simulated stars and planets come and go on Hesper's great galactic screen. The patterns are abstract and mean very little in astronomical terms to the year-captain—there is no way to achieve a direct view of the normal universe from within the nospace tube, and Hesper must work entirely by means of analogs and equivalents—but even so it reassures him in some obscure way to be reminded that those whose lives are totally confined by the unyielding boundaries of this small vessel sixteen light-years from the world of their birth are nevertheless not completely alone in the cosmos.

Sixteen light-years from home.

Not an easy thing to grasp, even for one trained in the mental disciplines that the year-captain has mastered. He can feel the force of the concept but not the real meaning. He can

Paco and Huw and Sylvia and Noelle and I, and all the rest of us aboard this vessel.

In the minds of all those myriad people who have come and gone upon the Earth before our time, when they look forward toward us and try to envision what our era must be like, we are the godlike glittering denizens of the barely imaginable future, leading lives of endless miracle. Everything is possible to us, or so it seems to them. But to those who are not yet born, and will not be for ages, we are the merest mud-crawling primitives, scarcely distinguishable from our hairy ancestors. That we have achieved as much as we have, given our pitiful limitations, is fascinating and perplexing to them.

To ourselves, though, we are only ourselves, people with some skills and some limitations: neither gods nor brutes. It would not be right for us to see ourselves as gods who sit at the summit of Creation, for we know how far from true that is; and yet no one ever sees himself as a pitiful primitive being, a hapless clumsy precursor of the greater things to come. For us there is always only the present. We are simply the people of the moment, living our only lives, doing our best or at least trying to, traveling from somewhere to somewhere aboard this unlikely ship at many multiples of the speed of light, and hoping, whenever we let ourselves indulge in anything as risky as hope, that this voyage of ours will send one new shaft of light into the pool of darkness and mystery that is the reality of human existence.

tell himself, *Already we are sixteen kilometers from home,* and find that concept easy enough to understand. *Already we are sixteen hundred kilometers from home* — a little harder, yes, but he can understand that too. What about *Already we are sixteen million kilometers from home?* That much begins to strain comprehension — a gulf, a gulf, a terrible empty dark gulf of enormous size — but he thinks he is able to wrap his mind about even so great a distance, after a fashion.

Sixteen light-years, though?

How can he explain that to himself?

Somewhere just beyond the tube of nospace through which the ship now travels lies a blazing host of brilliant stars, a wilderness of suns all around them, and he knows that his gray-flecked blond beard will have turned entirely white before the light of those stars glitters in the night sky of distant Earth. Yet only a few months have elapsed since the departure of the expedition. How miraculous it is, he thinks, to have come so far so swiftly.

Even so, there is a greater miracle. An hour after lunch he will ask Noelle to relay a message to Earth, summarizing the day's findings, such as they are, and he knows that he will have an acknowledgment from Control Central in Brazil before dinner. That seems a greater miracle to him by far.

He emerges from the dropchute and is confronted by the carefully ordered chaos that is the lower deck. Cluttered passageways snake off in many directions before him. He chooses the third from the left and proceeds aft, crouching a little to keep from banging his forehead on the multitudinous ducts that pass crisscrossingly just above him.

In the year-captain's mind the starship sometimes appears sleek, narrow, graceful: a gleaming silver bullet streaking across the universe at a velocity that has at this point come to exceed a million kilometers per second. But he knows that the actuality is nothing like that. In fact the ship is not remotely like a bullet at all. No Newtonian forces of action and reaction are driving it, nor does it have the slightest refinement of form. Its outlines are boxy and squat and awkwardly asymmetrical, a huge clunky container even more lopsided and outlandish in shape than the usual sort of spacegoing vessel, with an elaborate spidery superstructure of extensor arms and antennas and observation booms and other excrescent externals that have the appearance of having been tacked on in a purely random way.

ROBERT SILVERBERG

Yet because of the *Wotan*'s incredible speed and the serenity of its movements—the ship is carrying him without friction through the vast empty cloak of nospace at a pace already four times greater than that of light and increasing with every passing moment—the year-captain persists in thinking of it as he does, an imaginary projectile, sleek, narrow, graceful. There is a *rightness* to that which transcends mere literal sense. He knows better, but he is unable to shake that streamlined image from his mind, even though he is familiar with the true shape of the vessel inside and out. If nothing else, his routine movements through the labyrinthine interior of the starship each day provide constant and unending contradiction of his fanciful mental picture of it.

The tangled lower levels of the ship are particularly challenging to traverse. The congested corridors, cluttered with a host of storage domes and recycling coils and all manner of other utility ducts, twist and turn every few meters with the abrupt lunatic intricacy of a topological puzzle. But the year-captain is accustomed to moving through them, and in any case he is a man of extraordinary grace of movement, precise and fastidious of step. His outward physical poise reflects the deep strain of asceticism that is an innate part of his character. He is untroubled by the obstacles of these corridors—to him they have no serious existence, they are barely obstacles at all.

Lightfootedly he makes his way past a dangling maze of thrumming conduits and scrambles over a long series of swelling shallow mounds. These are the cargo nodules. In sheltered chambers beneath this level lies all the precious furniture of their journey: mediq machines, bone banks, data bubbles, pre-read vapor chips, wildlife domestication plaques, excavator arcs, soil samplers, gene replacement kits, matrix jacks, hydrocarbon converters, climate nodes and other planetary-engineering equipment, artifical intelligences, molecular replicators, heavy-machinery templates, and all the rest of their world-building storehouse. Below all that, on the deepest level of all, is the zygote bank, ten thousand fertilized ova tucked away snugly in permafreeze spansules, and enough additional sperm and unfertilized ova to maintain significant genetic diversity as the succeeding generations of the colony unfold.

He reaches a Y-shaped fork, where the passageway abruptly widens and takes the abrupt left turn into Hesper's little room. A blare of colored light confronts him, blue and green and dazzling incandescent red. Things blink and flash in comic excess. Hesper's screen is the center of the universe, toward which everything flows: from every corner of the firmament data comes streaming in torrents, and somehow it all is captured and reconstituted into visual form here. But only Hesper can understand it. Possibly not even he, the year-captain sometimes thinks.

The air in Hesper's room is warm and close, dense, moist jungle air. Hesper likes heat and always keeps humidity turned to the max. He is a small black-skinned man, with thin, perpetually compressed lips and a startling angular beak of a nose, who comes from some island on the far side of India. The sun must be very strong there; the fair-skinned year-captain imagines that he would find himself baked down to the bone in a minute, if ever he were to set foot in that land. Is it a place like that toward which all of Hesper's zealous scanning is bent, one with a sun of such ferocity?

"Look here, year-captain," Hesper says immediately. "Four new prospects!"

He taps the screen, here, here, here, here. Hesper is an eternal optimist. For him the galaxy brims and overflows with habitable worlds.

"How many does that make? Fifty? A hundred?"

"Sixty-one, within a sphere a hundred and thirty light-years across. Plausible suns, probable planetary configurations." Hesper's voice is light, high-pitched, inflected in a singsongy way. "Of course, I'm not yet ready to recommend an inspection of any one of them."

The year-captain nods. "Of course."

"But it won't be long, year-captain! It won't be long, I promise you that!"

The year-captain offers Hesper a perfunctory smile. One of these days, he knows, Hesper actually will find a planet or two that will be worth taking a look at—it's an article of faith for everyone on board that there *must* be such a world somewhere—but he understands that Hesper's early enthusiasms are just that, enthusiasms. Hesper is a quick man with a hypothesis. No matter: the voyage has just begun, really. The year-captain doesn't expect to be greeted here with any real discoveries, not yet. He simply wants to stare at the screen.

Hesper has told him, more than once, what the blazing swirls and squiggles on the screen are supposed to signify. The sequence of criteria for habitable worlds. The raw astronomical data, first. Each sun's place on the main sequence, the indications of the presence of planetary bodies in constructive positions. Mean orbital distances plotted against luminosity. And then a spectroscopic workup. Evidence for the presence of an atmosphere. The chemical components thereof: suitable or not? And then—biospheric analysis—conditions of thermodynamic disequilibrium, indicating the possible presence of transpiration and respiration—the temperature range, probable mean highs and lows—

The starship has data-gathering tentacles reaching far out into the incomprehensible void. A host of sensory receptors, mysteriously capable of piercing the nospace tube in which the ship travels and extending into the dark reality beyond, collects information tirelessly, information that is not actual realspace data but is somehow a usable equivalent of such data, and processes it into these bright designs. Over which this bubbly little man hovers, evaluating, discarding, reconsidering, unendingly searching for the ultimate new Eden that is the goal of their quest.

Hesper wants to discuss his newest prospects. The year-captain listens with half an ear. He wants nothing more just now than the simple relaxation that watching the screen affords. The abstract patterns, so very bright and cheerful. The wild swirls of color that whirl and flash like crazed comets. Is there any real meaning in them? Only Hesper knows. He devised this information-gathering system; he is the only one, really, who can decipher and interpret the mysterious factoids that the ship's sensors suck in. When the time comes, the year-captain will pay close attention to the little man's data. But this is not yet the time.

The year-captain stands and watches for a while, mindlessly, like a small child, taking innocent pleasure in the colors and patterns, admiring them for their own sake. There are few enough pleasures that he allows himself: this one is harmless and comforting. Stars dance on the screen in wild galliards and fandangos. He imagines that he identifies steel-blue Vega and emerald Deneb and golden Arcturus, but he knows that there is no way he can be correct. The patterns he sees here are not those of the constellations he watched so often soaring across the icy sky over Norway in his long vigils of the night. What Hesper views here is not the sky itself, nor even any one-to-one equivalent of it, but simply the nospace correlative of the sky, a map of energy sources in realspace as they have been translated into utterly alien nospace terms. No matter; let these seeming stars be any stars at all, let them be Markab or Procyon or Rigel or Betelgeuse or ones that have no names at all—let them, for all he cares, be nothing more than imaginary points of light. He wants only to see the dance.

He savors the light-show gratefully until his eyes begin to ache a little and the wild spectacle starts to weary his mind. Then he thanks Hesper gravely and goes out.

Noelle's cabin is neat, austere, underfurnished: no paintings, no light-sculptures, nothing to please the visual sense, only a few small sleek bronze statuettes, a smooth oval slab of green stone, and some objects evidently chosen for their rich textures—a strip of nubby fabric stretched across a frame, a sea urchin's stony test, a collection of rough sandstone chunks. Everything is meticulously arranged. Does someone help her keep the place tidy? She moves serenely from point to point in the little room, never in danger of a collision, moving this object a centimeter or two to one side, lifting another and fondling it a moment before returning it to the exact place where it had been. The supreme confidence of her movements is fascinating to the year-captain, who sits patiently waiting for her to settle down.

Her beauty fascinates him too. She is precisely groomed, her straight dark hair drawn tightly back from her forehead and held by an intricate ivory clasp. She has deep-toned Mediterranean-African skin, smooth and lustrous, gleaming from within. Her lips are full, her nose is narrow, high-bridged. She wears a soft flowing black robe with a border of silver stitching. Her body is attractive: he has seen her occasionally in the baths and knows of her full rounded breasts, her broad curving hips. She is light-boned, almost dainty, but classically feminine. Yet so far as he knows she has had no shipboard liaisons. Is it because she is blind? Perhaps one tends not to think of a blind person as a potential sexual partner. Why should that be? Maybe because one hesitates to take advantage of a blind person in a sexual encounter, he suggests, and immediately catches himself up, startled by the strangeness of his own thought, wondering why he should think of any sort of sexual relationship between adults as *taking advantage.* Well, then, possibly compassion for her handicap gets in the way of erotic feeling: pity too easily becomes patronizing, and that kills desire. He rejects that theory also: glib, implausible. Could it simply be that people fear to approach her, suspecting that she is able to read their inmost thoughts? Noelle has repeatedly denied any ability to enter minds other than her sister's. Besides, if you have nothing to hide, why be put off by her telepathy? No, it must be something else, and now he thinks he has isolated it: that Noelle is so self-contained, so calm, so much wrapped up in her blindness and her mind-power and her unfathomable communication with her distant sister, that no one dares to breach the crystalline barricades that guard her inner self. She is unapproached because she seems unapproachable: her strange perfection of soul sequesters her, keeping others at a distance the way extraordinary physical beauty can sometimes keep people at a distance. She does not arouse desire because she does not seem at all human. She gleams. She is a flawless machine, an integral part of the ship.

He unfolds the text he has prepared, the report that is to be transmitted to Earth today. "Not that there's anything new to tell them," he says to her, "but I suppose we have to file the daily communiqué all the same."

"It would be cruel if we didn't. We mean so very much to them."

The moment she begins to speak, all of the year-captain's carefully constructed calmness evaporates, and instantly he finds himself becoming edgy, oddly belligerent, distinctly off balance. He is bewildered by that. Something in the softness and earnestness of her sweet gentle voice has mysteriously annoyed him, it seems. Coils of sudden startling tension are springing up within him. Anger, even. Animosity. He has no idea why. He is unable to account for his reaction entirely.

"I have my doubts about that," he says, with a roughness that surprises him. "I don't think we matter at all."

This is perverse, and he knows it. What he has just said runs counter to all of his own beliefs.

She looks a little surprised too. "Oh, yes, yes, we do, we mean a great deal to them. Yvonne says they take our messages from her as fast as they come in, and send them out on every channel, all over the world and to the Moon as well. Word from us is terribly important to them."

He will not concede the point. "As a diversion, nothing more. As the latest curiosity. Intrepid explorers venturing into

the uncharted wilds of interstellar nospace. A nine-day wonder." His voice sounds harsh and unfamiliar to him, his
rhythms of speech coarse, erratic, words coming in awkward
rushes. As for his words themselves, so bleak and sardonic,
they astonish him. He has never spoken this way about Earth
and its attitude toward the starship before. Such thoughts
have never so much as crossed his mind before. Still, he finds
himself pushing recklessly onward down the same strange
track. "That's the only thing we represent to them, isn't it?
Novelty, vicarious adventure, a bit of passing amusement?"

"Do you really mean that? It seems so terribly cynical."

He shrugs. Somehow this ugly idea has taken possession of him, repugnant though his argument is, even to him.
He sees the effect that he is having on her—puzzlement turning to dismay—but he feels that he has gone in too deep now
to turn back. "Another six months and they'll be completely
bored with us and our communiqués. Perhaps sooner than
that. They'll stop paying attention. A year's time and they'll
have forgotten us."

She seems taken aback. Her nostrils flicker in apparent
alarm. Normally her face is a serene mask. Not now. "What a
peculiar mood you're in today, year-captain!"

"Am I? Well, then, I suppose I am."

"I don't see you as in any way a cynical man. Everything about you is the opposite of cynical. And yet here, today—saying such—such—" She falters.

"Such disagreeable things?"

"Yes."

"Perhaps I'm just being realistic. I try to be. A realist,
yes. Is a realist the same as a cynic?"

"Why do you feel you need to put labels on yourself?"

"That's an important part of being a realist."

"You don't know what real is. You don't know what you are, year-captain."

Her counterattack, if that is what it is, amazes him as much as his own outburst. This is a new Noelle, agitated, vehement. In just a few seconds the conversation has veered entirely out of control: much too charged, much too intimate. She has never spoken to him like this before. The same is true of him. He is saying things he doesn't believe; she is saying things that go far beyond the bounds of her normal quiet aloofness. It is as if there is a malign electricity in the air, a prickly field that distorts their normal selves, making them both unnaturally tense and aggressive.

The year-captain feels a touch of panic. If he disturbs the delicate balance of Noelle's consciousness, will she still be able to make contact with far-off Yvonne?

Yet he is unable to prevent himself from parrying once more: "Do *you* know what I am, then?"

"A man in search of himself is what you are. That's why you volunteered to come all the way out here."

He shakes his head briskly, futile though he knows such nonverbal language to be with her. "Oh, no, no, no. Too slick, Noelle. Too easy."

"They say you were a famous actor, once. Isn't that so? And after that, a biologist who made a great discovery on some moon of Jupiter, or maybe it was Saturn. Then a monk on a desert island somewhere. And now the captain of the first starship. There's no continuity in any of that that I can find. Who *are* you, year-captain? Do you really know?"

"Of course I do." But he does not care to amplify that response. Her words make no sense to him. He sees the logic of his jagged zigzagging career with perfect clarity; it is obvious to him how one thing has led inevitably to the next. He could explain all that to her, but something hardens in him. He is not willing to present an apologia for his life just now. That leaves him with nothing of any substance to say; and the best he can do is merely to throw her taunt back at her. "What about you?" he asks, still almost angrily. "Would you be able to answer such a question?"

"I think I could."

"Then tell me. The same things you were asking me. Show me how it's done, all right? What made *you* volunteer to come all the way out here, Noelle? What are *you* searching for? Come on. Tell me! Tell me!"

She lets the lids slide down over her unseeing eyes and offers no reply. She holds herself stiffly, hands tightly knitted, lips compressed, breath coming in ragged bursts. She moves her head from side to side three or four times, doing it very slowly, the way a wounded animal might try to shake off pain.

The year-captain says nothing: he has run out of sophomoric nonsense at last, and he is afraid that what he has already said has done terrible damage. He knows why Noelle is here, and she knows that he knows. How could he not? She is essential to the mission; her participation in it was less of a choice than the inevitable assumption of an unrefusable mantle, involving a terrible sacrifice of the one precious thing in her life. It was contemptible of him even to ask.

His throat is dry, his heart is pounding; his entire performance of these past few minutes amazes him. It is as though he has been possessed, yes. Transformed. He makes an effort to get back in touch with the self that he regards as his own, and, after a moment, seems to succeed in reaching some vestige of contact with the man he believes himself to be.

Can anything be salvaged now? he wonders.

As calmly as he can, he says into her tense silence,

ROBERT SILVERBERG

"This has all been very far out of line. I hope that you'll forgive me for the things I've said."

She remains silent. He sees a barely perceptible nod.

"I'm sorry that I upset you, Noelle. It was the last thing I intended when I came in here."

"I know."

"Shall I go?"

"There's a report to transmit, isn't there?"

"Do you think you'd be able to transmit it just now?"

"I'm not sure. I'm willing to try, though. Wait a little, all right?"

"Whatever you want."

She appears to be collecting herself. Her eyes are still closed, but he can see them moving about less rapidly beneath the lids. Unreadable furrows appear and vanish on her broad forehead. The year-captain thinks of the meditation exercises he learned to practice in his island days, under the bright Arctic sky of Lofoten. She must be doing something like that now herself, he thinks. He sits quietly, watching her, waiting.

Finally she looks at him, at any rate looks *toward* him, and says, after a moment, in a calm tone more like the one she normally uses, "How do you think they see us at home? As ordinary human beings doing an unusual job, or as superhuman creatures engaged in an epic voyage?"

"We don't really need to continue this discussion, do we, Noelle? It isn't getting us anywhere useful."

"Let's just finish it with this one last point. Tell me what you think. What do we seem like to them?"

"Right at this point, I suppose, as superhuman creatures engaged in an epic voyage."

"Yes. And later, you think, they'll regard us as being more ordinary—as being people just like themselves?"

He searches himself for his truest beliefs. He is surprised at what he finds, but he shares it with her anyway, even though it tends to support the dark, unexpectedly harsh words that had come blurting from him earlier. "Later," he says, "we'll become nothing to them. They'll forget us. What was important to them was the great global effort of getting this expedition launched. Now that it *is* launched, everything that follows is an anticlimax for them. We'll go on to live our lives, whatever they're going to be, and they'll proceed with theirs, pleasant and shallow and bland as always, and they and we will travel on separate and ever-diverging paths for all the rest of time."

"You really believe that?"

"Yes. I'm afraid I do."

"How sad that is. What a bleak finish you foresee for our grand adventure." Her tone tingles with a grace note of irony. She has become very calm; she may be laughing at him now. But at least there is no danger that he will unsettle her again. She has taken command. "One more question. You yourself, year-captain? Do you picture yourself as ordinary or as superhuman?"

"Something in between. Rather more than ordinary, but certainly no demigod."

"I think you are right."

"And you?"

"I regard myself as quite ordinary," she says sweetly. "Except in two respects. You know what they are."

"One is your—" He hesitates, mysteriously uncomfortable for a moment at naming it. Then he pushes ahead. "Your blindness. And the other, of course, is your telepathic communion with your sister."

"Indeed." She smiles. Radiantly. A long moment's

pause. Then she says, "Enough of this, I think. There's work to be done. Shall we send the report now?"

The speed with which she has regained her poise catches him off balance. "You're ready to go? You've been able to make contact with Yvonne?"

"Yes. She's waiting."

"Well, then." He is numb, hollow. She has completely routed him in whatever inexplicable duel it is that they have been waging here. His fingers tremble a little as he unfolds his notes. He begins slowly to read: "Shipday 117. Velocity . . . Apparent location . . ."

Noelle naps after every transmission. They exhaust her terribly. She was beginning to fade even before he reached the end of today's message; now, as the year-captain steps into the corridor, he knows she will be asleep before he closes the door. He leaves, frowning, troubled by that odd outburst of tension between them and by his mysterious attack of brutal "realism," from which he seems to be recovering almost at once, now that he is no longer in Noelle's presence.

By what right, he wonders, has he said that Earth will grow jaded with the voyagers? And that the voyage will have no ultimate consequence for the mother world? He was blurting idiotic foolishness and he knows it. The expedition is Earth's redemption, the most interesting thing that has happened there in two hundred years, the last best hope of a sleepy stagnant civilization smothering in its own placidity: it

matters to them, it matters terribly, he has no reason whatsoever to doubt that. All during the hundred years of prepara-
tion for this first interstellar journey the public excitement
had scarcely ever flagged, indeed had spurred the voyagers
themselves on at times, when their interminable training routines threatened *them* with boredom. And the fascination continues. The journey, eventless though it has been so far,
mesmerizes all those millions who remained behind. It is like
a drug for them, a powerful euphoric, hauling them up from
their long lethargy. They have become vicarious travelers;
later, when the new Earth is founded, they will be vicarious
colonists. The benefits will be felt for thousands of years to
come. Why, then, this morning's burst of gratuitous pessi-
mism? There is no evidence for the position he has so impul-
sively espoused. Thus far Earth's messages, relayed by
Yvonne to Noelle, have vibrated with eager queries; the curiosity of the home world has been overwhelming since the
start. Tell us, tell us, tell us!

And, knowing the importance of the endeavor they
have embarked upon, the voyagers have tried to make full
reply. But there is so little to tell, really, except in that one
transcendental area where there is so much. And how, really,
can any of that be told?

How can *this* —

He pauses by the viewplate in the main transit corridor,
a rectangular window a dozen meters long that provides direct
access to the external environment of the ship. None of Hesper's sophisticated data-gathering analog devices are in operation here: this is the *Wotan*'s actual visual surround. And what
it is, is the void of voids. The pearl-gray utter emptiness of
nospace, dense and pervasive, presses tight against the *Wotan*'s

skin. During the training period the members of the expedition had been warned to count on nothing in the way of outside inputs as they crossed the galaxy; they would be shuttling through a void of infinite length, a matter-free tube, and in all likelihood there would be no sights to entertain them, no backdrop of remote nebulas, no glittering stars, no stray meteors, not so much as a pair of colliding atoms yielding the tiniest momentary spark, only an eternal sameness, the great empty Intermundium, like a blank wall surrounding them on all sides. They had been taught methods of coping with that: turn inward, require no delights from the universe that lies beyond the ship, make the ship your universe. And yet, and yet, how misguided those warnings had proved to be! Nospace was not a wall but rather a window. It was impossible for those on Earth to understand what revelations lay in that seeming emptiness.

The year-captain, his head throbbing from his encounter with Noelle, now seeks to restore his shaken equanimity by indulging in his keenest pleasure. A glance at the viewplate reveals that place where the immanent becomes the transcendent: the year-captain sees once again the infinite reverberating waves of energy that sweep through the grayness, out there where the continuum is flattened and curved by the nospace field so that the starship can slide with such deceptive ease and swiftness across the great span of light-years. What lies beyond the ship is neither a blank wall nor an empty tube; the Intermundium is a stunning profusion of interlocking energy fields, linking everything to everything; it is music that also is light, it is light that also is music, and those aboard the ship are sentient particles wholly enmeshed in that vast all-engulfing reverberation, that radiant song of gladness, that is the universe. When he peers into that field of light it is manifestly clear to the year-captain that he and all his fellow voyagers are journeying joyously toward the center of all things, giving themselves gladly into the care of cosmic forces far surpassing human control and understanding.

He presses his hands against the cool glass. He puts his face close to it.

What do I see, what do I feel, what am I experiencing?

It is instant revelation, every time. The sight of that shimmering void might well be frightening, a stunning forcible reminder that they are outside the universe, separated from all that is familiar and indeed "real," floating in this vacant place where the rules of space and time are suspended. But the year-captain finds nothing frightening in that knowledge. None of the voyagers do. It is—almost, *almost!*—the sought-after oneness. Barriers remain, but yet he is aware of an altered sense of space and time, an enhanced sense of possibility, an encounter with the awesome something that lurks in the vacancies between the spokes of the cosmos, something majestic and powerful; he knows that that something is part of himself, and he is part of it. When he stands at the viewplate he often yearns to open the ship's great hatch and let himself tumble into the eternal. But not yet, not yet. He is far from ready to swim the galactic Intermundium. Barriers remain. The voyage has only begun. They grow closer every day to whatever it is that they are seeking, but the voyage has only begun.

How could we convey any of this to those who remain behind? How could we make them understand?

Not with words. Never with words.

Let them come out here and see for themselves!

He smiles. He trembles and does a little shivering wriggle of delight. His sudden new doubts all have fallen away, as swiftly as they came. The starship plunges onward through the great strange night. Confidence rises in him like the surging of a tide. The outcome of the voyage can only be a success, come what may.

He turns away from the viewplate, drained, ecstatic.

Noelle was the first member of the crew to be chosen, if indeed she could be said to have been chosen at all. Choice had not really been a part of it for her, nor for her sister. The entire project had been built about their initial willingness; had they not been who and what they were, the expedition would probably have gone forth anyway, but it would have been something quite different. Perhaps it would not have happened at all. The mere existence of Noelle and Yvonne was the prerequisite for the whole enterprise. They were central to everything; their consent was mainly a formality; and once it had been determined that Noelle and not Yvonne would be the one actually to travel on board the ship, her examination for eligibility was a mere charade.

Of those who had truly volunteered, Heinz was the first to win the formal approval of the Board, Paco was the second, Sylvia the third, then Bruce, Huw, Chang, Julia. The year-captain was one of the last to pass through the qualification process. The last one of all, technically, was Noelle, but of course, she was already a part of the project, as much so as the ship itself, and for many of the same reasons.

For each of them, but for Noelle, the process of qualifying was the same: simple, cruel, humiliating, insincere. Generally speaking, the crew members had been picked even before it had occurred to some of them that they might be interested in going. The world had become very small. Everyone's capacities were known. No one was particularly famous any more, but no one was obscure, either.

Certain formalities were observed, though. It was always possible that the covert *a priori* selection process had been mistaken in one or two instances, and no one wanted mistakes. Eleven hundred candidates were summoned to fill the fifty slots aboard the starship. They came from every part of the world, a carefully impartial and studiedly representative geographic sampling. Many of the old nations that had once been so distinct and noisily self-important still had some sort of tenuous existences, more as sentimental concepts than as sovereign entities now, but they had not completely evolved out of existence yet and it was a good idea to pay lip service, at least, to the continued quasi-fact of their quasi-status. Each of the formerly sovereign nations or historically significant fragment thereof contributed a few of its former citizens to the long list. And then, too, the candidates represented most or perhaps all—who could say, really? The old distinctions had often been so minute and dubious—of the planet's racial and ethnic and religious groups, insofar as such groups still existed and looked upon themselves as mattering in the small and cozy society that had evolved out of the turbulent, messy societies of the Industrial and immediately Post-Industrial epochs. In the cosmic scheme of things it no longer counted for very much that one person might like to think of himself as a Finn and another as a Turk, or a German or a Brit or a Thai or a Swede, nor was it really easy any more to fit most people into the old racial classifications that had once had such troublesome significance, nor had the world's innumerable theological distinctions survived very coherently into modern times. But there were those for whom—perhaps for philosophical reasons, or sentimental ones, or reasons of esthetics, or out of a lingering sense of historical connection, or a fondness for anachronisms, or just out of simple cantankerousness—there was still some value in valiantly claiming, "I am a Welshman" or "I am a communicant of the Roman Catholic Church" or "I carry the blood of the Norman aristocracy." Such people were considered quaint and eccentric; but there were plenty of them, even now. The world had come a long way, yes, yet ancient vestiges of the grand institutions and solemn distinctions of former civilizations still cropped out everywhere like fossil bones whitening and weathering in the sun. They had ceased to be *problems*, yes, but they had not fully ceased to be. Possibly they never would. And so the long list of candidates for the *Wotan* expedition was an elaborately representative one. The final group would be too, insofar as that was feasible. Formalities were observed, indeed.

There were five Examiners, distinguished and formidable citizens all, and they sat around a table on the top floor of a tall building in Zurich whose enormous wraparound windows offered a clear, crisp view that stretched halfway to Portugal. You stood before them and they asked you things that they already knew about you, things about your technical skills and your physical health and your mental stability and your willingness to say goodbye to the world forever, and to spend anywhere from one to five years, or perhaps even more, in intimate confinement with forty-nine other people, and you could tell from the way they were listening that they weren't really listening at all. After that they wanted you to speak only about your flaws. If you were in any way hesitant, they would list some for you, sometimes quite an extensive list indeed, and ask you to offer comment on your most flagrant failings, your choice of five. The whole interrogation lasted, in most cases, no more than fifteen or twenty minutes. Then they told you you were rejected. Every single candidate who came before the Board of Examiners was told that, calmly, straightforwardly, without show of regret or apology: "Sorry, you're off the list." They wanted to see what you would say then. That was the real examination; everything that had gone before had been mere maneuvering and feinting.

The ones who passed were the ones who had rejected the rejection. Some did it one way, some another. Points were given for arrogance, so long as it was sane and sensible arrogance. The man who eventually would become the expedition's first year-captain had simply said, "You can't be serious. Obviously I'm qualified. And I don't like it that you're playing games with me." Heinz, who was Swiss himself and indeed was the son of one of the Examiners, had taken a similar stance, telling them that it would be the whole world's loss if they stuck to their position, but that he had a high enough opinion of the human race to think that they would reconsider. Heinz had helped to design the still-unconstructed *Wotan;* he knew more of its workings than anyone. Did they really think that he was going to build it for them and then be left behind? Huw, who did indeed proudly call himself a Welshman, was another who reacted with the cool and confident attitude that the Examiners were making a big mistake. He had designed the planetgoing equipment with which the people of the *Wotan* would explore the new worlds: was he to be denied the right to deploy his own devices, and if so, who was going to handle the job of modifying them on-site to meet unanticipated challenges? And so on.

Most of the female candidates tended to temper their annoyance with a touch of sorrow or regret, partly for themselves but primarily—constructive arrogance again, only imperfectly concealed!—for the enterprise itself. Sylvia explained that she knew more about tectogenetic microsurgery than anyone else alive: how would the coming generations of starborn colonists be able to adapt to some not-quite-suitable planetary environment without her special skills? Giovanna, too, observed that it would be a great pity for the expedition to be deprived of her unique abilities—her primary specialty was metabolic chemistry, and there was something magical about her insight into the relationship between molecular structure and nutritional value. From Sieglinde, who had helped to work out some fundamental theorems of the mathematics of nospace travel, came the simple comment that she *belonged* aboard the ship and would not accept disqualification. Et cetera.

What the Examiners looked for—and found, in all of those whom they had chosen anyway before the examinations had even begun—was the expression of a justifiable sense of self-worth, tempered by philosophical realism. Anyone who raged or blustered or wept or begged would have been unanswerably rejected. But no one did that, none of the predesignated fifty.

At the end of the entire process it was Noelle's turn to come before the Examiners, and they played out their little charade with her too. They spoke with her for a while and then they gave her the ritual verdict, "Sorry, you're off the list," and she sat there in calm silence for a time, as though trying to comprehend the incomprehensible words they had just spoken, and then at last she said in her soft way, "Perhaps you would want to have my sister go, then." It was the perfect answer. They told her so. Her sister, they said, had given them the same response at the same point in *her* examination.

"Then neither of us will go?" Noelle asked, mystified.

"It was only a test of your reaction," they told her.

"Ah," she said. "I see." And she laughed—giggled, really—as she almost always did when she used that particular verb, and they, not sure of the meaning of her laughter, laughed along with her anyway.

Noelle had wanted to know, right at the end of her examination, how they had decided which sister would go and which would stay.

We flipped a coin, they told her.

She never found out whether that was really true.

N oelle lies in uneasy dreams. She is aboard a ship, an archaic three-master struggling in an icy sea. She sees it, she actually *sees*. The rigging sparkles with fierce icicles, which now and again snap free in the cruel gales and smash with little tinkling sounds against the deck. The deck wears a slippery shiny coating of thin, hard ice, and footing is treacherous. Great eroded bergs heave wildly in the gray water, rising, slapping the waves, subsiding. If one of those bergs hits the hull, the ship will sink. So far they have been lucky about that, but now a more subtle menace is upon them. The sea is freezing over. It congeals, coagulates, becomes a viscous fluid, surging sluggishly. Broad glossy plaques toss on the waves: new ice floes, colliding, grinding, churning: the floes are at war, destroying one another's edges, but some are entering into treaties, uniting to form a single implacable shield. When the sea freezes altogether the ship will be crushed. And now it has begun to freeze. The vessel can barely make headway. The sails belly out uselessly, straining at their lines. The wind makes a lyre out of the rigging as the ice-coated ropes twang and sing. The hull creaks like an old man; the grip of the ice is heavy. The timbers are yielding. The end is near. They will all perish. They will all perish. Noelle emerges from her cabin, goes above, seizes the railing, sways, prays, wonders when the wind's fist will punch through the stiff frozen canvas of the sails. Nothing can save them. But now! Yes! Yes! A glow overhead! Yvonne, Yvonne! She comes. She hovers like a goddess in the black star-pocked sky. Soft golden light streams from her. She is smiling, and her smile thaws the sea. The ice relents. The air grows gentle. The ship is freed. It sails on, unhindered, toward the perfumed tropics, toward the lands of spices and pearls.

"'Some say 'the world will end in fire,' " Elizabeth offers. In the lounge, the talk among those who are not playing *Go* has turned to apocalyptic matters. " 'Some say in ice.' "

"Are you quoting something?" Huw wants to know.

"Of course she is," says Heinz. "You know that Elizabeth's always quoting something." Long-limbed, straw-haired Elizabeth is the *Wotan*'s official bard and chronicler, among other things. Everyone on board has to be Something-Among-

Other-Things; multiple skills are the rule. But the center of Elizabeth's being is poetry. "I think it's Shakespeare," Heinz says.

"Not that old," says Giovanna, looking up from her game. "Only four or five hundred years, at most. An American."

"Frost," Elizabeth says. "Robert Frost."

"Is that a kind of ice?" someone asks.

"It's a name," says someone else.

" 'From what I've tasted of desire,' " Elizabeth says, and her tone makes it clear that she is reciting again, " 'I hold with those who favor fire.' "

The year-captain enters the room just then, and Paco glances toward him and says in his booming unfettered way, "And what about you, year-captain? How do you think the world's going to end? We've done the sun going nova, we've done the entropic heat-death, we've done the rising of the seas until everything has drowned. We've done plague and drought and volcanoes. Give us your take, now."

"Fimbulwinter," the year-captain says. "Ragnarok." The barbaric half-forgotten words leap instantly to his tongue almost of their own accord. The northern winds of his childhood sweep through his memory. He sees the frost-locked boreal landscape gleaming as though ablaze, even in the parsimonious winter light.

"The Twilight of the Gods, yes," Elizabeth says, and gives him a melting smile of unconcealed love, which the year-captain, lost in polar memories, does not see.

Faces turn toward him. They want to hear more. The year-captain says, reaching deep for the ancestral lore, "A time comes when the sun turns black. It gives no light, it gives

ROBERT SILVERBERG

no warmth, winter comes three times in succession with no summer between. This is the Fimbulwinter, the great winter that heralds the world's end. There is battle everywhere in the darkness, and brother slays brother for the sake of greed, and father lies with daughter, sister with brother, many a whoredom."

Elizabeth is nodding. She knows these ancient skaldic poems too. Half to herself she murmurs, rocking back and forth rhythmically, " 'An axe-age, a sword-age, shields shall be cloven. A wind-age, a wolf-age, ere the world totters.' "

"Yes," says the year-captain, shivering now, his mind swirling with the powerful ancient images. "A great wolf will swallow the sun, and another wolf the moon. The stars vanish from the heavens. Trees are torn up, and mountains fall, and all fetters and bonds are broken and rent. The sea bursts its bounds, and the Midgard Serpent stirs and comes up on the land and sprinkles all the air and water with his venom, and the Fenris-Wolf breaks free and advances with his mouth agape, his lower jaw against the Earth and the upper against heaven. Nothing is without fear anywhere in the world. For this is the day on which the gods will meet their doom."

He falls silent, playing out the final titanic battle in his mind, Thor putting the Serpent to death but dying himself of its venom, and the Wolf devouring Father Odin, only to have his gullet torn asunder by Vidar, and the demonic Surtr riding out of Muspelheim and casting fire over the Earth that burns all the world. But of these things the year-captain says nothing aloud. He feels he has had the center of the stage long enough just now. And an Arctic gloom has begun to seize his spirit. The ice, the darkness, the ravening wolves rising above the blazing world. And the Earth of his Viking forefathers is so far away, floating through the emptiness of the night, spinning eternally on its axis somewhere back behind him—a dot, a grain of sand. Nothing. Everything.

After a moment Elizabeth's voice continues the tale:

" 'Smoke-reek rages, and reddening fire. The high heat licks against heaven itself.' " Her mind is a crowded store-house of poetry. But even she is unable to remember the next line.

"And then?" Paco asks. He throws his hands upward and outward, palms raised. Paco is a small, compact-bodied man of great strength and personal force, and any gesture he makes is always more emphatic than it needs to be, just as his shoulders seem twice as wide as those of a man his height should be. "That's it? The End? Everybody's dead and there's nothing more? The curtain comes down and there's not going to be any next act, and we look around and see that the theater is empty?"

"Redemption, then," says the year-captain distantly. "Rebirth. The new world rising on the ashes of the old."

He isn't sure. Some details of his grandmother's stories have faded in his mind, after all these many years. But it must be so, the rebirth. It is that way in every myth, no matter what land it may come from: the world is destroyed so that it may be brought forth new and fresh. There would be no point to these tales, otherwise. Not if the Twilight of the Gods is followed simply by unending empty night. That way all of life would be reduced to the experience of any one mortal individual: we are each of us born into flesh and we live, well or not well as the case may be, and then we die, goodbye, and that's that for us, everything over. But that is only the individual case. New lives are being engendered even as ours is passing from us: an eternal cycle of rebirth and return. We end, yes, but the world of mortals goes on, death succeeded always by more life. So it must be with whole planets too. Sooner or later they may die, but new worlds are born from the dead husk of the old, and thus it all continues, world without end, always a new dawn beyond the darkness in which yesterday perished. There must never be a total and final end: never. Never.

"You know," Heinz says cheerfully—Heinz is always cheerful—"for us the world has already come to an end, really. Because we will never see it again. It is already becoming mythical for us. It was a dying world even before we left it, wasn't it? And now, so far as we're concerned, it's dead, and we are its rebirth. We, and all the ova and sperm sitting in cold storage down there in our tanks."

"If," says Paco. "Don't forget the Big If."

Heinz laughs. "There is no If. The sky is full of worlds, and we will find some. One good one is all we need."

In fact Heinz is right, they all agree: the world they had left behind them was essentially already dead—the human world, that is—even though some hundreds of millions of people were still moving about upon the face of it. It had passed successfully through all the convulsions of the twentieth and twenty-first centuries, the myriad acute crises of demography and nationalistic fervor and environmental decay, and had moved on into an era so stable and happy that its condition seemed indistinguishable from death, for what has ceased to grow and change has ceased to carry out the most important functions of life. Earth now was the home of a steadily dwindling population of healthy, wealthy, cautious, utterly civilized people, living the easy life in an easy society supported by automated devices of every sort. All their problems had been solved except the biggest one of all, which was that the solutions had become the problems and the trend-lines of everything were curving downward toward inevitable extinction. No one had expected that, really: that the end of striving and strife would in effect mean the end of life. But that was how it was working out. The last sputtering spark of Earth's vitality was here, carried aboard the *Wotan*, sailing farther out and out and out into the galactic gulfs with each tick of the clock.

An enormous irony, yes. A cosmic giggle. The world, free now of war and lesser conflicts, of inequalities, of disease, of shortages, was drifting downward on an apparently irreversible spiraling course. There was a lot of bland unexcited cocktail-party talk of the end of the human race within five or six hundred years, a notion with which hardly anybody seemed to care to disagree, and such talk was enough to make most people pause and contemplate matters of ultimate destiny for—oh, a good ten or fifteen minutes at a time.

The explosive population growth of the early industrial era had been curbed so successfully that virtually no children were being born at all. Even though the human life span now routinely exceeded a century, there was no region of the world where population was not steadily declining, because childbirth had become so uncommon that the replacement level was not being maintained. The world had become one vast pleasant suburb of well-to-do elderly childless folks.

Everyone was aware of the problem, of course; but everyone was eager for someone else to do something about it. The calm, mature, comfortable, emotionally stable people of the era had, as a general rule, very little interest in bearing or rearing children themselves, and such experiments in having children artificially generated and communally raised as had been carried out had not met with manifest success.

What the human race appeared to be doing, though no one said anything about it out loud, was to be politely allowing itself to die out. Most people thought that that was very sad. But what, if anything, was anybody supposed to do about it?

The *Wotan* was one answer to that question. A movement arose—it was the most interesting thing that had happened on Earth in two hundred years—aimed at founding a second Earth on some distant planet. Several dozen of the best and brightest of Earth's younger generation—men and women in their thirties and forties, mainly—would be sent out aboard an interstellar starship to locate and settle a world of some other star. The hope was that amid the challenges of life on an untamed primitive world the colonists and their starborn progeny would recapture the drive and energy that once had been defining characteristics of the human race, and thus bring about a rebirth of the human spirit—which, perhaps, could be recycled back to the mother world five hundred or a thousand years hence.

Perhaps.

Translating the hypothesis into reality required some work, but there were still enough people willing to tackle the job. The starship had to be designed and built and tested. Done and done and done. A crew of suitably fearless and adventuresome people had to be assembled. It was. The voyage had to be undertaken. And so it came to pass. A habitable world needed to be located. Scanning instruments were even now at work.

And then, if some reasonably appropriate world did

indeed turn up, a successful colony must be founded there, and somehow made to sustain itself, however difficult and hostile an environment the colonists might find themselves in—

Yes. The Big If.

Y ou promised to teach me how to play," Noelle says, pouting a little. They are once again in the ship's lounge, one of the two centers of daily social life aboard the *Wotan*, the other being the baths. Four games are under way, the usual players: Elliot and Sylvia, Roy and Paco, David and Heinz, Michael and Bruce.

The year-captain is fascinated by that sudden pout of Noelle's: such a little-girl gesture, so charming, so human. In the past few days she and he have passed through the small bit of tension that had so unexpectedly sprung up between them, and are working well together again. He gives the messages to her to transmit, she sends them to Earth, and back from her sister at the far end of the mental transmission line swiftly come the potted replies, the usual cheery stuff, predigested news, politics, sports, the planetary weather, word of doings in the arts and sciences, special greetings for this member of the expedition or that one, expressions of general good wishes—everything light, shallow, amiable, more or less what you would expect the benign stodgy people of Earth to be sending their absconding sons and daughters. And so it will go, the year-captain assumes, as long as the contact between Noelle and Yvonne holds. Of course, someday the sisters will no longer be available for these transmissions, and real-time contact between Earth and its colony in the stars will be severed when that happens, but that is not a problem he needs to deal with today, or, indeed, at all.

"Teach me, year-captain," she prods. "I really do want to know how to play the game. And I know I can learn it. Have faith in me."

"All right," he says. The game may prove valuable to her, a relaxing pastime, a timely distraction. She leads such a cloistered life, more so even than the rest of them, moving in complete tranquillity through her chaste existence, intimate with no one but her sister Yvonne, sixteen light-years away and receding into greater distances all the time.

He leads her toward the gaming tables. Noelle bridles only an instant as his hand touches her elbow, and then she relaxes with an obvious effort, allowing him to guide her across the room.

"This is a *Go* board," the year-captain says. He takes her hand and gently presses it flat against the board, drawing it from side to side and then up and down, so she can get some idea of the area of the board and also of its feel. "It has nineteen horizontal lines, nineteen vertical lines. The stones are played on the intersections of these lines, not on the squares that the lines form." He shows her the pattern of intersecting lines by moving the tips of her fingers along them. They have been printed with a thick ink, and evidently she is able to discern their slight elevation above the flatness of the board, for when he releases her hand she slowly draws her fingertips along the lines herself, seemingly without difficulty.

"These nine dots are called stars," he tells her. "They serve as orientation points." He touches her fingertips to each of the nine stars in turn. They, too, are raised above the board by nothing more than a faint thickness of green ink, but it seems quite clear that she is able to feel them as easily as though they stood out in high relief. All of her senses must be extraordinarily sharp, by way of compensation for the one that is missing. "We give the lines in this direction numbers, from one to nineteen, and we give the lines going in the other direction letters, from A to T, leaving out I. Thus we have coordinates that allow us to identify positions on the board. This is B10, this is D18, this is J4, do you follow?" He puts the tip of one of her fingers on each of the locations he names. She responds with a smile and a nod. Even so, the year-captain feels despair. How can she ever commit the board to memory? It's an impossible job. But Noelle looks untroubled as she runs her hand along the edges of the board, murmuring, "A, B, C, D . . ."

The other games have halted. Everyone in the lounge is watching them. He guides her hand toward the two trays of stones, the black ones of polished slate and the white ones fashioned of clamshell, and shows her the traditional way of picking up a stone between two fingers and clapping it down against the board. The skin of her hand is cool and very smooth. The hand itself is slender and narrow, almost fragile-looking, but utterly unwavering. "The stronger player uses the white stones," he says. "Black always moves first. The players take turns placing stones, one at a time, on any unoccupied intersection. Once a stone is placed it is never moved unless it is captured, in which case it is removed at once from the board."

"And the purpose of the game?" she asks.

"To control the largest possible area with the smallest possible number of stones. You build walls. You try to sur-round your opponent's pieces even while he's trying to sur-

ROBERT SILVERBERG

round yours. The score is reckoned by counting the number of vacant intersections within your walls, plus the number of prisoners you have taken." She is staring steadily in his direction, fixedly, an intense and almost exaggerated show of attention, all the more poignant for its pointlessness. Methodically the year-captain explains the actual technique of play to her: the placing of stones, the seizure of territory, the capture of opposing stones. He illustrates by setting up simulated situations on the board, calling out the location of each stone as he places it. "Black holds P12, Q12, R12, S12, T12—got it?" A nod. "And also P11, P10, P9, Q8, R8, S8, T8. All right?" Another nod. "White holds—" Somehow she is able to visualize the positions; she repeats the patterns after him, and asks questions that show she sees the board clearly in her mind.

He wonders why he is so surprised. He has heard of blind chess players, good ones: they must be able to memorize the board and update their inner view of it with every move. Noelle must have the same kind of hypertrophied memory. But playing *Go* is not like playing chess. When a chess game begins, the first player to move is facing fewer than two dozen possible moves. In *Go*, there are 361 potential moves in the first turn. There are more possible ways for a game of *Go* to unfold than there are atoms in the universe. The chessboard has just sixty-four squares, across which an ever-diminishing number of pieces is deployed, reducing and simplifying the number of options available to each player as the original thirty-two pieces dwindle down to a handful. The number of *Go* pieces also diminishes gradually as the game proceeds, but their absence makes the patterns on the board more complicated rather than simpler during the unfolding battle for territory.

Even so, Noelle seems to be grasping the essentials.

Within twenty minutes she appears to understand the basic
ploys. And there is no question that she is able to hold the
board firmly fixed on the internal screen of her mind. Several
times, in describing maneuvers to her, the year-captain gives
her an incorrect coordinate — the first time by accident, for the
board is not actually marked with printed numbers and letters,
and since it is a long time since he last has played, he mis-
gauges the coordinates occasionally — and then twice more de-
liberately, to test her. Each time she corrects him, gently
saying, "N13? Don't you mean N12?"

At length she says, "I think I follow everything now.
Would you like to play a game?"

In the baths later that day Paco and Heinz and Elizabeth discuss the year-captain's putative sex life. It is
one of their favorite speculative subjects. Most of the
sex that goes on aboard the ship, and there is quite a good deal
of it, takes place in complete openness, figuratively and often
literally. These people are the product of a highly civilized,
perhaps overcivilized, epoch. Very little is taboo to them. But
the year-captain, unlike virtually everyone else on board, is
scrupulous about his privacy.

"He doesn't have any sex and he doesn't want any,"
Paco insists. "He was a monk just before he joined us, you
know. That weird colony of meditating mystics up by the
North Pole somewhere off the coast of Scandinavia. And a
monk is still what he is, at heart. A man of ice through and
through. It shows in his face, that lean and grim thin-lipped

face with that little beard that he keeps cropped so short. And in his eyes, especially. Those terrible blue eyes. Like the blue ice of a glacier, they are. They show you the interior of the man himself."

"Wrong," Elizabeth says. "Ice outside, fire within."

"And you hold with those who favor fire," Paco says jeeringly. "Don't think I don't listen when you start quoting poetry."

Elizabeth, reddening down to her bony breast, sticks her tongue out at him.

"You're in love with him," Paco says. "Aren't you, Lizzy?"

Instead of answering, she turns the tank nozzle toward him and douses him with a foaming spray of hot water. Paco, more amused than annoyed, snorts and bellows like a breaching walrus and rises with a powerful thrust of his elbows, launching himself toward her, catching her around the middle, pulling her down into the tank and pushing her head under water. Elizabeth thrashes about in his grasp, wildly wigwagging her lean delicate arms, then frantically kicking her long frail legs in the air as Paco, roaring with laughter, up-ends her. Heinz, who is elongated and lean, with a sly ever-smiling face and a slippery, practically hairless body, glides forward and jams Paco under the surface with her, and for a couple of moments all three of them are splashing chaotically, forming an incoherent tangle of writhing limbs, the pale, thin Nordic Elizabeth and the stocky, swarthy Latin Paco and the gleaming, beautiful Teutonic Heinz. Then they bob to the top all at once, laughing, gasping merrily for breath.

Paco and Heinz and Elizabeth have been an inseparable triad for the past month and a half. The lines of attraction run among them in every direction, though not with uniform force: Elizabeth for both of the men in equal strong measure, Heinz being pleasantly fond of Elizabeth but fiercely passionate about Paco, Paco drawn strongly to Elizabeth by some sort of attraction of physical opposites but—somewhat to his own surprise—captivated by Heinz's easy self-confidence and omnivorous sexuality. So far the relationship has demonstrated remarkable three-sided stability, but, of course, no one expects it to last indefinitely. The voyage has really only just begun. Couples and triples will form and break apart and reform in new configurations, on and on and on, just as is the fashion on Earth but probably with greater rapidity, considering the limitation of choice in a population that at the moment numbers just fifty in a completely enclosed and utterly inescapable environment. Up until now none of the relationships that have formed aboard the *Wotan* has lasted more than about seven weeks. This one is approaching the ship record.

In the aftermath of the wrestling match they sit facing one another along the edge of the tank, unable to stop laughing: one will start and set off the other two, and around and around it goes. Elizabeth's pallid meager body is rosy now from the underwater frolic; her flesh glows, her small breasts heave. Paco studies her with a proprietary air, and Heinz amiably contemplates them both as if planning to spread his long arms about them and pull them in again.

The air in the small, brightly lit room is warm and steamy. A voluptuous abundant torrent of warm water splashes down from the fountainhead set in the tiled wall. No one worries about water shortages aboard the *Wotan:* every drop, urine and sweat and the vapor of everybody's breath included, is rigorously recaptured and purified and aerated and chilled and recycled, and not a molecule of it ever goes to waste. The baths are Roman in sensuousness if not in scale:

the room is compact but elegantly appointed, and there is a hot tank, a tepid one, and a frigid one, something for all tastes. Up to nine or ten people can use the baths at the same time, though in practice a certain amount of exclusiveness is afforded those who are in any sort of bonded relationship. Three small rooms adjacent to the tank chamber have beds in them. Much of the ship's erotic activity goes on in those rooms.

Elizabeth says in a serious tone, when the three of them are calm again, "I don't deny that I'm attracted to him. And not just for his body, though he's certainly a handsome man. But his mind—that mysterious, complicated, opaque mind of his—"

"The mind of a mystic," Paco says with unconcealed contempt. "The mind of a monk, yes."

"He's been a monk," Elizabeth retorts, "but he's been a lot of other things too. You can't pin him down in any one category. And I don't think he's as ascetic as you seem to believe. The Lofoten monastery isn't famous for vows of chastity."

"Oh, he's no ascetic," Heinz says. "I can testify to that."

Elizabeth and Paco whirl to gape at him. *"You?"* they say at the same time.

Heinz chuckles lazily. "Oh, no, not what you're thinking. He's not really my type. Too inward, too elusive. But I can see the passion in him. You don't have to go to bed with him to know that. It's there. Plenty of it. It streams from him like sunlight."

"There," Elizabeth says to Paco. "Ice outside, maybe, but fire within."

"And," Heinz continues, "I'm quite certain that he's been sleeping with somebody on board."

"Who?" Elizabeth asks, very quickly.

Another lazy chuckle. "Your guess is as good as mine, and mine is no good at all. I haven't been spying on him. I'm only saying that he moves around this ship like a cat, and knows every hidden corner of it better even than the man who designed it, and I'm certain that a man of his force, of his virility, is getting a little action somewhere, in some part of the ship that we don't even suspect can be used for some stuff, and with some partner who's keeping very quiet about what's going on. That's all."

"I hope you're right," says Elizabeth, forcing a broad lascivious grin not at all in keeping with the austere scholarly angularity of her face. "And when he's done with her, whoever she is, I'd gladly volunteer to be his next secret playmate."

"He doesn't want you," Paco says.

Elizabeth meets this casual dismissal of her fantasies with a disdainful wave of her hand. "Oh, I don't think you can be so sure of that."

"Oh, but I am, I am," Paco replies. "It's only too obvious. You keep sending him signals—everyone can see that, you stare at him like a lovesick child—and what does he send you in response? Nothing. Nothing. I don't mean to cast any personal aspersions, Liz. You know there are plenty of men who find you attractive. He doesn't happen to be one of them." Elizabeth is staring wide-eyed at him, and pain is visible in her rigid unblinking gaze. But Paco will not stop. "There's no—what is the term?—no chemistry between you and our year-captain. Or else he's a master at masking his emotions, but if he's that good at playing a part he should have had a more successful career as an actor than he did. No, he just isn't interested in you, my love. You must not be his type,

whatever that is. Just as he isn't Heinz's. There's no account-
ing for these things, you know."

Sadly Heinz says, "I think Paco's right. But not for the
same reasons, exactly."

"Oh?"

"You may or may not be the captain's type. Who can
say? I've already said I think he's got someone for casual sex,
and if we knew who he or she is, we'd have more of an idea
about his type. But you're up against another problem that
goes beyond his choice of casual bedmates. He sleeps with
someone, yes, very likely, but even so his emotions are focused
somewhere else, and that's too complicated a something for
you to deal with. The year-captain is in love, don't you realize
that? I'm not talking about sex now, but love. And it's a love
that's impossible to consummate."

"Yes, it's obvious. He's in love with himself," says Paco.

"You're such a filthy boor," Elizabeth says. She glances
toward Heinz. "What are you talking about? Who do you
imagine he's in love with?"

"The one untouchable person aboard this ship. The one
who floats through our lives like some kind of being from
another sphere of existence. I can see it written all over his
face, whenever he's within twenty meters of her. The blind
girl, that's who he wants. Noelle. And he's afraid to do anything about it, and it's agony for him. For God's sake, can't
you tell?"

"aptain?" Noelle says. "It's me, Noelle."

The year-captain looks up, startled. He is not expecting her. It is late afternoon, the last day of the voyage's fifth month. He is working alone in the control cabin, poring over a thick batch of documents that Zed Hesper has brought him: a new set of formal analyses of three or four of his best prospects for a planetary landing, set forth in much greater detail than Hesper has been able to supply previously.

For the first time, the year-captain has begun to pay serious attention to such things. Half his term of office is over, and he is thinking beyond his captaincy, to the time when he will have reverted to his primary specialty of xenobiology. He can't practice that aboard the *Wotan*. He needs an actual alien planet as his scene of operations. He has walked alien worlds before, not only Earth's neighbor planets but also the bleak strange moons of the gas-giant worlds beyond the orbit of Mars: Titan, Iapetus, Callisto, Ganymede, Io. The exultation of finding splotches of life on those cold forbidding worldlets, extraterrestrial microorganisms rugged beyond belief—supreme moments of his life, those were, the astounding discovery in the sulfurous landscape of Io, and then again on Titan, when he knelt and pointed into methane-ammonia snowdrifts at the tiny astonishing spots of burnt orange against the glaring white! And so he will certainly want to be a member of the first landing team, where his intuitive skills will be valuable on a world full of strange and perhaps challenging life-forms of unpredictably strange biochemical characteristics; but as year-captain he would be obliged to remain aboard the vessel while others take the risks outside. That is the rule of the ship.

It is time, therefore, for him to pick the site of the first landing and head for it in these closing months of the first year, while he is still in command. The die will be cast, that way. That way the timing will be right for him to hand his executive responsibilities on to his successor just as they arrive at their destination, and thus to be able to take part in the initial planetary expedition.

But here is Noelle, drifting silently, wraithlike, into the room where he is working. She looks older and less beautiful today than she usually seems to him: weary and drawn, so much so that she is almost translucent. She appears unusually vulnerable, as though a single harsh sound would shatter her.

"I have the return transmission from Yvonne," she tells him. There is an oddly timid, tentative inflection in her voice that is not at all like her. He wonders if something terrible has taken place on Earth. But what could possibly go awry on that torpid, tranquil world?

She hands him the small, clear data-cube on which she has archived her latest conversation with her sister on Earth. As Yvonne speaks in her mind, Noelle repeats each message aloud into a sensor disk, and it is captured on the cube.

He rests the cube on the palm of his hand and says to her, "Are you all right, Noelle? You look wiped out."

A faint shrug. "There was a little problem."

He waits. She seems to be having trouble articulating her thoughts.

"What kind of problem, Noelle?" he says finally.

"With the transmission. I had some difficulty receiving it. Or rather—what I mean to say is, it wasn't quite clear. It was—fuzzy."

"Fuzzy," the year-captain says. His voice is flat.

"Distorted. Not much, but some. A kind of static around the edges of the signal."

"Static," he says, flatly again, playing for time, trying to understand, though he does not really see how merely echoing her words will help him to do that. Yet what else can he do? "Mental static," he says, looking straight into her sightless eyes.

"That's the best word I can use for it."

Yvonne's mental tone, Noelle says, is always pure, crystalline, wholly undistorted. Noelle has never had an experience like this before. Plainly she is worried by it. Frightened, perhaps.

"Perhaps you were tired," he suggests gently. "Or maybe she was."

Noelle smiles. The year-captain knows that smile of hers by now: it is meant entirely to deflect unpleasantness. But it usually reflects a troubled inner state.

He fits the cube into the playback slot, and Noelle's voice comes from the speakers. It is not her customary voice; it is this new unfamiliar voice of hers, thin and strained and ill at ease; she fumbles words frequently, and often can be heard asking Yvonne to repeat something. The message from the mother world, what the year-captain can make out of it, is the customary chattery blather, no surprises. But this business of static disturbs him. Is this the beginning, he wonders, of the breakdown of their one communication link with Earth, the onset of a steady inexplicable degradation of the signal, leading inevitably to the isolation of the starship in a realm of total silence?

And what if it is? What if the telepathic link should fail, what if they should lose contact with Earth altogether? The transmissions between Yvonne and Noelle are nonrelativistic; they travel instantaneously across a cosmos in which light itself can go no faster than 300,000 kilometers per second and even this nonrelativistic faster-than-light starship crosses the topological folds of nospace at finite, though immense, velocity. Without the sisters, they would have to fall back on radio transmission to make contact with Earth: from their present distance a message would take two decades to get there.

The year-captain asks himself why that prospect should trouble him so. The ship is self-sufficient; it needs no guidance from Earth for its proper functioning, nor do the voyagers really derive any particular benefit from the daily measure of information about events on the mother planet, a world which, after all, they have chosen to abandon. So why care if silence descends? Why should it matter? Why not, in that case, simply accept the fact that they are no longer Earthbound in any way, that they are on their way to becoming virtually a different species as they leap, faster than light, outward into a new life among the stars? He is not a sentimental man. There are very few sentimental people on this ship. For him, for them, Earth is just so much old baggage: a wad of stale history, a fading memory of archaic kings and empires, of extinct religions, of outmoded philosophies. Earth is the past; Earth is mere archaeology; Earth is essentially nonexistent for them. If the link breaks, why should they care?

But he *does* care. The link matters.

He decides that it has to do with the symbolic function of this voyage to the people of Earth: the fact that the voyagers are the focal point of so much aspiration and anticipation. If contact is lost, their achievements in planting a new Earth on some far star, whatever they may ultimately be, will have no meaning for the people of the mother world.

And then, too, it is a matter of what he is experiencing on the voyage itself, in relation to the intense throbbing grayness of nospace outside: that interchange of energies, that growing sense of universal connectedness. He has not spoken with any of the others about this, but the year-captain is certain that he is not the only one who has felt these things. He and, doubtless, some of his companions are making new discoveries every day, not astronomical but—well, spiritual—and, the year-captain tells himself, what a great pity it will be if none of this can ever be communicated to those who have remained behind on Earth. We must keep the link open.

"Maybe," he says, "we ought to let you and Yvonne rest for a few days."

A celebration: the six-month anniversary of the day the *Wotan* set out for deep space from Earth orbit. The starship's entire complement is jammed into the gaming lounge, overflowing out into the corridor. Much laughter, drinking, winking, singing, a happy occasion indeed,

R O B E R T   S I L V E R B E R G

though no one is quite sure why they should be making such a fuss about the half-year anniversary.

"It's because we aren't far enough out yet," Leon suggests. "We still really have one foot in space and one back on Earth. So we keep time on the Earth calendar still. And we focus on these little milestones. But that'll change."

"It already has," Chang observes. "When was the last time you used anything but the shiptime calendar in your daily work?"

"Which calendar I use isn't important," Leon says. He is the ship's chief medical officer, a short, barrel-chested man with a voice like tumbling gravel. "As it happens, I use the shiptime calendar. But we still think in reference to Earth dates too. Earth dates still matter to us, after a fashion. All of us keep a kind of double calendar in our heads, I suspect. And I think we'll go on doing that until—"

"Happy six-month!" Paco cries just then. His broad face is flushed, his dark deep-set eyes are aglow. "Six months cooped up together in this goddamned tin can and we're still all on speaking terms with each other! It's a miracle! A bloody miracle!" He holds a tumbler of red wine in each hand. For tonight's party the year-captain has authorized breaking out the last of the wine that they brought with them from Earth. They will be synthesizing their own from now on. It won't be the same thing, though; everyone knows that.

Paco may not be as drunk as he seems, but he puts on a good show. He caroms through the crowd, bellowing, "Drink! Drink!" and bumps into tall, slender Marcus, the planetographer, nearly knocking him down, and Marcus is the one who apologizes: that is the way Marcus is. A moment later Sieglinde drifts past him and Paco hands his extra wineglass to her. Then he loops his free arm through hers. *"Tanz mit mir, liebchen!"* he cries. The old languages are still spoken, more or less. "Show me how to waltz, Sieglinde!" She gives him a sour look, but yields. It's a party, after all. They make a foolish-looking couple—she is a head taller than he is, and utterly ungraceful—but looking foolish is probably what Paco has in mind. He whirls her around through the crowd in a clumsy galumphing not-quite-waltz, holding her tightly at arm's length with a one-armed grip and joyously waving his wine-glass in the other.

The year-captain, who has come late to the party and now stands quietly by himself at the rear of the lounge near the tables where the *Go* boards are kept, sees Noelle on the opposite side, also alone. He fears for her, slim and frail as she is, and sightless, in this room of increasingly drunken revelers. But she seems to be smiling. Michael and Julia are at her side; Julia is saying something to her, and Noelle nods. Apparently she is asking if Noelle wants something to drink, for a moment later Mike plunges into the melee and fetches a glass of something for her.

There had been a party much like this six months before, on Earth, the eve of their departure. The same people acting foolish, the same ones being shy and withdrawn. They all knew each other so superficially, then, even after the year-long training sessions—names, professional skills, that was about it. No depth, no intimacy. But that was all right. There would be time, plenty of time. Already couples had begun to form as launch time drew near: Paco and Julia, Huw and Giovanna, Michael and Innelda. None of those relationships was destined to last past the first month of the voyage, but that was all right too. The ship's crew consisted of twenty-five men, twenty-five women, and the supposition was that they would all pair neatly off and mate and be fruitful and multiply on the new Earth to come, but in all likelihood only about half the group would do that at most, and the others would remain single to the end of their days, or pass through a series of intricate and shifting relationships without reproducing, as most people did on Earth. It would make little difference in the long run. There was a sufficiency of frozen gametes on board with which to people the new world. And one could readily enough contribute one's own to the pool without actually pairing and mating.

Partying was not a natural state for the year-captain. Aloof and essentially solitary by nature, marked also by his wintry years at the monastery in Lofoten, he made his way through these social events the way he had managed his notable and improbable career as an actor, stepping for the time being into the character of someone who was not at all like himself. He could pretend a certain joviality. And so he drank with the others at the launch party; and so he would drink here tonight.

The launch party, yes. That had called for all his thespian skills. The newly elected year-captain going about the room, grinning, slapping backs, trading quips. Getting through the evening, somehow.

And then the day of the launch. That had needed some getting through too. The grand theatrical event of the century, it was, staged for maximum psychological impact on those who were staying behind. The whole world watching as the chosen fifty, dressed for the occasion in shimmering, absurdly splendiferous ceremonial robes, emerged from their dormitory and solemnly marched toward the shuttle ship like a procession of Homeric heroes boarding the vessel that will take them to Troy.

How he had hated all that pomp, all that pretension! But of course the departure of the first interstellar expedition in the history of the human race was no small event. It needed proper staging. So there they came, ostentatiously strutting toward the waiting hatch, the year-captain leading the way, and Noelle walking unerringly alongside him, and then Huw, Heinz, Giovanna, Julia, Sieglinde, Innelda, Elliot, Chang, Roy, and on and on down to Michael and Marcus and David and Zena to the rear, the fifty voyagers, the whole oddly assorted bunch of them, the short ones and the tall, the burly ones and the slender, the emissaries of the people of Earth to the universe in general.

Aboard the shuttle. Up to the *Wotan,* waiting for them at its construction site in low orbit. More festivities there. All manner of celebrities, government officials, and such on hand to bid them farewell. Then a change of mood, a new solemnity: the celebrities took their leave. The fifty were alone with their ship. Each to his or her cabin for a private moment of—what? prayer? meditation? contemplation of the unlikeliness of it all?—before the actual moment of departure.

And then all hands to the lounge. The year-captain must make his first formal address:

"I thank you all for the dubious honor you've given me. I hope you have no reason to regret your choice. But if you do, keep in mind that a year lasts only twelve months."

Thin laughter came from the assembled voyagers. He had never been much of a comedian.

A few more words, and then it was time for them to go back to their cabins again. By twos and threes drifting out, pausing by the viewplate in the great corridor to have one last look at the Earth, blue and huge and throbbing with life in the center of the screen. Off to the sides somewhere, the Moon, the Sun. Everything that you take for granted as fixed and permanent.

The sudden awareness coming over them all that the *Wotan* is their world now, that they are stuck with each other and no one else for all eternity.

Music over the ship's speakers. Beethoven, was it? Something titanic-sounding, at any rate. Something chosen for its sublime transcendental force too. That added up to Beethoven. "Prepare for launch," the year-captain announced, over the music. "Shunt minus ten. Nine. Eight." All the old hokum, the ancient stagy stuff, the stirring drama of takeoff. The whole world was watching, yes. The comfortable, happy people of Earth were sending forth the last of their adventurers, a grand exploit indeed, ridding themselves of fifty lively and troubled people in the fond hope that they would somehow replicate the vigor and drive of the human species on some brave new world safely far away. "Six. Five. Four."

His counting was meaningless, of course. The actual work of the launch was being done by hidden mechanisms in some other part of the ship. But he knew the role he was supposed to play.

"Shunt," he said.

Drama in his voice, perhaps, but none in the actuality of the event. There was no special sensation at the moment the stardrive came on, no thrusting, no twisting, nothing that could be felt. But the Earth and Sun disappeared from the screen, to be replaced by an eerie pearly blankness, as the *Wotan* made its giddy leap into a matter-free tube and began its long journey toward an unknown destination.

Someone is standing beside him now, here at the six-month-anniversary celebration. Elizabeth, it is. She puts a glass of wine in his hand.

"The last of the wine, year-captain. Don't miss out." She has obviously already had her share, and then some. " 'Drink! For you know not whence you came, nor why: Drink! For you know not why you go, nor where.' " She is quoting something again, he realizes. Her mind is a warehouse of old poems.

"Is that Shakespeare?" he asks.

"The *Rubaiyat*," she says. "Do you know it? 'Come, fill the cup, and in the fire of spring the winter garment of repentance fling.' " She is very giddy. She rubs up against him, lurching a little, just as he puts the wine to his lips; but he keeps his balance and not a drop is spilled. " 'The bird of time,' " she cries, " 'has but a little way to fly—and lo! The bird is on the wing.' "

Elizabeth staggers, nearly goes sprawling. Quickly the year-captain slips his arm under hers, pulls her up, steadies her. She presses her thin body eagerly against his; she is murmuring things into his ear, not poetry this time but a flow of explicit obscenities, startling and a little funny coming from this bookish unvoluptuous woman. Her slurred words are not entirely easy to make out against the roaring background of the party, but it is quite clear that she is inviting him to her cabin.

"Come," he says, as she weaves muzzily about, trying to get into position for a kiss. He grips her tightly, propelling her forward, and cuts a path across the room to Heinz, who is pouring somebody else's discarded drink into his glass with the total concentration of an alchemist about to produce gold from lead. "I think she's had just a little too much," the year-captain tells him, and smoothly hands Elizabeth over to him.

Just beyond him is Noelle, quiet, alone, an island of serenity in the tumult. The year-captain wonders if she is telling her sister about the party.

Astonishingly, she seems aware that someone is approaching her. She turns to face him as he comes up next to her.

"How are you doing?" he asks her. "Everything all right?"

"Fine. Fine. It's a wonderful party, isn't it, year-captain?"

"Marvelous," he says. He stares shamelessly at her. She seems to have overcome yesterday's fatigue; she is beautiful again. But her beauty, he decides, is like the beauty of a flawless marble statue in some museum of Greek antiquities. One admires it; one does not necessarily want to embrace it. "It's hard to believe that six months have gone by so fast, isn't it?" he asks, wanting to say something and unable to find anything less fatuous to offer.

Noelle makes no reply, simply smiles up at him in that impersonal way of hers, as though she has already gone back to whatever conversation with her distant sister he has in all probability interrupted. She is an eternal mystery to him. He studies her lovely unreadable face a moment more; then he moves away from her without a further word. She will know, somehow, that he is no longer standing by her side.

There is trouble again in the transmission the next day. When Noelle makes the morning report, Yvonne complains that the signal is coming through indistinctly and noisily. But Noelle, telling this to the year-captain, does not seem as distraught as she had been over the first episode of fuzzy transmission. Evidently she has decided that the noise is some sort of local phenomenon, an artifact of this particular sector of nospace—something like a sunspot effect, maybe—and will vanish once they have moved farther from the source of the disturbance.

Perhaps so. The year-captain isn't as confident of that as she seems to be. But she probably has a better understanding of such things than he has. In any event, he is pleased to see her cheerful and serene again.

What courage it must have taken for her to agree to go along on this voyage!

He sometimes tries to put himself in her place. Consider your situation carefully, he thinks, pretending that he is Noelle. You are twenty-six years old, female, sightless. You have never married or even entered into a basic relationship. Throughout your life your only real human contact has been with your twin sister, who is, like yourself, blind and single.

R O B E R T   S I L V E R B E R G

Her mind is fully open to yours. Yours is to hers. You and she are two halves of one soul, inexplicably embedded in separate bodies. With her, only with her, do you feel complete. And now you are asked to take part in a voyage to the stars without her—a voyage that is sure to cut you off from her forever, at least in a physical sense.

You are told that if you leave Earth aboard the starship, there is no chance that you will ever see your sister again. Nor do you have any assurance that your mind and hers will be able to maintain their rapport once you are aloft.

You are also told that your presence is important to the success of the voyage, for without your participation it would take decades or even centuries for news of the starship to reach Earth, but if you are aboard—and if, *if*, contact with Yvonne can be maintained across interstellar distances, which is not something that you can know in advance—it will be possible for the voyagers to maintain instantaneous communication with Earth, no matter how far into the galaxy they journey.

The others who undertake to sail the sea of stars aboard the *Wotan* will be making painful sacrifices too, you know. You understand that everyone on board the ship will be leaving loved ones behind: mothers and fathers, perhaps, or brothers and sisters, certainly friends, lovers. There will be no one in the *Wotan*'s complement who does not have some Earthbound tie that will have to be severed forever. But your case is special, is it not, Noelle? To put it more precisely, your case is unique. Your sister is your other self. You will be leaving part of yourself behind.

What should you do, Noelle?

Consider. Consider.

You consider. And you agree to go, of course. You are

needed: how can you refuse? As for your sister, you will naturally lose the opportunity to touch her, to hold her close, to
derive direct comfort from the simple fact of her physical
presence. You will be giving that up forever. But is that really
so significant? They say you must understand that you will
never "see" her again, but that's not true at all. Seeing is not
the issue. You can "see" Yvonne just as well, certainly, from a
distance of a million light-years as you can from the next
room. There can be no doubt of that. If contact can be maintained between them at two or three continents' distance—and
it has—then it can be maintained from one end of the universe
to another. You are certain of that. You have a desperate need
to be certain of that.

You consult Yvonne. Yvonne tells you what you are
hoping to hear.

*Go, love. This is something that has to be done. And everything
will work out the right way.*

Yes. Yes. Everything will work out. They agree on that.
And so Noelle, with scarcely a moment's hesitation, tells them
that she is willing to undertake the voyage.

There was no way, really, that she could have known
that it would work. The only thing that mattered to her, her
relationship with her sister, would be at risk. How could she
have taken the terrible gamble?

But she had. And she had been right, until now. Until
now. And what is happening now? the year-captain wonders.
Is the link really breaking? What will happen to Noelle, he
asks himself, if she loses contact with her sister?

For a moment, right at the beginning, sitting in her cabin aboard the *Wotan* as it lay parked in orbit above the Earth with launch only an hour or two away, Noelle had given some thought to such matters too, and in that moment she had nearly let herself be overwhelmed by panic. It seemed inconceivable to her, suddenly, that she would really be able to maintain contact with her sister across the vast span of interstellar space. And she could not imagine what life would be like for her in the absence of Yvonne. A sword suddenly descending, cutting the thread that had bound them since the moment of their birth, and even before. And then that dreadful silence — that awful unthinkable isolation — she was astonished, suddenly, that she had ever exposed herself to the possibility that such a thing might happen.

What am I doing here? Where am I? Get out of this place, idiot! Run, home, home to Yvonne!

Wild fear swept her like fire in a parched forest. She trembled, and the trembling turned into an anguished shaking, and she clasped her arms around her shoulders and doubled over, sick, miserably frightened, gasping in terror. But then, somehow, some measure of calmness returned. She closed her eyes—that always helped—took deep breaths, compelled herself to unfold her clasped arms and stand straight, forced the knotted muscles of her shoulders and back to uncoil. It would all work out, she told herself fiercely. It would. It would. Yvonne would be there after the shunt just as before.

It was time to go back to the lounge. The captain was going to make a speech to the assembled crew just before the launch itself. Coolly Noelle moved through the corridors of the ship, touching this, stroking that, drawing its strange sterile air deep into her lungs so that she would begin to feel native to it, familiarizing herself with textures and smells and highly local patterns of coolness or warmth. She had already been aboard twice before, during the indoctrination sessions. They had built the starship up here in space, for it was a flimsy thing and could not be subjected to the traumas of the acceleration needed to lift it out of a planetary gravitational field. For months, years, hordes of mass-drivers had come chugging up from bases on the Moon, hauling tons of prefabricated matériel as the great job of weaving and spinning went on and on. And gradually the members of the crew had been chosen, brought together here, shown their way around the strange-looking vessel that would contain their lives, perhaps, until the end of their days.

Yvonne will still be there once we have set out, she told herself. Why should the link fail?

There was no reason to think that it would; but none to think that it would necessarily hold, either. She and Yvonne were something new under the sun. No body of experimental study existed to cover the case of telepathic twin sisters separated by a span of dozens of light-years. Noelle had nothing but faith to support her belief that the power that joined their

ROBERT SILVERBERG

minds was wholly unaffected by distance, but her faith had been secure up till that moment of sudden panic just now. She and Yvonne had often spoken to each other from opposite sides of the planet without difficulty, had they not?

Yes. Yes. But would it be so simple when they were half a galaxy apart?

The last hours before departure time were ticking down. The ship was full of people, not all of them actual members of the crew. Noelle felt their presences all around her: men, a lot of them, deep voices, a special sharpness to their sweat. Some women too. The rustle of different kinds of garments, thin robes, crisp blouses, the clink of jewelry. Everybody tense: she could smell it, a sharpness in the air. She could hear it in the subliminal hesitations of their voices.

Well, why not be tense? Switches would be thrown and incomprehensible forces would come into play and the starship would vanish with all hands into nowhere.

There had been test voyages, of course. This project was almost a century old. The unmanned nospace ships, first, going out on short journeys into absolute strangeness and successfully sending radio messages back, which arrived after the obligatory interval that radio transmission imposes. And then two manned journeys into interstellar space, small ships carrying unimaginably courageous volunteers—the *Columbus* and the *Ultima Thule,* names out of antiquity given new gloss. The *Columbus* had traveled eleven light-months, the *Ultima Thule* fourteen; and both had returned safely. The second of those voyages had been carried out seven years ago. Members of its crew had spoken to them, trying to explain what nospace travel would feel like to them. No one had grasped anything of what they were saying, least of all Noelle.

Now the *Wotan*—more ancient mythology, a ship

named for some shaggy savage indomitable headstrong god of the northern forests—was ready to go. And am I? Noelle wondered. Am I?

Final speeches. Much orotund noise. Drums and trumpets. The exit of the high governmental officials who had come aboard to see them off. The year-captain—they had elected him yesterday, the dour Scandinavian man with the wonderfully musical voice—telling them to prepare themselves for departure, by which he meant, apparently, to say any sort of prayers that they might find meaningful, or at least to do whatever it was they did to compose their minds as they prepared to make the irrevocable transition from one life to another.

—*Yvonne? Do you hear me?*
—*Of course I do.*
—*We're about to get going.*
—*I know. I know.*

There was no sensation of acceleration. Why should there be? This was no shuttle ride from Earth to the Moon, or to some satellite world. There was no propulsive engine aboard other than the relatively insignificant braking motor to be used when they reached their destination; no thrust was being applied; none of the conventional patterns of acceleration were being established. Some sort of drive mechanism was at work in the bowels of the ship, yes; some sort of forces was being generated; some kind of movement was taking place. But not Newtonian, not in any way Einsteinian. The movement was from space to nospace, where relativity did not apply. Mass, inertia, acceleration, velocity—they were irrelevant concepts here. One moment they had been hanging in midspace only a few thousand kilometers above the face of the Earth, and in the next they were floating, silent as a comet,

ROBERT SILVERBERG

through a tube in a folded and pleated alternative universe that ran adjacent to and interlineated with the experiential universe of stars and planets, of mass and force and gravitation and inertia, of photons and electrons and neutrinos and quarks, of earth, air, fire, and water. Caught up in some unthinkable flux, hurled with unimaginable swiftness through an utter empty darkness a thousand times blacker than the darkness in which she had spent her whole life.

It had happened, yes. Noelle had no doubt of it. There had been an instant in which she seemed to be at the brink of an infinite abyss. And then she knew she was in nospace. Something had happened; something had changed. But it was unquantifiable and altogether undefinable. Forces beyond her comprehension, powered by mysterious energies that spanned the cosmos from rib to rib, had come abruptly into play, hurling the *Wotan* smoothly and swiftly from the experiential universe, the universe of space and time and matter, into this other place. She knew it had happened. But she had no idea how she knew that she knew.

—*Yvonne? Can you hear me now, Yvonne?*

The reply came right away, with utter instantaneity. Not even time for a moment of terror. There was Yvonne, immediately, comfortingly:

—*I hear you, yes.*

The signal was pure and clear and sharp. And so it remained, day after day.

Throughout the strange early hours of the voyage Noelle and Yvonne were rarely out of contact with each other for more than a moment, and there was no perceptible falling off of reception as the starship headed outward. They might have been no farther from each other than in adjacent rooms. Past the orbital distance of the Moon, past the million-kilometer mark, past the orbital distance of Mars: everything stayed clear and sharp, clear and sharp. The sisters had passed the first test: clarity of signal was not a quantitative function of distance, apparently.

But—so it had been explained to them—the ship at this point was still traveling at sublight velocity. It took time, even in nospace, to build up to full speed. The process of nospace acceleration—qualitatively different, *conceptually* different, from anything that anyone understood as acceleration in normal space, but a kind of acceleration all the same—was a gradual one. They would not reach the speed of light for several days.

The speed of light! Magical barrier! Noelle had heard so much about it: the limiting velocity, the borderline between the known and the unknown. What would happen to the bond between them, once the *Wotan* was on the far side of it? Noelle had no real idea. Already she was in a space apart from Yvonne, and still could feel her tangible presence: that much was immensely reassuring. But when the starship had crossed into that realm where even a photon was forbidden to go? What then, what then? No one had discussed these things with her. She scarcely understood them. But she had always heard that traveling faster than light involved paradox, mystery, strangeness. There was an element of the forbidden about it. *It was against the law.*

That terrible tension rose in her all over again. One more test—the final one, she hoped—was approaching. She had never known such fear. As they entered the superluminal universe it might become impossible for her mind to reach back across that barrier to find Yvonne's. Who could say? She had never traveled faster than light before. Once more she contemplated the possibility of an existence without Yvonne.

ROBERT SILVERBERG

She had never known a lonely moment in her life. But now — now —

And again her fears were proven needless. Somewhere during the day they reached the sinister barrier, and the starship went on through it without even the formality of an announcement. They had, after all, been outside Einsteinian space since the first moment of the voyage; why, then, take notice of a violation of the traffic laws of another universe, when they were here, already safely journeying across no-space?

Someone told her, later in the day, that they were moving faster than light now.

Her awareness of Yvonne's presence within her had not flickered at all.

—It's happened, she told her sister. *Here we are, wherever that is.*

And swiftly as ever came Yvonne's response, a cheery greeting from the old continuum. Clear and sharp, clear and sharp. Nor did the signal grow more tenuous in the weeks that followed. Clear and sharp, clear and sharp. Until the first static set in.

Hesper is in his element. The year-captain has called a general meeting of the crew, and Hesper will lecture them on his newest findings and conclusions. The year-captain has resolved to make his move. He will declare that Hesper has identified a world that holds potential for settlement—several, as a matter of fact—and that they will immediately begin to direct their course toward the most promising of them with the intention of carrying out an exploratory landing.

Large as the *Wotan* is, and it is very large indeed as spaceships go, there is no chamber aboard the ship big enough to contain all fifty voyagers at the same time. The general meeting is held in the great central corridor on the uppermost deck, spilling outward from the gaming lounge. People sprawl, lean, cling to the rungs on the sides of the walls.

Hesper, standing before them with his arms folded cockily, flashes the brightest of grins, first-magnitude stuff, and says, "The galaxy is full of worlds. This is no secret. However, we ourselves have certain limitations of form that require us to find a world of appropriate mass, appropriate orbital distance from its sun, appropriate atmospheric mix, appropriate—"

"Get on with it," Sieglinde calls. She is famous for her impatience, a brawny, heavy-breasted woman with close-cropped honey-colored hair and a brusque, incisive manner. "We know all this stuff."

Hesper's brilliant grin vanishes instantly. The little man glowers at her.

"For you," he says, "I have found just the right planet. It is something like Jupiter, but really *large*, and it has a mean temperature of six thousand degrees Kelvin at its surface, beneath fifty thousand kilometers of corrosive gases. Will this be satisfactory? As for the rest of us—"

Sieglinde continues to mutter, but Hesper will not be turned from his path. Relentlessly he reminds everyone once again that the sort of world they need to find is the sort of world that they would be capable of living on. Hesper spells this tautological platitude out in terms of temperature, gravitational pull, atmospheric composition, solar luminosity, and all the obvious rest, and then he asks if there are any questions. Sieglinde says something uncomplimentary-sounding in German; Zena nudges her and tells her to hush; the others remain silent.

"Very well," Hesper says. "Let me show you now what I have found."

He touches switches and conjures up virtual images at the far end of the corridor, where the beams of a communicator node intersect.

Hesper tells them that what they see is a star and a solar system. Hesper's star seems not to have a name, only an eight-digit catalog number. So evidently it hadn't ever registered on the consciousnesses of those old Arab astronomers who had given Rigel and Mizar and Aldebaran and all those other stars such lovely poetic designations, somewhere back a thousand or two years ago. All it has is a number. But it has planets. Six of them.

"This is Planet A," he announces. The assembled voyagers behold a small bright dot of light with six lesser dots arrayed in orbits around it. He explains that this is merely the decoding of a reality-analog, not in any way an actual telescopic image. But it is a reliable decoding, he assures everyone. The instruments with which he pierces the veil of the nospace tube are as accurate as any telescope. "Main sequence sun, type G2. Type G and perhaps Type K are the only acceptable stars for us, of course. This is a yellow-orange sun, G2, not uncomfortably different in luminosity from our own. I call your attention to the fourth planet." A small gesture of a finger: one of the six small dots expands until it fills the visual field. Now it is a globe, green faintly banded with blue and red and brown, dabs of white above and below. It has a cheerily familiar look. "Here we see it, not a direct image, of course, but an enhanced transformation of the data. Its diameter, by all indications, is Earthlike. Its distance from its primary is such that small ice caps are present at the poles. The spectral reading indicates a strong dip in brightness at 0.76 micron, which is a wavelength at which molecular oxygen absorbs radiation. Nitrogen is also present—somewhat overabundantly, in truth, but not seriously so. The temperature range seems to be within human tolerability. Also we have indications of the presence of water, and the distance of this world from its primary is such that water would be capable of existing on its surface. Now, notice also the sharp absorption band at the far red end of the visible spectrum—0.7 micron, approximately. Green light is reflected, red and blue are absorbed. This is a characteristic of chlorophyll."

"So what time do we land?" Paco calls out.

Unperturbed, Hesper continues blandly: "We note also the minute presence of methane, one part in 1.5 million. That is not much methane, but why is there any? Methane rapidly oxidizes into water and carbon dioxide. If this atmosphere were in equilibrium, all the methane would have been gone long ago. Therefore we must not have an equilibrium here, do you see? Something is generating new methane to replace that which is oxidized. Ongoing metabolic processes, perhaps? The presence of bacteria, or larger organisms? Life, anyway, of one sort or another. Every indication thus far points toward viability."

"And if the place is already inhabited?" asks Heinz. "What if they don't want to sell us any real estate?"

"We would not, of course, intrude on a planet that has intelligent life of its own. But that can readily be determined while we are still at a distance. The emission of modulated radio waves, or even the visual signs of occupation —"

"How far is this place from our present location?" Sylvia wants to know.

Hesper looks puzzled. He spreads the fingers of his precise little hands and glances uncomfortably toward the year-captain.

The year-captain says, "There's no easy way of answering that. While we're in nospace we don't have spatial coordinates relating to anything but Earth."

"In relation to Earth, then," Sylvia says.

"About ninety-five light-years," Hesper tells her.

There is murmuring in the corridor. "Ninety-five light-years" is a phrase that carries the weight of serious distance.

"We should be able to reach it," says the year-captain, making a quick and probably slightly hazy estimate, "in about seven months."

Hesper says, "The other prime prospect, Planet B, which is eighty-six light-years from Earth, has similar characteristics, although with perhaps keener indications of the presence of organic molecules." A new virtual pattern springs into the air in the hallways, eleven pips of light clustered about their bright little star. He begins to speak once more of spectral lines, insolation levels, temperature gradients, probable size and gravitational pull, electromagnetic emissions, and all the other criteria they must consider.

Somebody cautiously asks if they have enough information to make a decision about a landing.

The year-captain says they do. Enough to allow him to recommend a reconnaissance mission, at any rate. And what they don't know now, they will be able to learn by sending down drone surveillance vehicles before deciding whether to undertake an actual manned exploration. But first they must agree to take the steps that will bring them out of nospace and carry them to the vicinity of the designated world. There are certain risks in that; there will be risks every time they move from nospace to normal space or back again. But those are risks that must be taken.

He calls for the motion. He proposes a survey of Hesper's Planet A; and if A proves unsuitable, a look at Planet B.

No one is opposed. They have come out here, after all, to find a place to live.

Playing *Go* seems to ease the tensions of Noelle's situation. She has been playing daily for weeks now, as addicted to the game as any of them, and by now she has become astonishingly expert at it.

The year-captain was her first opponent. Because he had not played in years he was rusty at first, but within minutes the old associations returned and he found himself setting up chains of stones with skill. Although he had expected her to play poorly, unable to remember the patterns on the board after the first few moves, she proved to have no difficulty keeping the entire array on her mind. Only in one respect had she overestimated herself: for all her precision of coordination, she was unable to place the stones exactly, tending rather to disturb the stones already on the board as she made her moves. After a while she admitted failure and henceforth she would call out the plays she desired—M17, Q6, P6, R4, C11—and he would place the stones for her. In the beginning he played unaggressively, assuming that as a novice she would be haphazard and weak, but soon he discovered that she was adroitly expanding and protecting her territory while pressing a sharp attack against his, and he began to devise more cunning strategies. They played for two hours and he won by sixteen points, a comfortable margin but nothing to boast about, considering that the year-captain was an experienced and adept player and that this was her first game.

The others were skeptical of her instant ability. "Sure she plays well," Paco muttered. "She's reading your mind, isn't she? She can see the board through your eyes and she knows what you're planning."

"The only mind open to her is her sister's," the year-captain said vehemently.

"How can you be sure she's telling the truth about that?"

The year-captain scowled. "Play a game with her yourself. That ought to tell you whether it's skill or mind reading that's at work."

Paco, looking sullen, agreed. That evening he challenged Noelle to a game; and later he came to the year-captain looking abashed. "She plays very well. She almost beat me, and she did it fairly."

The year-captain played a second game with her. She sat almost motionless, eyes closed, lips compressed, calling out the coordinates of her moves in a quiet steady monotone, like some sort of clever automaton, a mechanical game-playing device. She rarely needed much time to decide on her moves and she made no blunders that had to be retracted. Her capacity to devise game patterns had grown with incredible swiftness just in those first few days: no more than thirty minutes into the game he found that she had him nearly shut off from the center, but he recovered the initiative and managed a narrow victory. Afterward she lost once more to Paco and then to Heinz, but again she displayed an increase of ability, and in the evening she defeated Chang, a respected player. Now she became invincible. Undertaking two or three matches every day, she triumphed over Leon, Elliot, the year-captain, and Sylvia. *Go* had become something immense to her, something more than a mere game or a simple test of mental agility. She focused her energy on the board so intensely that her playing approached the level of a religious discipline, a kind of meditation. On her fourth day of play she defeated Roy, the ship's reigning champion, with such economy that everyone was dazzled. Roy could speak of nothing else that evening. He demanded a rematch and was defeated again.

And now she plays almost all the time. She sits within a luminous sphere of Noelleness, a strange otherworldly creature lit by that eerie inner glow of hers, and finds some kind of deep and abiding peace in a universe of black and white stones.

So it is decided. We are to make our first planetary visit. The first of how many, I wonder, before we discover our new home? Will we find a world on this first attempt that's almost good enough but perhaps has one or two more or less serious drawbacks, and will that cause us to get embroiled in a long, dreary battle over whether to stay or leave? We don't want to pick a place that doesn't really work, of course. But what's our definition of a place that works? A planet that's 99.77 percent identical to Earth?

ROBERT SILVERBERG

Blue skies, fleecy clouds, green forests, easy gravitation, a pleasant climate, ripe and nicely edible fruit on every vine, lots of easily domesticated useful animals close at hand? We aren't going to find a place like that. If we hold out for a perfect simulacrum of Earth, we're going to be roaming the galaxy for the next fifty thousand years.

What we're going to have to settle for is some place that's 93 percent Earthlike, or 87 percent, or maybe only 74 percent. Obviously we need an oxygen-based atmosphere and plenty of available water, and we aren't going to be able to manage if the biochemistry of the place is pure poison to our systems, or if the gravitation is so strong that we can't take a step without falling on our noses. But we will need to understand that wherever we settle, we're going to have to make changes in the environmental conditions to the limit of our ability to effect them, and probably we're also going to have to make significant genetic changes in ourselves to the point where there's likely to be some serious debate over whether our children can really be considered human.

Will people be willing to settle for a planet like that on the first or second or even tenth try? Or will they vote again and again to reject what we find and look elsewhere for something a little better? We can waste our entire lives looking for the perfect world, or even the almost perfect one.

An autocratic year-captain could force them to settle for the first plausible-looking planet we find, simply by decree. But the year-captain isn't supposed to be that kind of an autocrat. And in any case I'm not going to be year-captain, am I, by the time we reach Planet A. My year will be up. They could reelect me, I suppose, if I agreed, and then I could do whatever was within my powers to influence our decision about where we found our colony. But if I want to be part of the landing team, somebody else has to be elected captain. And I do want to be part of the landing team. I can't have it both ways.

Who will succeed me? Heinz? Roy? Sieglinde? I don't immedi-

ately see an ideal candidate. That makes me uncomfortable. And anything at all can happen once this collection of prima donnas starts to vote, which makes me feel even more troubled about the whole idea of handing the job over to someone else.

One other thing to consider. Are we really going to be able to jump in and out of nospace with the greatest of ease? This is experimental equipment we're flying here. We aren't entirely sure about its stress tolerance. It may have plenty of surprises waiting for us. Apparently there's a mathematical angle too, which has only now begun to surface in something I heard Sieglinde and Roy discussing. The stardrive, it seems, is governed by probabilistic phenomena that aren't fully understood, that in fact are scarcely understood at all. Whenever we make a jump in or out of nospace there's a small but distinct possibility that the ship will do something completely unexpected. It might just happen on any given shunt that something critical will have gone awry that is beyond our capacity to correct, and we won't be able to make the equipment work any more, so that we wind up stuck wherever we happen to be, whether that's in nospace or out of it. Come to think of it, we might find that the first time we try to get back into normal space we simply can't do it.

That's quite a screed of worries, for one little journal entry. But it's of some therapeutic value, I suppose, to set all this stuff down. In actuality I'll deal with all of these problems the way I deal with everything, tackling them one at a time in the appropriate order. No need to worry about our rejecting a nearly suitable world until we've found one. No need to worry about whether the shunt mechanism will fail until it does. As for choosing the next year-captain, I ought to trust to the common sense and good judgment of my companions, instead of fretting about my own supposed indispensability and the likelihood that they will replace me with some clown.

What matters right now is simply to locate Planet A in some kind of Einsteinian-universe coordinates, get ourselves as close as we

R O B E R T   S I L V E R B E R G

can to it before we leave nospace, and shunt back into the real continuum within easy exploring range of Planet A's star's solar system.

We're supposed to know how to do that. If we can't manage it,
none of the other problems are going to be very important.

And so we get started on the grand quest. I don't seriously
believe we're going to find our New Earth on the very first try. Still,
nothing ventured, nothing gained. And there's a chance—small, but
real—that we'll find what we need right away. Both of these two
planets look as though they just may be the real thing, insofar as we
can tell very much about that at these distances and with the scanning
equipment at our disposal. What we have to do now is go out and take
a close look.

The morning transmission. Noelle, sitting with her
back to the year-captain, listens to what he reads her
and sends it coursing over a gap that now spans
more than twenty light-years. "Wait," she says. "Yvonne is
calling for a repeat. From 'metabolic.'"

He pauses, goes back, reads again:

"Metabolic balances remain normal, although, as earlier re-
ported, some of the older members of the expedition have begun to show
trace deficiencies of manganese and potassium. We are, of course,
taking appropriate corrective steps, and—"

Noelle halts him with a brusque gesture. The year-
captain waits. She bends forward, forehead against the table,
hands pressed tightly to her temples.

"Static again," she says. "It's worse than ever today."

"Are you getting through at all?"

"I'm getting through, yes. But I have to push, to push, push. And still Yvonne asks me for repeats." She lifts her head and stares at him, her eyes locking on his in that weird intuitive way of hers. Her face is taut with tension. Her forehead is furrowed, and it glistens with a bright film of sweat. The year-captain wants to reach out to her, to hold her, to comfort her. She says huskily, "I don't know what's happening, year-captain."

"The distance—"

"No!"

"Better than twenty light-years."

"No," she says again, a little less explosively this time. "We've already demonstrated that distance effects aren't a factor. If there's no falling off of signal after a million kilometers, after one light-year, after ten light-years—no measurable drop in clarity and accuracy whatever—then there shouldn't be any qualitative diminution suddenly at any greater distance. Don't you think I've thought about this?"

"Of course you have, Noelle."

"It's not as if we're getting out of earshot of each other. We were in perfect contact at ten light-years, perfect at fifteen. Those are already immense distances. If we could manage that, we ought to be able to manage at any distance at all."

"But still, Noelle—"

"Attenuation of signal is one thing, and interference is another. An attenuation curve is a gradual slope. Remember, Yvonne and I have had complete and undistorted mental access from the moment we left Earth until just a short while ago. And now—no, year-captain, it can't be attenuation. This has to be some sort of interference. A purely local effect that we're encountering in this region of the galaxy."

"Yes, like sunspots, I know. Perhaps when we head out for Planet A, things will clear up."

"Perhaps," Noelle says crisply. "Let's start again, shall we, year-captain? Yvonne's calling for signal. Go on from *'manganese and potassium.'*"

"—manganese and potassium. We are taking appropriate corrective steps—"

T he year-captain visualizes the contact between the two sisters as an arrow whistling from star to star, as fire speeding through a shining tube, as a river of pure force coursing down a celestial wave guide. He sees the joining of those two minds as a stream of pure light binding the moving ship to the far-off mother world. Sometimes he dreams of them both, Yvonne and Noelle, Noelle and Yvonne, standing facing each other across the cosmos with their hands upraised and light streaming from their fingertips, and the glowing bond that stretches across the galaxy between the two sisters gives off so brilliant a radiance that he stirs and moans and presses his forehead into the pillow.

✳️ I have a funny idea," Sieglinde says, and everyone looks up, for Sieglinde is not noted for funny ideas. Nor is there anything at all comic in the unusually thin, high, strained tone in which she is speaking now. But something has been building up in her for the past half hour, and now it comes erupting forth. "What if we throw the switch and the ship doesn't want to come out of nospace?" she asks. "What if we find that we simply can't reach this Planet A, or any other realspace destination? What do we do then? Do we have a fallback plan?"

This is the first brainstorming session for the group that is planning the change of course. They are meeting in the control cabin. Intelligence readouts embedded in the curved wall glow all around them, soft emanations of pulsing light, amethyst and amber and jade. Sieglinde and Roy and Heinz and Paco and Julia and the year-captain have been talking for two hours straight and they are all getting tired and a little silly now.

"If that happens, then we find a nice nospace planet

somewhere and we settle down there instead," Paco answers. "That's our fallback plan."

Roy gives him a glowering stare. "What you say is absurd and irrelevant. There aren't any nospace planets. Such a thing is a logical impossibil—"

Heinz, smiling as always but displaying an edge of controlled annoyance, says to Sieglinde, "Why do you even ask these things? This is a meeting to discuss a survey mission into realspace. You're conjuring up imaginary demons for us. The stardrive wasn't designed to fail. It will not fail."

"And if it does?" Sieglinde asks.

"Heinz is right," says the year-captain wearily. "It won't fail. It simply won't. You can count on that."

"I count on nothing," Sieglinde says, speaking in a throaty mock-dramatic way. Maybe she *is* trying to be funny. But her eyes are strangely bright. She seems possessed by some powerful contrary energy that will not relent. "Anything may happen. We are dealing with tremendous physical forces and we still have relatively little experience with this equipment. And we work with stochastic processes here. Do you understand what I am saying? Each jump we make is in effect a gamble. The odds are in our favor each time, of course. But with each jump there is always the possibility of the random event, whenever the stardrive is changed from one state to another. It is here in the equations: the random factor, the fatal probability. The more often we jump, the more often we expose ourselves to that small but real probability. And on one of our jumps we may leap from one nospace to another instead of returning to realspace, or experience something even worse. It is possible."

"Not highly probable, though," says Heinz. "The odds favor us, you say."

"Not highly probable, no, but possible, distinctly possible, and what is possible is worth a little thought when that possibility can be fatal to our endeavor. You are an engineer, Heinz; you deal in tangible things, in absolute concepts of what works and what does not. I am a mathematician. We are more poetic than you, do you understand me? I deal in axioms and certainties; but I also know that beneath the axioms lie only assumptions, and beneath the assumptions lies—chaos!"

"Rely on faith, then, if you can't trust your own equations," says the year-captain. "We all took a leap into the dark when we signed on. If you didn't think the drive would work properly, you should have stayed home."

"I say only that there is a finite chance that it will not."

"And therefore—?"

"And therefore, as I have just said, the more jumps we make, the greater the likelihood that one of them will be a bad one. And so I argue that we ought not to make any shunt that is not absolutely necessary. By which I mean that we should not attempt a realspace reentry without complete assurance that the world we have picked is likely to be a place where we'll want to settle, because the risk of moving from one reality state to another is so great that we will want to attempt it only when there is a high order of probability that the risk is worth taking."

Paco says, in what is for him an uncharacteristically subdued and thoughtful tone, "You know, there's something to that. The odds that any given Earth-size planet has anything like Earthlike living conditions are—what? A hundred to one against? So we may find ourselves having to make a hundred jumps, five hundred, a thousand, if we don't get lucky right away. Which multiplies the shunt risks enormously, if I follow Sieglinde correctly. If there's any real likelihood that the drive might fail, we ought to be damned sure ahead of time that whatever place we're jumping to is—"

Julia, who has the actual responsibility for operating the nospace drive, says irritably, "This is a stupid conversation, and we're not supposed to be stupid people. Why are we even discussing this? There's been a vote and we're going to take a look at Planet A, because we have good reason to believe that it's the sort of place that we came out here to find, as far as we can tell without actually getting up close to it and taking a good look, and that's all there is to it. Heinz is right. Sieglinde is pulling demons out of nowhere. When we make our next shunt, the stardrive will behave exactly as we want it to behave, and you all know it. And even if there's some slight mathematical risk hanging on each jump, we've already reached agreement that Planet A is a place worth taking risks to find. Our job is to find the way to Planet A, not to debate hypothetical nightmare scenarios."

"Yes, we are not stupid," says Heinz. "But we are restless. We live in a confined place and we think too much. And if we think long enough, eventually we begin to think stupidly. Enough of this, Sieglinde. We will never find any place to live at all, if we are too terrified of these probability problems to undertake even a single survey mission. You knew all this when we set out. Why did you wait until now to say anything? If somebody else had raised this string of last-minute objections while you were trying to get on with the work at hand, you'd be trying to cut off his head by now." He turns to the year-captain. "Rule her out of order, will you? And then let's adjourn."

"What do you say, Sieglinde?" the year-captain asks. "Can we drop this, please?"

The big woman shrugs. The manic force has gone out

of her as suddenly as it came. She has made her little bit of
trouble and is ready to relent. She looks tired and defeated,
and to the year-captain's relief she seems as ready to be done
with this as the rest of them. The point she has raised is a
troublesome one, but, as Heinz has observed, this is not the
moment to be discussing it. And in an almost toneless voice
Sieglinde says, "Whatever you want, captain. Whatever you
want."

Until now the starship, in the absence of any specific
destination, has been following an essentially undi-
rected path through the nospace tube, simply traveling away from Earth rather than toward some particular
star. Its course, such as it is, has been chosen to carry it into
one of the more densely populated areas of the immediate
sector of the celestial sphere in which Earth's sun is located;
but the intent of the planners of the voyage was that the
voyagers would at some point redirect the ship toward a star
they would choose themselves on the basis of planetary data
collected in the course of the journey.

Now that time has arrived. The *Wotan* must swing its
course through nospace toward the star that is the primary of
Zed Hesper's Planet A; and when it has reached the vicinity of
that star, it must break itself out of the nospace tube in which
it has been traveling and return to the Einsteinian continuum,
so that surveillance of Planet A may be carried out by ordinary spacefaring methods, an orbital circuit in a probe ship,
direct visual inspection, and then perhaps an actual landing if

ROBERT SILVERBERG

the survey of surface conditions from nearby is in any way encouraging.

Nospace travel is a fundamentally nonlinear phenomenon. If you propose to make a surface journey between two cities on Earth that are three thousand kilometers apart—Los Angeles and Montreal, let us say—you will expect to cover a distance of three thousand kilometers during the course of the trip, no more, no less, and the elapsed time of the journey will be a function of the average time it takes to cover *one* kilometer, multiplied by three thousand. There are no shortcuts; there are no exceptions to the rule that one must travel a distance of three thousand kilometers in order to make a journey of three thousand kilometers. Not so in nospace. Linear measurements applicable in the classical continuum have no meaning there. Spatial relationships between points in the universe that have been determined by conventional means are irrelevant in nospace. Nospace is all shortcuts, nothing *but* shortcuts. In that special space, flattened and curved and doubled and redoubled upon itself as it is, the logic of linear travel is useless and paradoxes abound. Dimensions are collapsed and transformed; the infinite universe is infinitely adjacent to itself; all normal understanding of such concepts as "near" and "far," "here" and "there," "toward" and "away from" must be discarded. In nospace it may be quicker to travel between two stars five hundred light-years apart than between two that are close neighbors. There may—there is at least theoretical basis for the notion—be no clear and consistently calculable relationship between realworld distance between two points and nospace transit time between those points at all.

There are, however, proxies and equivalents. With the aid of appropriate computational power one can plot a set of transformations that will carry one through nospace along quasi-geodetic lines corresponding to actual realspace vectors and allow one actually to reach a preselected destination. At least, so the governing equations of nospace travel demonstrate, and in the brief experimental flights of the *Columbus* and then the *Ultima Thule* those equations were found to hold true.

The *Columbus*, after making a journey of not quite one light-year from Earth in a period of eleven Earth-days, was able successfully to reenter Einsteinian space, accurately measure its distance from its starting point, and, returning to nospace without difficulty, carry out its homeward voyage in the same span of time. The *Ultima Thule*, going in a different direction, found itself a little more than a light-year from home after just nine days: it, too, was able to move out of nospace and back into it and to aim itself satisfactorily toward Earth. Despite Sieglinde's sudden willful skepticism, the year-captain prefers to think that there is every reason to believe that the *Wotan* would have just as little difficulty redirecting itself in nospace in order to head itself toward the Einsteinian location of the star it meant to visit, and then in leaving nospace to execute a survey of the habitability of that star's planet. He understands her point that there is some risk with every shunt and that the more shunts they make, the greater is the number of times they place themselves in jeopardy. But they must find a world where they can live; and for that, the taking of certain risks is unavoidable. She is simply overwrought. He has no regrets about quashing her objection to the survey shunt.

The year-captain, *ex officio*, is the head of the team that will calculate and achieve this maneuver. But he is no expert on such things; the real work of the group will be done by five other crew members. Roy and Sieglinde will handle the mathematical aspects. Paco is the master navigator. Julia programs

ROBERT SILVERBERG

and operates the star drive. Heinz, the ship's designer, is the prime generalist who comprehends all of the specialties of the other members of the team; he will be the interface, the grand communicator, the true captain of the enterprise.

This first meeting of the group has been only a preliminary one. Hesper was there for the beginning of it. He has shown the others where, in normal-space reckoning, the star of Planet A is located, according to the set of correlatives that he has worked out. After Hesper goes, there is much consulting of star-maps and the ship's navigation circuitry. There will be need for much more, before the actual jump is attempted. Ultimately the drive intelligence itself is going to do the real work of getting them there; but the intelligence, clever though it is, is as finite as the minds of its makers. It has only limited ability to compensate for bungled instructions. They must figure out precisely what it is they want to do before they authorize the drive intelligence to do it. Or as precisely as they are able to manage. And then pray. But to whom? And with what hope that their prayers will be heard?

Sieglinde's outburst convinces the year-captain that the meeting has gone on long enough. He keeps them together only a few minutes more, so that he can summarize this day's work and get a consensus vote for the log. Then he adjourns.

Sieglinde is the first to leave, a fraction of a second later, striding from the room without a word, the implacable stride of a Valkyrie. She was poorly named, the year-captain thinks: Brünnhilde should have been her name, not Sieglinde. Paco and Roy go out together, arm in arm, bound for the lounge and their millionth game of *Go*. Julia trails after them.

Heinz alone remains with the year-captain. He stands before him, rocking lightly back and forth on the balls of his feet. "Are you worried?" he asks, after a moment.

The year-captain looks up. "About what?"

"Sieglinde's hypothesis. Drive malfunction."

"No. Not in the slightest. Should I be?"

Heinz smiles oddly, as though he is smiling within his smile. "That drive will take us from one end of the galaxy to another, a thousand times in and out of nospace and no problem. I promise you that."

Their eyes meet for a moment. The year-captain searches them. It is always hard to tell whether Heinz is being sincere. His eyes are blue like the year-captain's, but much more playful, and of an altogether different kind of blueness, a soft sky-blue greatly unlike the fierce ice-blue of the year-captain's. Both men have fair Nordic hair, but again there is a difference, Heinz's being thick and flowing and a burnished glowing gold in color, whereas the year-captain's is stiff and fine and almost silver, not from aging but from simple absence of pigment. They are oddly similar and yet unalike in most other ways too. The year-captain does not regard Heinz as a friend in any real sense of that word; if he were to allow himself friends, which has always been a difficult thing for him, Heinz would probably not be one of them. But there is a certain measure of respect and trust between them.

The year-captain says, after a little while, "Is there something else you want to tell me?"

"To ask, rather."

ROBERT SILVERBERG

"Ask, then."

"I've been wondering if there's some difficulty involving Noelle."

The year-captain takes great care to show no change of expression. "A difficulty? What sort of difficulty?"

"She seems to be under unusual stress these days."

"She is a complicated person in a complicated situation."

"Which is true of us all," Heinz says easily. "Nevertheless, she's seemed different somehow in recent days. There was always a serenity about her—a saintliness, even, if you will allow me that word. I don't see it any more. The change began, I think, about the time she started playing *Go* with us. Her face is so tightly drawn all the time now. Her movements are extremely tense. She plays the game with some sort of weird scary intensity that makes me very uneasy. And she wins all the time."

"You don't like it that she wins?"

"I don't like it that she's so intense about it. Roy used to win all the time too, but that was simply because he was so good that he couldn't help winning. Noelle plays *Go* as if her life depends on it."

"Perhaps it does," the year-captain says.

Heinz shows just a flicker of vexation now at the year-captain's constant conversational parrying. It is a standard trait of the year-captain's, these repetitions—his automatic manner of responding, his default mode—and most people are accustomed to it. It has never seemed to bother Heinz before.

He says, "What I mean, captain, is that I think she may be approaching a breakdown of some sort, and I felt it was important to call that to your attention."

"Thank you."

"She is more high-strung than the rest of us. I would not like to see her in any sort of distress."

"Neither would I, Heinz. You have my assurance of that."

An awkward silence then. At length Heinz says, "If it were possible to find out what's bothering her, and to offer her whatever comfort would be useful—"

"I appreciate your concern," the year-captain says stonily. "Please believe me when I say that I regard Noelle as one of the most important members of the expedition, and I am doing everything in my power to maintain her stability."

"Everything?"

"Everything," the year-captain says, in a way intended unmistakably to close the conversation.

Noelle dreams that her blindness has been taken from her. Sudden light surrounds her, phenomenal white cascades of shimmering brilliance, and she opens her eyes, sits up, looks about in awe and wonder, saying to herself, This is a table, this is a chair, this is how my statuettes look, this is what my sea-urchin shell is like. She is amazed by the beauty of everything in her room. She rises, going forward, stumbling at first, groping, then magically gaining poise and balance, learning how to walk in this new way, judging the positions of things not by echoes and air currents any longer, but rather by the simple miracle of using her eyes. Information floods her. She walks around her room, picking things up, stroking them, matching shapes with actual

appearances, correlating the familiar feel of her objects with
the new data coming to her now through this miraculously
restored extra sense. Then she leaves the cabin and moves
about the ship, discovering the faces of her shipmates. Intuitively she knows who they all are. You are Roy, you are
Sylvia, you are Heinz, you are the year-captain. They look,
surprisingly, very much as she had always imagined them:
Roy fleshy and red-faced, Sylvia fragile, the year-captain lean
and fierce, Heinz handsome and constantly smiling, and so on
and so on, Elliot and Marcus and Chang and Julia and Hesper and Giovanna and the rest, everyone matching expectations. Everyone beautiful. She goes to the window of which all
the others talk, the one that provides a view of nospace, and
looks out into the famous grayness. Yes, yes, the scene
through that window is precisely as they say it is: a cosmos of
wonders, a miracle of complex pulsating tones, level after level
of incandescent reverberation sweeping outward toward the
rim of the boundless universe. There is nothing to see, and
there is everything. For an hour she stands before that dense
burst of rippling energies, giving herself to it and taking it into
herself, and then, and then, just as the ultimate moment of
illumination toward which she has been moving throughout
the entire hour is coming over her, she realizes that something
is wrong. Yvonne is not with her. Noelle reaches out with her
mind and does not touch Yvonne. Again. No. No contact.
Can't find her. She has somehow traded her special power for
the mere gift of sight.

Yvonne? Yvonne?

All is still. Where is Yvonne?

Yvonne is not with her. This is only a dream, Noelle
tells herself, and I will soon awaken from it. But she cannot
awaken. She cries out in terror. And then she feels Yvonne at

last. "It's all right," Yvonne whispers, across the immensities of space and time. "I'm here, love, I'm here, I'm here, just as I always am," comes Yvonne's soft voice, rising out of the great whirlpool of invisible suns. Yes. All is well. Noelle can feel the familiar closeness again. Yvonne is there, right there, beside her. Trembling, Noelle embraces her sister. Looks at her. Beholds her for the first time.

I can see, Yvonne! I can see!

Noelle realizes that in her first rapture of sightedness she had quite forgotten to look at herself, although she had rushed about looking at everything and everyone else. It had not occurred to her. Mirrors have never been part of her world. But now she looks at Yvonne, which is, of course, like looking at herself, and Yvonne is beautiful, her hair dark and silken and lustrous, her face smooth and sleek, her features finely shaped, her eyes—her blind eyes!—alive and sparkling. Noelle tells Yvonne how beautiful she is, and Yvonne smiles and nods, and they laugh and hold one another close, and they begin to weep with pleasure and love, out of the sheer joy of being with each other, and then Noelle awakens, and of course the world is as dark as ever around her.

Heinz goes out, finally. *Finally.*

There are exercises that the year-captain learned in Lofoten, spiritual disciplines designed to restore and maintain tranquillity. He makes use of them now, breathing slowly and deeply, running through each of the routines. And then he runs through them all over again.

ROBERT SILVERBERG

The conversation with Heinz has seemed interminable and has been deeply embarrassing, and it has left the year-captain feeling greatly annoyed, as annoyed as his fundamentally controlled and equable nature will allow him to be. Does Heinz think the year-captain has failed to notice Noelle's disturbed state? Does Heinz think he has failed to care about it? Heinz knows nothing, presumably, of the recent difficulties in communication between the sisters. It is not his business to know about that. But the year-captain knows; the year-captain is aware of the existence of a problem; the year-captain does not need the assistance of Heinz in order to discover that an important member of the expedition is experiencing problems. And in any case, what does Heinz want him to *do* about it? Does he have some suggestion to make, and, if so, why has he not made it? That damnable sly smile of Heinz's seemed always to imply that he was holding something back that would be very useful for you to know, if only he cared to let you in on the secret. It was easy enough to think that there was less behind that smile of his than you might suspect. But was that true?

The year-captain wonders whether everyone aboard, one by one, is about to undergo some maddening transformation for the worse. Already Noelle is losing the ability to communicate with her sister on Earth; the blunt and straightforward Sieglinde has unsettlingly chosen to challenge the reliability of the theorems that she herself helped to write; and now the easygoing and irreverent Heinz is tiresomely eager to explain the year-captain's own responsibilities to him. What next? What next, he wonders?

The year-captain is particularly bothered by Heinz's sudden little burst of pious helpfulness because it has kept him from a badly needed therapeutic engagement of his own. Julia is waiting for him in their secret place of rendezvous in a dark corner of the cargo deck.

Julia and the year-captain are lovers. They have been since the third week of the voyage, after she had extricated herself from her brief and unsatisfying fling with Paco. So far as he knows, no one but he and she are aware of their relationship, such as it is, and he prefers to keep it that way. Among the people of the *Wotan* he has a reputation for asceticism, for a certain monkish ferocity of discipline, and, rightly or wrongly, he has come to feel that this enhances his authority as captain.

The truth is that the year-captain feels the pull of physical desire at least as often as anyone else on board, and has been doing something about it with great regularity, as any sane person would. But he does it secretly. He finds pleasure and amusement in the knowledge that he has managed to maintain a private life within the goldfish bowl that is the ship. There are times when the year-captain feels that he is committing the sin of pride by allowing others to think that he is more ascetic than he really is; at the very least, there is something hypocritical about it, he realizes. He has chosen, however, to lock himself into this pattern of furtive behavior since the beginning of the voyage, and now it seems to him much too late to do anything about changing it. Nor does he really want to, anyway.

So he sets out once more down the corridor to the dropchute, descends to the lower levels, moves with his usual feline grace through the tangle of stored gear that clutters those levels, and, pressing his hand against the identification plate that gives access to the deepest storage areas, steps through the opening hatch into the secret world of the ship's most precious cargo, its bank of genetic material.

ROBERT SILVERBERG

Not many people have Need-to-Enter access to this area coded into the ship's master brain. Chang does—he is the custodian of the *Wotan*'s collection of fertilized and unfertilized reproductive cells—and so does Sylvia, the ship's other genetic specialist. But the expedition is a long way from any point where the birth of children aboard ship would be a desirable thing, and neither of them has reason to come down here very often. Michael, whose primary job is maintenance of all of the ship's internal mechanical functions, is another one who can enter this part of the vessel without the year-captain's specific permission. There are two or three others. But most of the time the unborn and indeed mostly still unconceived future colonists of the as yet undiscovered New Earth sleep peacefully in the stasis of their freezer units, unintruded upon by visitors from above.

Julia is not someone who should be authorized to come to this part of the ship. Her responsibilities center entirely on the functioning of the stardrive, and no element of the stardrive mechanism is located anywhere near here. The year-captain has added her palmprint to the section's Need-to-Enter list for purely personal reasons. He has given her the ability to pass through that hatch because hardly anyone else has it, which makes this an excellent location for their clandestine meetings. The chances of their being disturbed here are very small. And if ever they should be, why would anyone care that the year-captain has illicitly permitted his lover to join him down here? He suspects that his little crime, such as it is, would be taken merely as a welcome indication that he is human, after all.

This is a dark place, lit only by little pips of slave-light that jump into energized states along the illuminator strands set overhead as he passes beneath them, and wink out again when he has gone by. To the right and the left are the cabinets in which germ plasm of various sorts is stored. The plan of the voyage calls for no births aboard ship at all during the first year; then, if it seems desirable in the context of what position the ship has attained and what potential colony-worlds, if any, have been located, births will be authorized to shipboard couples interested in rearing children. There is room on board for up to fifty additional passengers to be born en route. After that, no more until a planetary landing. The stored ova and spermatozoa are to be kept in the cooler until that time as well. A mere twenty-five couples, no matter how often their couplings are rearranged, will not be able to provide sufficient genetic diversity for the peopling of a new world. But all those thousands of stored ova and the myriad sperm cells will be available to vary the genetic mix once the colony has been established.

A single small light illuminates the year-captain's love nest, which is an egg-shaped security node, just barely big enough for two people of reasonable size to embrace in, that separates one of the sectors of freezer cabinets from its array of monitoring devices. The year-captain peers in and sees Julia stretched out casually with her arms folded behind her head and her ankles crossed. Her clothes are stacked in the passageway outside; there is no room in the little security node to get undressed.

"Was there a problem?" she asks.

"Heinz," says the year-captain, wriggling quickly out of his tunic and trousers. "There was something he felt I ought to be told about, so he stayed after the meeting and told me. And told me and told me."

"Something serious?"

"Nothing I didn't already know about," he replies.

ROBERT SILVERBERG

He is naked now. She beckons to him and he crawls in beside her. Julia hisses with pleasure as he curls up around her cool, muscular body. It is an athlete's body, a racer's body, taut-bellied, flat-buttocked, not a gram of excess flesh. Her thighs are long and narrow, her arms slender and strong, with lightly corded veins strikingly prominent along them. She swims an hour each day in the lap-pool on the recreation level. Occasionally the year-captain joins her there, and although he is not unlike her in build, an athlete too, his body hardened and tempered by a lifetime of discipline, he invariably finds himself breathing hard after fifty or sixty turns in the pool, whereas Julia goes on and on without a single break in rhythm for her full hour and when she climbs from the water she seems not to have exerted herself at all.

Their couplings are like athletic events too: dispassionate excursions into passion, measured and controlled expenditures of erotic energy, uncomplicated by emotion. Julia is easy to arouse but slow to reach consummation, and they have evolved a way of embracing and gliding into a steady, easy rocking rhythm that goes on and on, as though they are swimming laps. It is a kind of pleasant, almost conversational kind of copulation that gradually moves through a series of almost unquantifiable upticks in pace, each marking a stage in her approach to the climax, until at last he will detect certain unmistakable terminal signals from her, soft staccato moaning sounds, a sudden burst of sweat-slickness along her shoulders, and he will whip himself onward then to the final frenzied strokes, taking his cues from her at every point and letting go in the ultimate moment, finally, of his own carefully governed self-control.

The year-captain knows that what he and Julia do with one another has nothing to do with love, and he is aware that even sex for the sake of sex itself can be considerably more gratifying than this. But he is indifferent to all of that. Love is not unimportant to him, but he is not interested in finding it just now, and the physical satisfactions he achieves in Julia's arms may fall short of some theoretical ideal but they do serve to keep him tuned and balanced and able to perform his administrative duties well, which is all that he presently seeks.

She is uttering the familiar staccato moans now. His fingertips detect the first onrush of preorgasmic sweatiness emerging from the pores of her upper back.

But a curious thing happens this time. Ordinarily, when he and Julia are making love and they have just reached this point in the event, he invariably topples into a trancelike state in which he no longer feels capable of speech or even thought. His mind goes blank with the sort of shimmering blankness that he learned how to attain in his years at the Lofoten monastery—the same blankness that he sees when he looks through the viewplate at the reverberating nothingness of the nospace tube surrounding the ship. After he has arrived at that point, all his mental processes are suspended except those elementary ones, not much more than tropisms, that are concerned with the mechanics of the carnal act itself.

But today things are different. Today when he reaches the blank point and begins the hectic ride toward their shared culmination, the image of Noelle suddenly bursts into his mind.

He sees her face hovering before him as though in midair: her dark, clear sightless eyes, her delicate nose, her small mouth and elegantly tapering jaw. It is as though she is right here in the cubicle with them, floating not far in front of his nose, watching them, watching with a kind of solemn childlike curiosity. The year-captain is jolted entirely out of his trance.

ROBERT SILVERBERG

He is flooded at this wrongest of moments by a torrent of mysterious conflicting emotions, shame and desire, guilt and joy. He feels his skin flaming with embarrassment at this disconcerting intrusion into the final moments of his embrace of Julia, and he is certain that his sudden confusion must be dismayingly apparent to his partner; but if Julia notices anything unusual, she gives him no hint of that, and merely goes on moving steadily beneath him, eyes closed, lips drawn back in a grimacing smile, hips churning in the steady ever-increasing rhythmic thrusts that carry her closer to her goal.

All the preparations have been carried out and they are ready now to alter the trajectory of the starship so that it will take them toward Hesper's Planet A. What this requires is largely a mathematical operation. Conventional line-of-sight navigation is not a concept that applies in any way to the starship, traveling as it does through space that is both non-Einsteinian and non-Euclidean. The ship, however tangible and substantial it may seem to its tangible and substantial occupants, is in fact nothing more than a flux of probabilities at this point, a Heisenbergian entity at best, not "real" at all in the sense of being subject to the Newtonian laws of action and reaction or any of the other classical concepts of celestial mechanics. Its change of course must be executed by means of equivalences and locational surrogates, not by applications of actual thermodynamic thrust along some particular spatial vector. The changing of signs in a cluster of equations rather than the changing of the direction of acceleration through an outlay of physical energy is what is needed.

So Roy and Sieglinde do the primary work, plotting Hesper's star data against Paco's computations of the *Wotan*'s presumed location in Einsteinian space and calculating the appropriate nospace equivalents. Paco then converts their figures into navigational coordinates intended to get the ship from *here* to *there* and presents his results to Julia, who—working in consultation with Heinz—enters the necessary transformations in the stardrive intelligence. Whereupon the intelligence produces a simulation of the flight plan, indicating the course to be taken and the probable consequences of attempting it. The final step is for the year-captain, who bears ultimate responsibility for the success of these maneuvers, to examine the simulation and give his approval, whereupon the drive intelligence will put it into operation.

All this, except for the last, has been accomplished.

The year-captain does not pretend to any sort of expertise in nospace travel. His considerable skills lie in other fields. So it is largely by means of a leap of faith rather than any intellectual process that he allows himself to announce, after Julia and Heinz have shown him the simulation diagrams, "Well, I'm willing to go with it if you are."

What else can he say? His assent, he knows, is nothing but a formality. The jump must be made—that has already been decided. And he has to assume that Julia and Heinz have done their work properly. That all of them have. These calculations are matters that he does not really understand, and he knows he has no real right to an opinion. This far along in the operation he can only say yes. If he is thereby giving assent to catastrophe, well, so be it: Julia and Heinz and Paco and Roy and Sieglinde will partake of the catastrophe along with all the others, and so will he. He is in no position to recalculate and emend their proposal.

"When we make the course change," he says, "are we going to be aware that anything special is happening, and if so, what?"

"Nothing will be apparent," Julia tells him. "Nothing that we can feel, anyway. You mustn't think of what we'll be doing in terms of acceleration effects. You mustn't think in terms of any sort of phenomenological event that makes sense to you."

"But will it make sense to you?" he asks.

"It'll make sense," Julia replies. "Not to me, not to you, maybe not even to Sieglinde and Roy. We don't need to have it make sense. We only need to have it work."

"And it will."

"It will. It will."

Well, then, it will. The year-captain sends for Noelle.

"It's time to let Earth know about the course change," he tells her. "We're going to be redirecting the ship toward the star of Planet A a little later this day. Our first planetary surveillance mission is getting started."

Noelle nods gravely. "The people at home will find that news very exciting, I'm sure." She says that in the most unexcited way possible, as if she is reading it from a script she has never seen before, and not reading it very well.

The year-captain's last few encounters with Noelle have been uncomfortable ones. That odd business of having her face pop so vividly into his mind like that, just as he was settling into the home stretch with Julia, was still bothering him the next time he saw the actual Noelle, and evidently she was able to pick up traces of his discomfort—from his body odor, maybe? from some edge on his voice?—for she had said, at once, "Is something wrong, year-captain?" Which he had taken pains to deny. But she knew. She knew. She never missed a nuance. It was hard, sometimes, to banish the suspicion that she could read anybody's mind, and not just her sister's. Most likely not; most likely she simply had greatly heightened senses of smell and hearing to compensate for the one sense that was missing, as was so often the case among the blind. The suspicion lingered all the same. He disliked holding on to it, but it was difficult for him to discard it. And he hated the thought that his mind might be wide open to hers, all his carefully repressed and buried cowardices and selfishnesses and hypocrisies and, yes, shameful lusts on display, waving like banners in the breeze.

The uneasiness between them had not diminished in the ensuing days. He found it disturbing in some way to be alone with her, and she was disturbed by his disturbance, and that was upsetting to him, and so it went shuttling back and forth between them in infinite regress, like a reflection trapped between two mirrors. But neither of them ever said a word about it.

"Is this a good time for you to try to send the message?" the year-captain asks.

"I can try, yes," she says, a little hesitantly.

The interference has been growing worse, day by day. Neither Noelle nor Yvonne has any explanation for what is happening; Noelle clings without much conviction to her sunspot analogy for lack of any better answer. The sisters still manage to make contact twice daily, but the effort is increasingly a strain on their resources, for nearly every sentence must be repeated two or three times, and whole blocks of words now do not get through at all. Noelle has begun to look drawn, even haggard. The only thing that seems to refresh her, or at least divert her from this failing of her powers, is her playing of *Go*. She has become a master of the game, awarding even the masterly Roy a two-stone handicap; although she occasionally loses, her play is always distinguished, extraordinarily original in its sweep and design. When she is not playing she tends to be remote and withdrawn, as she is right now as she stands before the year-captain in his working quarters: head downcast, shoulders slumped, arms dangling, blind eyes no longer even attempting contact with his. She has become in all aspects a more elusive person than she had been before the onset of this communications crisis.

Her deepening solitude must be frightful. The year-captain often yearns to extend some sort of comfort to her that would take the place of the ever more tenuous contact with her sister: to sweep her into his arms, to hold her close, to permit her to feel the simple proximity of another human being. But he does not dare. He is afraid of giving offense, or perhaps of frightening her. And he is afraid, also, of certain upwelling inchoate emotions of his own. He has no idea how far things might go once he lets them begin, and he fears letting them begin.

Noelle's classic beauty no longer seems quite so marmoreal to him. He has started, since the time that that apparition of her intruded on his lovemaking with Julia, to admit to himself the existence of a feeling of something as uncomplicated as desire for her. Why else had she entered his mind at that moment in the cubicle, if not that hidden feelings, feelings to which even he himself had had no access up till now, were beginning to break through to the surface?

But he keeps his distance. He does not dare to touch her. He does not dare.

"Tell them," he says, "that the transverse journey across

nospace will take approximately four and a half ship-months, after which—"

"Wait. Too fast."

"Sorry."

She seems to be shivering. Some part of her mind, he knows, is linked to a woman essentially identical to herself who happens to be some twenty-odd light-years away, even as she seems to be focusing her attention on him. Who is more real to her, the identical twin far away on Earth, or the odd, edgy, troubled man just a hundred fifty centimeters distant from her in this cabin aboard this starship?

"The transverse journey across nospace," he says again, and waits.

"Yes."

"Will take approximately four and a half ship-months—"

"Yes. All right."

"After which the *Wotan* will have reached the vicinity of—"

"Wait. Please."

A ripple of something not much unlike pain crosses her face. This is hurting her, this unclarity, the effort of maintaining the weakening link to Yvonne. The year-captain clenches his fists and presses his knuckles together until they pop. Waits. Waits.

"Go ahead," Noelle says. "Now."

"Will have reached the vicinity of the G-type star which—"

"Wait. I'm sorry. It's bad today."

He waits.

They finish sending the message eventually. Noelle seems to be at the verge of tears by the time they are done.

ROBERT SILVERBERG

Her breath is coming in ragged bursts. Her dusky, lustrous skin has taken on a ghostly subcutaneous pallor. But after a moment she manages a sort of a smile.

"Yvonne says she'll tell everyone the news right away. She says it sounds wonderful. She wishes us all the luck in the world. No. In the *universe*."

Indeed, at the next transmission Noelle learns from Yvonne that the news of the Planet A surveillance mission has generated tremendous excitement everywhere on Earth. The reaction to the bulletin has been extreme, a kind of worldwide intoxication, a frenzied communal agitation such as has not been experienced by the staid people of Earth in centuries. It is as though the voyagers have announced not merely a surveillance mission but the actual discovery of a habitable New Earth. Yvonne says that they demand further reports at once: descriptions of the new planet's climate and topography and other geographical details, conjectures about its possible flora and fauna.

The year-captain is pleased that the news from the *Wotan* is having the appropriate beneficial psychological effect on the citizens of the home world. But he knows he must clarify the actual situation, and quickly, before their unrealistic expectations become embedded so deeply that it will be difficult for them to deal with the possible, even probable, disappointment that awaits.

"Tell them," he instructs Noelle, "that it's too soon to start setting off fireworks—that this is probably only the first of many worlds that we're going to have to explore before we find one that we can settle."

It takes her more than an hour to send that one brief message. The communications difficulties seem to be growing worse all the time.

Huw holds his smooth black *Go* stone lightly in the center of one broad fleshy fingertip, waggles the finger two or three times with great seriousness, as though trying to estimate the weight of the tiny polished disk, and says, apropos of nothing that anybody has been discussing this morning in the lounge, "Has he decided, I wonder, which of us are actually going to make the landing on Planet A?"

"Well, he'll be one of them, for sure," Leon replies. He is Huw's opponent, doing poorly, and waiting with ill-concealed impatience for Huw to make his move. "That's his big specialty, isn't it, planetary exploration?"

Huw grunts and puts his stone down with a great flourish, clapping it against the board in a way that makes an emphatic, almost belligerent click. He has only recently surrendered to the *Go*-playing addiction, which by now is almost universal on board. Practically everyone except Hesper, Sieglinde, and a couple of the others has taken to spending three or four hours a day in the gaming lounge.

It is only a couple of ship-weeks now until the *Wotan* is due to reach the nospace vicinity of the solar system in which Planet A is the feature of greatest interest, and then must shunt back into realspace for the direct-vision survey work. A great many unanswered questions will begin to receive their answers at that point, not the least of which is whether the starship has traveled in the right direction through nospace and whether it will be able successfully to return to realspace at all; and shipboard tensions have begun to run a little higher than usual as the moment of truth approaches.

"During his term of office the year-captain isn't allowed to leave the ship for any reason whatsoever, unless we've come to our final destination," Chang says from across the room. "It's in the Articles of the Voyage."

"His year is almost up," Leon says. "Once he's out of office he'll be free to take part in the exploration mission. My bet is that he'll name himself to the landing party as one of his last official acts."

"Why do you think he'll leave office when his year is up?" Paco asks. "What if he puts himself forward for reelection? I think he'd win. Who else would want that bloody job, anyway? And there's nothing in the rules preventing a year-captain from succeeding himself when his year is up."

"Is he so power-hungry that he would want a second term, do you think?" Julia says.

"Nobody in his right mind would want a second term," Paco tells her. "Or even a first one. But is he necessarily in his right mind? Are any of us? Would anyone in his right mind have agreed to go on this voyage in the first place?"

Calmly, Heinz, who is playing a game with Sylvia at the far side of the lounge, says, "My opinion is that a second term is the last thing he wants. I think he would very much prefer to be part of the landing party, and, as Chang says, having a second term would disqualify him from joining that. So he intends to step down. But if he does, who are we going to elect in his place?"

The question lands with sudden force among them, like a fist slamming down on everyone's gaming board. There is a long moment of surprised silence in the lounge. Has this abruptly become an impromptu nominating convention? In that case, why is no one speaking out?

"What about you, Heinz?" Chang says at last.

"Don't speak foolishness. I'm not a reliable person. Not in the way a captain needs to be."

"Well, then, who would you suggest?"

"I'm not suggesting anyone. I simply raised the question." Heinz looks around at each of the others. "What about you, Sylvia? A year as captain—why not? You don't have any other urgent responsibilities at this stage in the voyage. Or you, Paco? You say you wouldn't want the job, but you'd be a nice contrast with him, all sound and fury in place of chilly Nordic restraint. And what about Sieglinde, maybe? She'd nominate herself, I suspect, if we gave her half a chance." They all laugh at that. Sieglinde is not a popular member of the expedition. "Or you, Huw," Heinz says, grinning and pointing at the heavyset red-faced Welshman. "You'd make a damned good captain."

"No. Not on your life. If I took the job, I would then face the same problem that he does, of the year-captain's not being permitted to take part in a planetary exploration mission," Huw reminds him. "And this entire conversation began with my question about the possible makeup of the planetary landing mission, if there is indeed to be one. Of course, I'm intending to be part of it. So obviously there's no chance I'd let myself be put forth for captain."

"Who would we pick, then?" someone asks.

Again, silence. There is no clearly apparent consensus

R O B E R T   S I L V E R B E R G

candidate and they all know it. They have all become accustomed to the captaincy of the incumbent in these eleven months; he seems well fitted to the role, and it seems a useful employment of his strange restless intensity. Many have voiced the hope that he will simply remain in office, which would spare the rest of them the bother of having to do the job and also keep him safely busy. Which is why discussions of the upcoming expiration of the year-captain's term have been few and far between, and why this one has rapidly petered out.

Huw says, "If we may return to the question of the makeup of the landing party now—"

"Play your stone, Huw," Leon grunts.

Huw flamboyantly sweeps a black stone out of the pile of loose ones and slaps it almost without looking against the board, capturing a little group of Leon's that evidently had been left undefended for some time now. Leon gasps in surprise. Huw says, addressing the others, "The exploration team ought to consist, I would think, of three people, no more, no less. Obviously we can't send one person down alone, and two is probably too few to deal with the risks that might arise. On the other hand, we mustn't risk any big percentage of our total complement in any landing. Three is probably the right number."

"You've put a lot of thought into this, haven't you?" Leon says sourly.

Huw ignores him. "The ideal exploration party, it seems to me, would include one biologist, one planetographer, and, of course, one man to operate and do necessary maintenance work on the vehicle the party uses. The year-captain is the expert on alien biologies: he's an obvious choice, though we could send Giovanna or even Elizabeth if for some reason the year-captain can't or won't go. As for the planetographer—"

"I don't think we should let any women be part of the group," Paco says firmly.

The unexpected remark cuts across Huw's line of discourse so completely that Huw falls silent and his mouth gapes open two or three times, fishlike. Everyone turns to stare at Paco. He is beaming in a very self-satisfied way, as though he has just demonstrated the existence of a fourth law of thermodynamics.

There are four women in the lounge: Julia, Innelda, Giovanna, Sylvia. Julia and Innelda and Giovanna seem too astonished to reply. It is Sylvia, finally, who speaks up. "Bravo, Paco! What a marvelously medieval idea! The bold, brave knights go forth to check out the country of the dragons, and the ladies stay home in the castle. Is that it?"

Paco's self-congratulatory glow dims. He gives her a surly look.

"That's not what I mean at all," he says.

"No?"

"No. It's purely a matter of genetic diversity, don't you see?" The room has become very quiet. Paco hunches forward and begins to count off points on his fingers. "Look. We have twenty-five live wombs on board, to put matters in the most basic possible way. Twenty-five walking ovum banks, twenty-five potential carriers of fetuses. That is to say, we've got only you twenty-five women available among ourselves with which to get the population of New Earth started. There's plenty of sperm available around here, you know. One man could fertilize a whole army of women, if necessary. It's potential mothers who are scarce, and we don't want to make them any scarcer.

Each woman on board represents an irreplaceable four per-cent of all the women we'll be bringing to the new world. Each of you is an irreplaceable pool of genetic information, in other words. And an instrument of embryo nurture. The chance of losing even one of you on a risky exploration mission is too big a gamble to take. Q.E.D."

Innelda and Julia and Giovanna begin to speak all at once. But it is Sylvia's light, clear voice that carries through the hubbub:

"You're an idiot, Paco. One live womb more or less, as you so prettily put it, one instrument of embryo nurture, won't make any statistical difference in the long run. The handful of fertile men and women aboard this ship aren't going to be a significant factor in populating New Earth, and you know it. What really matters is the gene bank downstairs and the *ex utero* genetic machinery. We've got barrels of fertile ova stored safely away down there. And plenty of sperm too, thank you. That's where the genetic diversity of New Earth is going to come from, not from us. Naturally we don't want to lose any members of the expedition, but to claim that the women of the voyage are such sacred and special carriers of life that it's folly to risk them in a planetside mission is nonsense, Paco, down-right stupid nonsense!"

"So you'll volunteer for the first landing, then?" Paco asks her.

"Has anybody called for volunteers? I would go if I were asked. Of course I would. But you who worry so much about our precious genetic heritage and our irreplaceable in-struments of embryo nurture might stop and think a little about the logic of risking one of the two people on board who have a thorough understanding of how to operate our gene bank."

"I take it that what you're saying is that you aren't willing to go," Paco says cheerfully. It is apparent to everyone now, by the light in his eyes and the lopsided smile on his face, that he is simply goading her for the sake of a little fun.

Sylvia is a small and fairly timid woman, and this is an unusual situation for her. The stress of it is already beginning to show. "I *said* I would go if I were asked! But it would be idiotic to ask me. *You* go, Paco. All you're good for is navigating and producing sperm. You said yourself that we have plenty of sperm available, so we can get along without yours in case you get killed down there. And if it's a planet good enough to settle on, we won't need a navigator any more anyway."

Julia and Giovanna applaud. So do Heinz and David, after a moment. Even Paco grins.

Huw, who can be an extremely patient man, has been waiting with extreme patience while all this takes place. Now he says doggedly, as though the entire Paco–Sylvia interchange had never taken place, "If I may continue, then: three of us make up the landing party. The year-captain is the biologist. Marcus or Innelda will do the planetographic analysis, I suppose. And, naturally, I will drive the surface vehicle in which we will travel, and look after it in case of a breakdown. What do you think?"

"What the year-captain thinks is a better question," Heinz says. "But your list sounds good to me. Why don't you go down the hall right now and let him know that you've picked his landing crew for him?"

"I mean to," Huw replies. "Just as soon as I finish this game."

He puts down his next stone. Leon stares sadly at the

board and offers a countermove into Huw's territory, but Huw heads it off with three quick moves that leave Leon's stones encircled in a sea of black. Heinz and Paco come over to watch. Leon is one of the most experienced players on board, and Huw is still regarded as a novice; but Huw is murdering him with the aplomb and panache of an expert. He is playing now with the unsparing swiftness of the formidable Roy; he is playing almost on the extraordinary level that Noelle herself, the ship's unquestioned champion these days, has attained. Leon seems rattled. He makes his moves too hastily, and Huw replies to each one with some crushing new onslaught. Two new enclosures sprout on the board, black stones throttling white. Leon peers at them for a time and shakes his head.

"I resign," he says. "This is hopeless."

"Indeed," Huw agrees. He offers Leon his hand. "A good game, doctor. Thank you."

"You're welcome," Leon says, not very cordially.

"You will all excuse me, please," says Huw. "I will speak with the year-captain now."

Huw rises to go out of the lounge. He is a big, thickly built man, rumpled and inelegant-looking, who walks with the ponderous but confident rolling stride of someone accustomed to walking the deck of a seagoing vessel. As he crosses the room, he pauses to pat Paco appreciatively on the back, as though expressing admiration for his clowning. But also he blows a kiss in Sylvia's direction. Then he proceeds down the corridor to the control cabin, where the year-captain is usually to be found.

Huw and the year-captain are old friends, if anyone can be said to be a friend of the year-captain's. They are the only

two members of the expedition who actually have worked
together in any sort of way before they were chosen for the
voyage.

Unlike the year-captain, who has chosen to reinvent
himself every ten or twelve years with an entirely new career,
Huw has devoted himself single-mindedly to planetary reconnaissance since he was a very young man. He is by nature an
explorer. Some vagrant gene in his makeup has sparked an
insatiable curiosity in him, not at all typical of his era: he seeks
to move outward, ever outward, journeying through the
realms of the universe, seeing everything that is there to be
seen. The moons and planets in the vicinity of Earth first, of
course. But it had always been his intention to be part of the
first interstellar mission, which was already in the planning
stages before he was born, and so he has spent his life design-
ing, building, and testing equipment for use in the exploration
of unfamiliar environments. Huw is a descendant, so he likes
to claim, of Prince Madoc of Wales, who in the twelfth century set out with two hundred followers westward into the
Atlantic and came to a land unknown, where he saw many
strange things. And returned to Wales and recruited colonists,
and went back to the land on the far side of the Atlantic to
found a settlement of God-fearing Welshmen in the New
World and to convert the Aztecs and other heathen to Chris-
tianity.

Was it so? Of course it was, Huw would say. The
account of Madoc's voyage was right there in the chronicle of
Caradoc of Llancarfan, the *Historie of Cambria now called Wales*,
and who was he to call the learned Caradoc a liar? It was well
known, Huw would tell you, it was a fact beyond question,
that certain Aztec words were much like Welsh, and that Indi-
ans as far north as the Great Plains had been found to be

ROBERT SILVERBERG

speaking the pure Welsh tongue like true Silurians when the later European explorers arrived. And did Madoc's blood truly run in Huw Morgan's veins? Who could say it did not? There wasn't a Welshman alive who couldn't trace his ancestry, one way or another, to the glorious kings of olden days, and Madoc had been one of the greatest of those kings: there was no questioning of that.

And so this jovial ruddy-faced son of Madoc had gone up from the green and placid precincts of happy Earth to ride in a silver bullet across the sun-blasted plains of Mercury, he had prowled the parched wastelands of Mars, he had risked even the corrosive atmosphere of Venus. He was a designer and builder of the equipment that protected him, the sealed and armored land-rovers, the doughty spacesuits. When he was done with Venus the moons of the outer worlds attracted him. Outward, ever outward: and it was on Ganymede of Jupiter that his path and that of the man who one day would be the year-captain of the *Wotan* first intersected.

They knew of each other, of course. Earth's population in these latter days was so small, and the number of those of their particular cast of mind so few, that they could hardly not have heard of each other. But even a small world like Earth is quite big enough for two roving men to move about freely without bumping into one another, especially if they are periodically making excursions to adjacent planets.

Life was what the man who one day would be the year-captain of the *Wotan* was looking for. Not his own life; he had already found that, knew precisely where its center was located. But life outside himself, far outside, the life of other worlds. Mercury had none: the sun had baked it clean in the horrific intervals of daylight between the long spells of terrible night. The hidden landscape of Venus was too difficult to explore with any thoroughness, though it was not beyond hope that some organisms comfortable in blast-furnace heat under a carbon-dioxide sky might have evolved there. Still, none could be found. And on Mars—grim, red, dusty Mars—microfossils four billion years old spoke of ancient bacteria and protozoa, but it did not seem as if they had left any living descendants on that harsh and uninviting world.

The moons of Jupiter and Saturn, though—Io, Callisto, Iapetus, Titan, Ganymede—

"I'm going to Ganymede to look for microbes," the man who would be year-captain said, five minutes after his first meeting with Huw. "Build me an ice-sled and a proton-storm suit. And come with me."

They were very different kinds of men. Huw, cheerful and outgoing and exuberant, was surprised to find himself drawn so strongly to someone so remote, inaccessible, unsympathetic. It was the attraction of opposites, perhaps. They were mirror images of one another. And yet they wanted the same thing.

Huw was puzzled by the odd combination of flightiness and profundity that was the Scandinavian man's mind: the curious episode of the career in the theater with which he had interrupted his scientific work, for example, a thing that made no sense to Huw, and the peculiar medieval yearnings toward some sort of transcendental consummation that he occasionally expressed, and which also seemed pure foolishness to Huw. But despite all that, they quickly found themselves drawn toward one another. They both were fearless, hungry, determined to seek things that lay outside the placidities of the tame housebroken civilization into which they had been born.

So they went to Ganymede together.

Ganymede was the biggest of Jupiter's moons, an immense ice-ball, cratered by billions of years of battering from space, grooved by the heavings of fierce internal forces. There had been an atmosphere here once, though now it lay in frozen heaps: ammonia, methane. Together the two men skated in Huw's cunningly shielded sled in eerie pale sunlight over fields of muddy brown ice beneath the mighty eye of Jupiter. The great planet, ceaselessly spewing primordial energy, spit angry swarms of protons against them, but the magnetic fields of their suits deflected the onslaught. Could anything live, endure, replicate, under such a bombardment? In theory, perhaps, yes. They found no sign of life on Ganymede, though, nor on big Callisto nearby. Not a microbe, not the merest speck. Nothing.

But volcanic Io was a different matter. An ocean of molten sulfur with a frozen surface; ice of sulfur dioxide forming white frost clinging to a silicate landscape; geysers spouting fiery plumes of elemental sulfur fifty kilometers high that came raining down as sulfuric snow, pastel yellow and orange with undertones of blue; and volcanoes everywhere, eternally belching, sending dense clouds of sulfur-dioxide debris booming skyward that tumbled back to ground like a rain of cannonballs. Here, on the night side of this dire turbulent terrain, under a black sky glittering faintly with the lethal electrical discharges from Jupiter's huge relentless magnetosphere, the two explorers collected the first extraterrestrial life ever found: sturdy one-celled entities, closer in nature to bacteria than anything else, sulfur-loving things, bright dots of scarlet against yellow ice, spreading slowly and happily across the face of the frightful little world of which they were the supreme and absolute rulers.

Huw danced wildly, ecstatically, around those little colored splotches, flinging high his hands, shouting thick-tongued nonsensical syllables that he wanted to believe were Welsh. His companion remained motionless, regarding him quizzically.

"Come on, damn you," Huw cried. "Dance! Dance! A celebration of life, damn you!" He took the other man by the hand, pulled him along with him, led him in a reluctant lurching acknowledgment of their great discovery.

And then it was on to Titan for them, Saturn's chilly Titan, big enough to have held its atmosphere, a place where methane sleet fell steadily out of a hazy hydrogen-cyanide sky. Luck was with them here too. By the gloomy shores of hydrocarbon lakes, under a thick layer of faintly glowing lemon-colored smog, they stared at sprinkles of orange against a gray shield of ammonia-methane ice. These, too, were living creatures. Biological processes of some sort were taking place here, anabolism, catabolism, ingestion, respiration, reproduction, whatever. Living creatures, altogether different from those of Io and unutterably different from anything native to Earth.

Those two sets of alien splotches are still the only forms of extraterrestrial life that the human race has ever discovered, and the two men who found them stand face-to-face now in the control cabin of the *Wotan*.

"We've been talking about the people who'll be going on the landing party," Huw says.

"There's been no decision about a landing party," the year-captain replies evenly.

"We can at least speculate about the makeup of the party."

"You can at least do that. But we don't have any assurance yet that we'll want to make a landing at all."

"If we do," Huw says. "Let's assume that much, shall we, old brother?"

"All right. If we make a landing, then."

"If we do," Huw says, "my feeling is that a group of three is our best bet: a biologist, a planetographer, and—"

The year-captain says, "Do I understand that you're proposing yourself as a candidate for my job, Huw?"

Huw, bewildered, shakes his head. "Why do you say that?"

"Naming the landing party is my prerogative. Here you've already worked out the proper number of people to go, and, I assume, the names of the actual personnel as well. Captain's work. All right: you want to be captain, Huw, you can be captain. We'll call a ship assembly and I'll nominate you as my successor, and then you can pick anybody you like to go down for a look at Planet A. Assuming that you regard it as desirable to make a landing in the first place."

Huw is still shaking his head. "No, you don't understand—I'm not trying to—I don't want—I wouldn't want—"

"To be captain?"

"Not at all. Not in the slightest bit. We both know that the captain can't be part of the landing party. Listen, man, for Christ's sake, I am not trying to usurp your captainly prerogatives and I most assuredly don't want to be the next captain myself. I simply came down here to have a little preliminary discussion with you about the makeup of a possible landing party, and—"

"All right," the year-captain says, as calmly as though they are discussing whether it is getting close to time for lunch. "So tell me who you think ought to be the ones to go."

Huw, flustered and crimson-faced, says, "Why, you

and me, of course. Me to drive the buggy, you to examine the biological situation. And Marcus or Innelda to work out the overall planetary analysis. That's a big enough party to do the job, but not so big that we'd be putting an enormous proportion of the whole expedition at risk in one basket."

The year-captain nods. But he says nothing. He sits there silently, inscrutable as ever. Perhaps he is considering the best reply to make to what Huw has said; perhaps he is simply sitting there with his mind blanked out in the proper Zen-monk fashion, allowing Huw to fidget. Indeed, Huw fidgets. Huw thinks he knows this man better than anyone else alive, and perhaps that is true. But, even so, he does not know him nearly well enough. He has transgressed on some inviolable boundary here, he realizes, but he is not sure what it is.

After a very long while the year-captain says, "You and me and Marcus. Or Innelda. All right. Certainly those are qualified personnel. And who is to become the next captain? Have you worked that out too?"

"Man, man, I don't give a bloody damn who is captain! What I care about is the landing party! You and me, old brother, the way it was on Io, on Callisto, on Titan—!"

"Yes. You and me. And Marcus or Innelda. We agree on that. It's a logical group, yes, Huw. But also we will need a new captain." He smiles, but to Huw the smile seems no warmer than the landscape of Callisto or Ganymede. "We should hold the election immediately, I think. And then, once my successor is chosen, I'll name the members of the landing party as my last act in office, and they will be the ones that you've proposed. You really want to go, do you, Huw?"

"Stop playing idiotic games with me. Of course I do!"

"Then find me a new year-captain," the year-captain says.

At Lofoten I was taught how to put all vestiges of ego aside and live as a purely unattached entity, undistracted by irrelevant yearnings and schemes. And thereby to be a more perfect being, who will be more nearly likely to attain the dissolution of self that is the highest goal of the disciplined mind.

I absorbed the teachings fully, yes, I did, I did. Even though the nagging feeling remained in me that by trying to make myself perfectly unattached I was in fact acting out the ultimate in self-aggrandizement, because I was setting out to try to turn myself into a god, and what is that if not self-aggrandizement? I remember how my Preceptor smiled as I told him all that. Obviously he had been down the same path himself. It was, he said, the paradox of striving toward unstrivingness, a circular trap, and there was no way out of it except right through the middle of it. Scheme as hard as you can to free yourself of the need for scheming. Drive yourself ever onward toward liberation from the slavery of goals. Exert merciless self-discipline in the pursuit of freedom from compulsive achievement.

Well, so be it, I told myself. You are an imperfect being seeking to follow a course of perfection, and it's altogether likely that you'll hit a few problems along that way. I did my best, given the inherent *limitations of the material I was required to work with, and by and large I think that the Lofoten experience got me closer to whatever it is that I'm searching for than anything I had previously done. But look at me now! Oh, just look! Where is all my nonattachment? Where is my freedom from fruitless and distracting striving?*

I want to be part of the team that lands on Planet A.

I want it desperately. Desperately.

I feel excitement gathering in me night and day as we get closer to that place. I feel it in my fingertips, in my throat, in my chest, in my balls. A new world! The *new world, for all we know! If it is to be the place where we build our settlement, then the first ones of us who set foot on it will become figures of myth in millennia to come, culture-heroes, even gods. Do I want my remote descendants to think of me as a god? Apparently I do. Oh, Lofoten, Lofoten, you seem even farther away than you actually are! All those salutary plunges into icy pools, all that naked sprinting through the snow, all the fasting, all the meditation, the focusing of the mind on that clear white light, and yet here I am hungry for godhood, and how idiotic it is, how contemptible, how absurd. Yet undeniable. I want to go down there.*

Which means I must find someone to replace me as captain. But who? Who? No one is stepping forward. No one seems even re-motely interested. They are quite content to let me remain in the job. Like sheep, all of them, and none wants to be shepherd in my place. I should have thought of all this when I first let myself in for this year-captain business. Perhaps I did; perhaps I thought that it would be just another valuable spiritual discipline for me, to take on the responsibil-ity of running the ship. Perhaps I had in mind, even, the great incre-ment of virtue that would accrue to me by denying myself the right to be part of an exploring party. Certainly I'm capable of such nonsense. And now I have trapped myself in it.

Noelle reports that the transmission difficulties she has been

ROBERT SILVERBERG

experiencing in recent weeks have seemingly cleared up during the course of our move to this sector of space. Perhaps her "sunspot" theory really was correct, and some wholly local force was filling her mind with static back there. We'll see. It's a positive development, anyway, and those are always welcome. She still seems very tense and strange, though. Sits there in the lounge half the day and half the night, playing Go as though playing Go is the most important thing in the universe, taking on all comers and beating them with the greatest of ease. What a mystery that woman is! In this ship of strange creatures she is surely the strangest by some distance.

Unless Paco has botched his calculations, we are just a few days away now from the vicinity of Planet A. Given the uncertainties of my own situation, I find myself half hoping that the place will be so obviously unsuitable for colonization that we won't even want to take an exploratory look at it. But that's contemptible idiocy. Ten to one we'll be sending a team down to prowl around. Huw, certainly. And Innelda, I think. And—me? That remains to be seen, I guess. The extent of my fear that I won't be eligible to go is a good measure of the failure of my Lofoten training, and my anxiety level in that area is, well, embarrassingly high.

What I need to do now is call everyone together and hold an election. And get this thing settled before I lose whatever respect for myself I may happen to have.

"The Articles of the Voyage specify that a simple majority is sufficient to elect," the year-captain says. "In the event of there being more than two candidates, a simple plurality will be sufficient, providing it represents more than thirty-three percent of the total population of the ship. I call now for nominations."

As is the case when all fifty of them are assembled in general meeting, they are gathered in the great central corridor of the top deck, fanned out in several directions from the place where the year-captain stands. His back is against the gray bulkhead that forms the corridor's aft end. From there he can face them all. His eyes rove this way and that, looking onward from Leon to Elliot to Huw, from Giovanna to Sylvia to Natasha, from David to Marcus to Zena to Heinz.

No one says anything.

Chang and Roy, Noelle and Elizabeth, Paco, Hesper, Marcus, Bruce. Jean-Claude. Edmund. Althea. Leila. Imogen. Charles. The year-captain looks here, he looks there. Expressionless faces look back at him.

"The post of year-captain becomes vacant in five days," the year-captain says, though that fact hardly comes as news to them. "I call for nominations to the post of year-captain."

An ocean of uneasy faces. Frowns, sidewise glances. Silence. Silence.

Paco says, finally, "I nominate Leon."

"Declined," says Leon, almost before Paco has finished speaking the words that place his name in nomination. "I can't be ship's doctor and year-captain as well."

"Why is that?" the year-captain asks. "Holding the one responsibility doesn't preclude holding the other."

"Well," Leon says, glowering, "in my mind it does. I don't want the job. Declined."

"Very well. Do I hear another nomination?"

His eyes begin roving again. Innelda, Sieglinde, Julia, Giovanna. Michael. Celeste. Chang and Elizabeth, Hesper and Marcus, Paco and Heinz. Imogen. Zena.

Someone. Anyone.

Elizabeth says out of another long stark silence, "I nominate you to succeed yourself."

The year-captain closes his eyes just for a moment. "I don't choose to retain the office," he says quietly.

"There's nobody better qualified."

"Surely that isn't so. Surely. I decline the nomination." He looks around again, a little desperately, now. No one says anything. The wild thought crosses his mind that this is a conspiracy of the whole group, that they are determined by their obstinacy to force him to reassume the captaincy by default. He will not let them do that to him. He will not.

"Well, then," he says, "I'll place some names in nomination myself. There's nothing in the Articles preventing me from doing that, is there?"

This is unexpected. Startled glances are interchanged. Everyone looks troubled. There is no one in front of him, except perhaps Noelle, who does not show visible signs of fearing to be among those who are named.

"Heinz," the year-captain says. "I nominate Heinz."

Cool as usual, Heinz says, "Oh, captain, you know that that's a bad idea."

"Is that a refusal?"

Heinz shrugs. "No. No, I'll let the nomination stand. What the hell, why not? But anybody who votes for me is crazy."

"Are there any other nominations?" the year-captain asks. "If I hear none, nominations are closed." He stares at them almost imploringly. Heinz is an impossible candidate, and surely they all know that; the year-captain has put his name in nomination only for the sake of getting the process moving. But what if no one rescues the situation now? Can he blithely allow the captaincy to go to Heinz?

Rescue comes from an unlikely quarter. It is Heinz himself who says, smiling wickedly, "I nominate Julia."

There are gasps at his audacity. But it is just the sort of thing, the year-captain thinks, that one would expect from Heinz. He looks toward Julia. Heinz has taken her by surprise. Her handsome face is flushed with sudden color.

"Do you accept?" he asks her.

Flustered though she is, she hesitates only a moment. "I accept, yes."

The year-captain feels a flood of relief, and something much like love for her, for that. "Thank you," he tells her, trying to maintain a purely businesslike tone. "Are there any further nominations? Or does someone want to make a motion that nominations be closed?"

ROBERT SILVERBERG

Paco says, troublesome to the end, "I nominate Huw."

"Declined," Huw snaps back. And swiftly says, "I nominate Paco."

"You bastard," Paco says amiably, and nearly everyone laughs. Not, however, the year-captain, who sees the proceedings degenerating rapidly into farce and does not like that at all. He glances from one to another of them, trying to silence the laughter that is still rolling nervously around the group. His gaze comes to rest on Noelle. She is the only calm one in the group. As usual she stands by herself, her expression serene and impassive, as though she is present at this meeting only in body and her mind is actually on some remote planet at this very moment. Perhaps it is. Very likely she is in contact with Yvonne and is reporting on the election to her as it unfolds.

"Will you allow your nomination to stand?" the year-captain asks Paco.

"Sure. I might even vote for myself too."

The year-captain fights back his anger. "We have three nominees, then," he declares in his most solemn official tone. Any more than three, he knows, and it will be difficult or perhaps impossible to achieve the prescribed 33 percent plurality, the seventeen votes required to elect. "A motion to close nominations, please."

"So moved," Elizabeth says.

"Seconded," says Roy.

They will vote by notifying the ship's intelligence of their choices. The year-captain, watching them line up at the terminals, runs through quick calculations in his mind. The women, he thinks, will mostly vote for Julia, not merely because she, too, is a woman, but because they mistrust the flip, irreverent manner of Heinz and generally dislike Paco's coarse jeering attitude toward most matters of importance. Probably most of the men will take the same position. So Julia will be the new year-captain. It is not a bad outcome, he feels. She is a calm and decisive person, certainly capable of handling the job. Heinz, in a spirit of mockery, has done him a great favor: the year-captain can feel only gratitude. And he is grateful to Julia, too, for allowing the nomination to stand, busy as she already is with her responsibilities on the drive deck. She is doing it for him, he knows. She understands, though he has never spoken of it with her, how eager he is to lay down his captaincy and go forth to Planet A's surface as part of the exploratory mission.

The voting takes just a few minutes. The year-captain, who is the last to vote, casts his own vote for Julia.

"Very well," he says, looking up at the grid through which the voice of the ship's intelligence emerges. "Let's have the totals, please."

And the intelligence tells them that Julia has received five votes, Heinz has received two, Paco has received one. The other forty-two votes are abstentions.

For an instant the year-captain is stunned. He can scarcely find his voice. Then his Lofoten training somehow kicks in, and he manages to say, almost calmly, "We have failed of a proper plurality, it seems."

"What do we do now?" Zena asks. "Take another vote?"

"That would be useless," the year-captain says, slowly, heavily. He stares at their faces, once again struggling with the rage that he knows he dares not allow himself to express. "You've made your position plain enough. Nobody here wants the job."

"We want *you* to have the job!" Elizabeth cries.

ROBERT SILVERBERG

"Yes. Yes. I do see that. Thank you. Thank you very much."

Some of them look frightened. He must be letting the fury show, he realizes.

"So be it," he says. "The election has failed. I yield to what you apparently want of me. I will stay in office a second year."

In their secret place belowdecks Julia attempts to offer him consolation for the bitter outcome of the election. But his Lofoten skills have carried him through the crisis; he has already begun to reconcile himself to the loss of the Planet A trip. There will be other worlds to visit beyond this one, and someday he will no longer be year-captain and will be allowed to go down and explore them; or else this will be the planet where they are going to settle, in which case he will be seeing it soon enough. Either way, there is no real reason for him to grieve. So the year-captain accepts, and gladly, the comfort of her breasts, and her lips, and her thighs, and of the warm place between them; but Julia's words of sympathy he brushes gently aside. He does tell her, though, how touched he was by her gesture of willingness to take the captaincy from him so that he would be able to join the landing party. What he does not speak of is that sensation that seemed so much like love for her that passed through him at the moment of her acceptance of the nomination. It was, he has subsequently come to see, not really love at all, only a warm burst of gratitude. Love and gratitude are different things; one does not fall in love simply as a response to favors received. He is fond of Julia; he likes and respects her a great deal; he certainly takes great pleasure in all that passes between them in their little private cubicle. But he does not think he loves her, and he does not want to complicate their relationship with discussions of illusory states.

Noelle, unworldly as she often seems to be, shows surprising awareness of the meaning and consequences to him of the election. "You're terribly disappointed, aren't you, at not being able to be part of the landing mission?" she says when they meet the next morning for the daily transmission to Earth.

"Disappointed, yes. Not necessarily *terribly* disappointed. I very much wanted to go. But I'll survive staying behind."

"Do you mind very much having to be year-captain for a second term?"

"Only insofar as it keeps me from leaving the ship," he says. "The work itself isn't anything I object to. I simply accept it as something I have to do."

She turns toward him, giving him that forthright straight-in-the-eyes look of hers that so eerily seems to deny the fact of her blindness. "If one of the others had been elected year-captain," she says, "then you and I wouldn't be meeting like this any more. I would be getting briefings from Julia or Paco or Heinz about the messages to send to Earth."

That startles him. He hadn't considered that possibility at all.

"I'm glad that didn't happen. I would miss you," she says. "I like being with you very much."

Her quietly uttered words unsettle him tremendously. The statement is too simple, too childlike, to carry with it any deeper meaning. Of that he is certain, or at least wants to be certain. She has said it as though they are playmates and this is their daily game, the loss of which she would regret. And yet she is not a child, is she? She is a woman, twenty-six years old, a beautiful and intelligent and mysterious woman. *I like being with you very much.* Yes. Yes. The simple straightforward phrase makes something stir in him, something disturbing and turbulent and troublesome, the strength of which is all out of keeping with the innocence of her words. He stares at her smooth, broad forehead, seeking some understanding of what may be going on behind it. But she is utterly opaque to him, as she has always been.

Noelle getting her briefings from Heinz—Noelle and Paco—

There is some sort of leap of connections within the year-captain's whirling mind and he finds himself wondering whether Noelle has had any sort of intimate involvement with anyone aboard ship, other than her daily meetings with him. Sexual, emotional, anything. Mostly she spends her time in her cabin, so far as he knows, except for the hours each day that she is in the gaming lounge playing *Go,* or the time consumed in taking meals, bathing, official meetings, and so forth. Certainly there has been no gossip about her going around. But what does that mean? He doesn't think there's been any gossip about him and Julia, either. The starship is big—the biggest spacegoing vessel ever built, it is, by a couple of orders of magnitude—and it is full of nooks, crannies, hideaways. All sorts of undetected things might be going on. Noelle and Paco? Noelle and Huw? Noelle and Hesper, for God's sake, down in Hesper's little chamber of flashing colored lights that she would never be able to see?

All these wild thoughts astound him. He finds himself suddenly lost in a vortex of crazy nonsense.

Nothing is going on, he tells himself. Not that it should matter to you one way or the other.

Noelle leads a life of complete chastity. There are no probable alternatives. She comes occasionally to the baths, yes—everyone does that—and sits there unselfconsciously naked in the steamy tub, but what of it? She does not flirt. She does not join in the cheerfully bawdy byplay, the double entendres and open solicitations, of the baths. She has never been known to go into one of the little adjacent rooms with anyone. On board this ship she lives like a nun. She has always lived that way. Very likely she is a virgin, even, the year-captain thinks.

A virgin. Strange medieval concept. The word itself seems bizarrely antiquated. No doubt there *are* such creatures somewhere—past the age of twelve or thirteen, that is. But one doesn't ever give them much thought, any more than one thinks about unicorns.

Whatever else she may be, Noelle is certainly an island unto herself. She and faraway Yvonne dwell joined in an indissoluble union, into which no one else is ever admitted by either sister. If she is indeed a virgin, then the virginity, perhaps, may be essential to the manifestation of her telepathic powers. Untouched, untouchable. And so she would not ever—she has not ever—

What in God's name is happening here?

This is all craziness. His head is full, suddenly, of absurd puerile speculations and suspicions and theories. He is behaving exactly like the lovesick adolescent that he never was. Why? Why? He wonders just how much Noelle means to him. Certainly she fascinates him. Is he in love with her, then? At the very least, her strangely impersonal beauty exerts a powerful effect on him. Does he want to go to bed with her? Then go to bed with her, he tells himself. If she's interested, of course. If she is not in literal truth the nun he was just imagining her to be.

The year-captain is grateful now for Noelle's blindness, which keeps her from seeing the way his face must look as all this stuff goes coursing through his mind.

As he struggles to regain his equilibrium, she says, "Is there anything wrong?"

She can tell. Of course. She doesn't need to see his face. She is equipped with a horde of secret built-in receptors that bring her a steady stream of messages about the way he is breathing, the chemical substances that are flowing from his pores, and all the other little physiological betrayals of internal psychological states that a sufficiently keen observer is able to detect even without eyesight. The naturally augmented auxiliary senses of the blind.

"I was just thinking," he says, not entirely dishonestly, "that I would miss these sessions with you too. Very much, as a matter of fact."

"But we don't have to miss them now."

"No. We don't."

He takes her hand between his and presses it there, lightly, for a moment. A small gesture of mild affection, nothing more. Then he suggests they get down to work.

"I've been getting mental static again," she says.

"You have? Since when?" He is glad that the subject is changing, but this is a jarring, unwelcome shift.

"It began during the night. A feeling like a veil coming over my mind. Coming between me and Yvonne."

"But you can still reach her?"

"I haven't tried. I suppose so. But I thought everything was better, and now—"

"We've been traveling between stars the past few months," he points out. "Now we're getting close to one again."

"When I was on Earth," Noelle says, "I was only ninety-three million miles from a star, and Yvonne and I had no transmission problems whatever, even when we were far apart."

"Even when you were as far apart as you could get on Earth," he says, "you and your sister were standing side by side, compared to the distances between you out here."

"I still don't think distance has anything much to do with it. I think it's something connected with stars, but I don't know what it can be. Stars that are not the sun, maybe. But I don't really understand." Now she is the one who takes his hand, and holds it rather more firmly than he had been holding hers a moment ago. "I hate it when anything gets between me and Yvonne. It scares me. It's the most terrifying thing I can imagine."

The time has arrived now to emerge from nospace and set about reaching a decision about whether to attempt a landing on the world that Zed Hesper has labeled Planet A. Now is the moment when they will discover whether the *Wotan* can indeed jump in and out of nospace in any controllable way; and once that test is behind them, they will be able to learn whether the information that Zed Hesper's instruments have brought them—all that impossibly detailed data about stars and planets and atmospheric composition and polar ice-caps—constitutes a genuine report on real components of the real universe, or is merely a set of imaginary constructs having no more connection with reality than the chants and potions of a prehistoric sorcerer.

Julia has the responsibility for the first part of the business, bringing the starship out of nospace. Accomplishing that is mostly a matter of giving the drive intelligence the appropriate orders in the appropriate command sequence, and then giving the command—in the presence of the year-captain, and with him supplying the proper official countersign—that activates the whole series of orders. And then waiting to see whether what happens next is anything like what is supposed to happen.

So is it done, step by step. And it comes to pass that the maneuver is successful.

It seems at first as if nothing has happened. There had been no perceptible sensation when they originally shunted into nospace, and there is none coming out, either. No sense of being turned inside-out (or outside-in), no banshee wails in the corridors, no flashing of gaudy colors up and down the visual spectrum and perhaps a little way beyond.

Indeed, there is no indication whatever that anything has changed aboard the *Wotan*. Except that—suddenly, astoundingly, miraculously—the throbbing gray nothingness of interlacing energy fields which was all that any of them had had to look at for the past year is gone from the viewplate, and the voyagers find themselves staring at jet-black sky, a dazzling golden sun not very much different from the one under which they had been born, and a bright scattering of planets. One, two, three, four, five, six planets, so it seems.

That is a stunning sight, after a full year of staring at the majestic but featureless woolly wrapper of nospace that has surrounded the ship like a second skin. The voyagers who stand by the viewplate break into cheers, applause, giddy laughter, even a few sobs.

The year-captain is on the phone to Zed Hesper, who remains holed up in his scanning room down below. "What do you say, Hesper?" the year-captain asks. "Is this the place, or is this the place?"

This is the place, Hesper opines. They have accurately navigated the murky seas of nospace—Paco must be congratulated—and are sitting right in the middle of the solar system that contains his Planet A. Planet A itself is the fourth of the six worlds of this G2 sun, Hesper reminds him.

But it is not so easy to tell, at least not merely by glancing into the viewplate, which of the six planets is the fourth from its primary. If the *Wotan*'s position in relation to this solar system were optimally inclined to the plane of its ecliptic at a nice ninety-degree angle, one could perhaps casually line the planets up in their actual order of distance from the sun just by peering at the screen. But the *Wotan* is not so conveniently positioned. At the place where they have emerged from nospace the voyagers have a skimming, edge-on, rim-shot kind of view of this solar system. And each of the six worlds is chugging along in its own orbit, naturally, some of them at perihelion at the moment and others at aphelion, and from the point of view of the *Wotan*, confronting the whole system on the skew as it is, they are strewn randomly around the sky.

Hesper knows which of the six is Planet A, though. Hesper knows all manner of things of this sort. He tells the year-captain, and the year-captain brings the eye of the view-plate to focus on the world they hope to explore.

It looks like a world.

It looks like *the* world. The world of their dreams; their home away from home; the New Earth that they have crossed this immense gulf to find.

All of Hesper's data-analogies and equivalencies have turned out to be smack-on-the-nose accurate. It is a miracle, the information that the sharp-nosed little man has managed to conjure out of the scrambled nospace numbers with which he works. Planet A seems to be exactly what he said it would be, an Earth-size world, more or less, with what appear to be blue oceans and patches of green vegetation and brown soil. There is a sprawling tentacular ice cap at the northern pole and a smaller, more compact cap at the southern one. There seem to be thin clouds scudding through what seems to be an atmosphere.

"Break out the champagne!" Paco yells. "We're home!"

But there is no champagne, the supply that they brought from Earth having been exhausted the night of the six-month anniversary party and the newly synthesized batch still undergoing its second fermentation; nor are they "home," however much this place may superficially resemble Earth; nor is there any guarantee that they will be able to settle here. Far from it. The year-captain can't help thinking that the odds against their finding the right planet on the first attempt are about the same as those of four poker players being handed royal flushes on the same deal.

Still, all the early signs are promising. And the year-captain is neither surprised nor greatly displeased by Paco's boisterousness. Boisterousness is one of Paco's specialties. Besides, they have at least managed successfully to find their way to this place. That calls for a little jubilation, whether or not the planet turns out to be one they can use.

Julia has some more work to do now: braking the starship in such a way that it will glide down into orbit around Planet A. Because nospace travel takes place outside the classical Newtonian conceptual framework of the laws of motion, the "acceleration" that the stardrive imparted to the *Wotan* during its journey and the "velocity" that the ship thereby attained bear no relation to the starship's movements now that it has departed from nospace. It is traveling, in fact, at the same speed it had been making at the instant it shunted from realspace to nospace in its departure from Earth. Since it had been positioned at that time in orbit not far above the surface of Earth, it is still moving now at its former orbital velocity. The starship is essentially still in orbit around Earth. But Earth is no longer nearby.

So Julia must make the necessary adjustments. The *Wotan* is not equipped for extended travel through realspace, but the braking motor with which the starship is equipped will be sufficient for a maneuver of this sort. It is a simple operation; Julia copes with it with ease.

Meanwhile Marcus and Innelda, whose main areas of expertise are in planetary survey work, are doing an instrument analysis of the world that they hope to explore. There is no sense expending the reaction mass needed to launch a drone probe, let alone sending a manned expedition down there, if Hesper's readings of Planet A's atmospheric makeup and gravitational force and other significant characteristics are incorrect.

But Hesper's figures continue to be right on the mark. The gravity is reasonable, even alluring: .093 Earth-norm. A handy nitrogen-oxygen atmosphere, a little shorter on oxygen and heavier on nitrogen than might be ideal, but probably breathable. Traces of carbon dioxide, argon, neon, helium, none of these deployed in perfect Earthlike proportions but basically close enough to be okay. No sign of free atmospheric hydrogen, which would be a bad thing, indicating disagreeably low temperatures. Definite and heartening presence of water vapor in the air, not a lot, but enough. A dry place, mostly, this planet, but dry like Arizona, not dry like Mars. And there is just a touch of methane, too, precisely as Hesper had predicted—indicating a strong likelihood that the processes of life are going on down there. Not a certainty—the methane could be bubbling up out of subterranean vents, perhaps—but nevertheless there's a decent probability that living things are growing and eating and digesting and farting, maybe, and dying and decaying, all of which are methane-producing processes, on the cheerful turf of Planet A.

Innelda and Marcus turn in a positive report. Everything their instruments have told them leads to the conclusion that Planet A is a good bet for colonization. There is water at least in moderation; there is air that is recognizable as air; the gravity is okay; at least in a general way the place appears to be capable of sustaining life, Earth-type life. But on the other hand, it is not possible to detect the presence of higher life-forms already in possession of the place. There are no cities visible from up here, no roads, no construction of any sort. No radio emission comes from Planet A, or anything else in any part of the whole electromagnetic spectrum. No artificial satellites are in orbit around it. All this is to the good. It is not the intention of the voyagers to move in on thriving alien civilizations and conquer them, or even to wheedle permission with gifts of beads and mirrors to settle among them. The Articles of the Voyage specifically state that the *Wotan* is to refrain from making landings on any world that is seen to be inhabited by apparently intelligent beings, leaving the definition of "intelligent" up to the year-captain, but making it quite clear that any sort of intrusion on a going civilization is definitely to be avoided.

There are, presumably, enough habitable but uninhabited worlds available within relatively easy reach to make such an intrusion not only morally undesirable but also unnecessary. This may or may not be the case, the travelers realize, but it is a good working assumption with which to begin their galactic odyssey. There are those on board who have already pointed out that policies can always be revised, much farther down the line, if circumstances demand such a revision.

The year-captain is suspicious, of course, of the encouraging data that Marcus and Innelda have brought him. It is inherent in his wary nature that he will believe that it is much too good to be true that the very first planet they have located should conveniently turn out to be suitable for colonization. Unless, of course, every solar system in the galaxy has one or two Earth-type planets in it—but in that case, why have there been no signs thus far of intelligent life anywhere in the galactic neighborhood? If there are millions or even billions of Earth-type worlds in the galaxy, is it at all probable that Earth itself should be the only one of those worlds to evolve a civilization?

So, then: Is Earth, that green and pleasant world, the one-in-a-billion galactic fluke, and, if so, how come they have struck a second such fluke so easily? Or are there planets of this kind all over the place and it is the human race itself that is the improbable statistical anomaly? The year-captain has no idea. Perhaps there will be some answers later on, he thinks.

R O B E R T   S I L V E R B E R G

But he is made definitely uneasy by the swiftness with which they have discovered this apparently habitable but evidently uninhabited world.

The action now shifts to Huw's department. He is the chief explorer; he will mount and launch an unmanned probe to provide them with actual and tangible samplings of the planetary environment that awaits them.

The *Wotan* carries three robot drones, and has the technological capacity to assemble others if anything happens to these. But constructing replacements for the original three would require a considerable redeployment of the ship's resources of matériel and energy, and Huw understands very clearly that every effort must be made to bring each drone back successfully from a launching. He runs simulated landings nonstop for three days before he is ready to send one of the little robot vessels forth.

The outing, though, is carried off perfectly. The drone emerges smoothly from the belly of the starship and spirals downward to its target with absolute accuracy. Taking up an orbital position some 20,000 kilometers above the surface of Planet A, it carries out an extensive optical reconnaissance, sending back televised images that continue to provide confirmation for the belief that no higher life-forms are to be found down there.

After circling Planet A for one entire ship's day—making several orbital adjustments during that time to ensure full visual coverage of the planet's land surface—the drone enters landing mode and descends to the great rolling savannah in the heart of the biggest and driest of Planet A's four continental landmasses. There—guided by Huw, who is sitting at a set of proxy controls aboard the *Wotan*—it adapts itself to surface locomotion by extruding wheels and treads and sets out over a circular route with a radius of a hundred kilometers, gathering at Huw's command atmospheric samples, soil, water, minerals, bits of vegetation, all manner of interesting odds and ends. Having accomplished this, it goes airborne again and moves on to the opposite hemisphere, where conditions are more or less the same though a trifle less barren, and takes a second set of samples. Then Huw, well satisfied with the robot drone's accomplishments, keys in the command that summons it back to the *Wotan.*

For nine working days a team of seven expedition members, garbed head to toe in space gear as a cautionary measure, analyzes the drone's haul in one of the sterile isolation rooms on the *Wotan's* laboratory level. The year-captain, who has allocated the biological research to himself, finds bacteria in the soil samples, various kinds of protozoa in the water, and several heavily armored little ten-legged insectlike creatures in one of the drone's collecting jars. He stares at these with awe and reverence: they are the first multicelled extraterrestrial beings ever discovered, though he suspects and hopes that they will not be the last.

Biological analysis reveals nothing obviously toxic in the soil samples or in the water. Analysis of the air samples indicates the strong likelihood that the atmosphere of Planet A will be accessible to lungs that have evolved in the air of Earth. The bacteria, when cultured in juxtaposition with microorganisms of terrestrial origin, engage in no interaction with them whatever, neither killing them nor being killed by them. This may or may not be a good sign—it remains to be seen whether the biochemistry of Planet A will be compatible with that of Earth, and the indifference of one set of bacteria to the other would raise the possibility that human settlers will be unable to digest and assimilate the foodstuffs that they find on this world.

Other little troublesome questions necessarily must go unanswered at this point. Are there airborne viruses somewhere down there, carrying fascinating new diseases? A few well-spaced scoops of atmospheric samples won't necessarily reveal that. What about lethal amino acids in the meat of the Planet A equivalents of sheep and cattle, if there happen to be any such animals? Or murderous alkaloids in the local versions of apples and asparagus? The drone samples can't tell them any of that. These are matters that can only be discovered the hard way, in the fullness of time, by direct experience.

Huw says, "All that's left to do now is for us to send down a manned expedition, captain."

The year-captain is aware of that already. Still, Huw's words give him a good jab in the solar plexus. He hopes he has not allowed his pain to show. He has, by now, chosen the team that will descend to make the reconnaissance, and, of course, he is not a member of that team. And, Lofoten training or not, he will probably always continue to feel occasional moments of dark regret over the necessity of remaining behind.

"We only want volunteers for this mission, of course," the year-captain says. "Huw, do I hear you volunteering to be the leader?"

Huw grins broadly. "You have persuaded me to do my duty, old brother."

"Innelda?" says the year-captain. "What about you?"

Innelda, slim, imperious, almond-eyed, is taken no more unawares by the request than was Huw. Everybody on board has been trained to some degree in the techniques of analyzing alien landscapes—their lives ultimately may depend on the quickness with which they react to unfamiliar conditions—but Innelda's knowledge in that area isn't just part of her survival training, it is her scientific specialty.

"And finally," the year-captain says—there is great suspense involved in this choice; everyone is wondering about it—"we want to know something about the plant and animal life down below. Its biochemistry, primarily. Whether we're going to be able to make use of anything for food, or will have to set up alternative food-sources using genetic manipulation of the foodstock we've brought with us from Earth." His glance comes to rest on Giovanna. "This falls into your domain, I would think," he tells her.

The general reaction is one of surprise. Not that he would ask the biochemist Giovanna to make the journey—she is at least as qualified for the third slot as the year-captain himself, and perhaps more so—but that he has chosen two women for the group. Everyone has heard by this time of Paco's primordial little pronunciamento about the inadvisability of risking useful wombs by letting any women at all go down to Planet A. And here is the year-captain sending not just one woman but *two*, a full 8 percent of the ship's female complement. Is this some sort of direct rebuke of Paco? Or does the year-captain actually agree with Paco's thesis, and is this the year-captain's furious way of telling them all that his only recourse, now that they have prevented him from undertaking the trip, is to send Giovanna?

Nobody knows, and no one is going to ask, and the year-captain plainly is not going to say. Huw, Innelda, and Giovanna it will be, and that is that. Huw and Giovanna, everyone recalls now, were lovers in the earliest days of the

ROBERT SILVERBERG

journey; they are still good friends; doubtless they will work well together. The choice meets with general approval.

What is actually uppermost in the year-captain's mind, however, is the simple fact that he is risking three priceless and irreplaceable lives on this enterprise. Men, women: that makes no difference to him. But he doesn't want to lose anyone, and there is the possibility that he will, and he hates that idea. The trick is to choose a landing party made up of people who will be useful down there yet whose loss, if they should be lost, will not seriously cripple the ship.

The planetary mission is absolutely necessary, of course. So far everything about Planet A's habitability has checked out admirably, at least from this modest distance, and it is now incumbent on them to send someone down there who can learn at close range what the place is like. And those who are sent may very well not come back. There is always the possibility that ugly and even fatal surprises will be waiting on that alien world for the first human explorers. More to the point, though, there is risk even in the brief journey down from orbit. The drone probe in which the mission is to be made has been designed for maximum simplicity and reliability of operation, and it has been tested and retested, naturally. But it is only a machine. Machines fail. Some of them fail quickly and some of them fail only after thousands or hundreds of thousands of operations; but failure modes often are uncomfortably random things, and even a mechanism designed to fail no more often than once in a hundred billion times may nevertheless fail the very next time it is used.

Failure—an explosion en route, a bad landing, a bungled lift-off—would mean loss of personnel. The *Wotan*'s personnel are not readily expendable, although some, just now, are less indispensable than others. The year-captain has given much thought to that in making his choices. There is a considerable degree of redundancy of skills aboard ship, yes, but certain people are more vital to the present purposes of the voyage at this point than others, and it would be a heavy blow to lose any of those. Huw is one of those—nobody is better equipped than Huw to cope with the unpredictabilities of an alien world's terrain—but for that very reason he has to be part of this first mission. The year-captain hopes he comes back, of course, for there will almost certainly be other missions of this sort beyond it and Huw will be needed for those. But there is no avoiding sending Huw out on this one. Giovanna and Innelda would be serious losses, but there are others on board who could do their work almost as well. If they had been unwilling or unable to go, he might have chosen any of eight or ten others. But some had never been on the year-captain's list. The ones he would not risk under any circumstances at this stage in the voyage are Hesper and Paco and Julia and Leon, Hesper because he is the one who finds them their worlds, Paco is the one who aims the ship toward them, Julia the one who makes the ship follow the path that Paco has chosen, and Leon the one who keeps them in the prime of health while they wait to reach their new home. Since it is not at all sure at this moment that Planet A will be acceptable, other planets may need to be found, other galactic jumps must be planned for. Without the basic skills of those four, there is not likely ever to be demand for the skills of the others on board, the gene-bank operators and the agronomists and the construction engineers and such.

There is one other non-expendable person: Noelle. The year-captain regards it as unthinkable to be sending Noelle out on a journey like this one. *Noelle, you are a rare and precious*

ROBERT SILVERBERG

flower. You are Earth's salvation, Noelle. I would never place you at risk, never. Never.

The year-captain summons her now. "Is transmission quality all right today?"

The interference effect has been coming and going lately. The frequency of its occurrences is without discernible pattern. In any case it seems to have no connection with their position in space or with their proximity to any particular star.

This is one of the better days, Noelle tells him.

"Good," he says. "Send forth the word, then. Let them know, back there on Earth, that we're about to make our first planetary landing. Tell them to keep their fingers crossed for us. Maybe even to pray for us, if they can. They could look up how it's done in some of the old books."

Noelle is staring at him in bewilderment.

"Pray?"

"It means asking for the special favor of the universal forces," he explains. "Never mind. Just tell them that we're sending three of our people out to see whether we've found a place where we can live."

For Huw this is the big moment of his career, the time when he takes the center of the stage and keeps it for all time. He is about to become the first human being to set foot on a planet of another star.

He has spent the past three days reconfiguring the largest of the *Wotan's* three drone probes for manual operation. Unlike the probe that has already gone down to Planet A, and a second one just like it that is also on board, this one is big enough to hold a crew of three or four people, and is intended for follow-up expeditions precisely of this sort. It is default-programmed for proxy operation from the mother ship, but Huw intends to be his own pilot on the trips to and from the planetary surface. And now, after three days of programming and simulations and rechecks, he has pronounced the little vessel ready to go.

There has been one change in the personnel of the mission since the original three were named. During some celebratory horseplay in the baths involving Heinz, Paco, Natasha, and two or three others, Innelda has slipped on a soapy tile—she says she was pushed, somebody's sly hand on her rump—and has badly sprained her leg. Leon says that she will be able to move about normally within five or six more days; but at the moment the best she can do is hobble, and Huw is unwilling to delay the expedition until she recovers, and the year-captain has backed him on that. So Marcus, whose planetographic expertise duplicates Innelda's in many ways, has been chosen to replace her. Innelda is irate at missing her chance, but her protests to the year-captain fall on deaf ears. She will discover, before very long, that whoever it was who gave her that rude shove in the baths has done her a considerable favor; but that is the kind of thing that becomes apparent only after the fact.

The space suit—clad figures of Huw, Giovanna, and Marcus constitute a grand and glorious procession as they march through the bowels of the ship toward the drone-probe hangar. Virtually everyone turns out to see them off, everyone except Noelle, who is drained and weary after her morning colloquy with her distant sister and has gone to lie down in her cabin, and the still-angry Innelda, who is sulking in *her* cabin

ROBERT SILVERBERG

like brooding Achilles. Huw leads the way, waving majestically to the assembled onlookers like the offshoot of the great Prince Madoc of Wales that he believes himself to be. Certainly his Celtic blood is at high fervor today. What is a little trip to Ganymede, or even Venus, next to *this*?

He and Giovanna and Marcus settle into their cozy slots aboard the probe. Hatches close. Pressurizing begins. The *Wotan*'s launch bay opens and the probe slides forward, separates itself from its mother ship, emerges into open space.

A tiny nudge of acceleration, the merest touch of Huw's finger against the control, and the probe breaks from orbit and begins to curl planetward. Soon enough the brown-blue-green bulk of Planet A is the only thing the three explorers can see from the port in front of their acceleration chairs. It is astonishing how big the planet looks as they near it. It is only an Earth-size planet, but it looms like a Jupiter before them. A year in the seclusion that is nospace has given them the feeling that the *Wotan* is the only object in the universe. But now there is another one.

Though Huw is definitely in charge, and can override anything at any moment, the real work of calculating the landing orbit is being done by the *Wotan*'s drive intelligence. That's only common sense. The intelligence knows how such things are done, and its reaction time is a thousand times quicker than Huw's. So he watches, now and then nodding approvingly, as the landing operation unfolds. They are coming down near the coast of the least parched of the four desertlike continents. The climate appears to be the most temperate here, milder than in the interior and, so it would seem, blessed with somewhat higher precipitation levels. Huw is planning a trek to the ocean shore to try to get a reading on what sort of marine life, if any, this place may have.

The ground, visible a few hundred kilometers below, seems pretty scruffy here, though: dry buff-brown fields, isolated patches of low contorted shrubs, a few minor blunt-nosed rocky outcroppings, but nothing in the way of really interesting geological formations. To the east, low hills are evident. Planet A does not appear to have much in the way of truly mountainous country. To Huw the landscape looks elderly and a little on the tired side. It is a flattened, eroded landscape, well worn, one that has been sitting out here doing nothing very much for a very long time.

Not really a promising place to found New Earth, he thinks. But we are here, and we will see what there is to see.

"Touchdown," he tells the year-captain, sitting up there 20,000 kilometers away in the control cabin of the *Wotan,* as the drone makes a nice unassisted landing right in the heart of a large, broad, shallow bowl-shaped formation, perhaps the crater of some ancient cosmic collision, set in a great dry plateau.

The landscape, Huw observes, does not seem all that wondrously Earthlike when viewed at very close range. The sky has a faint greenish tinge. The position of the sun is not quite what he would expect it to be: out of true by a few degrees of arc, just enough to be bothersome. The only living things in sight are little clumps of yellow-headed shrubs arrayed here and there around the sides of this sloping basin; they have peculiar jet-black corkscrew-twist trunks and oddly jutting branches, and they, too, seem very thoroughly otherworldly. Even the way they are situated is strange, for they grow in long, tight elliptical rings, perhaps a hundred bushes to each ring, and each ring spaced in remarkable equidistance from its neighbors. As though this is a formal garden of some weird sort. But this is a desert, on an apparently uninhabited world, not anybody's garden at all. Something feels wrong to him about these spacing patterns.

The surrounding rock formations, jagged black pyramidal spires fifty or sixty meters high, have the same nonspecific *wrongness*. They announce, however subtly, that they have undergone processes of formation and erosion that are not quite the same as those the rocks of Earth have experienced.

It is understood that Huw will be the first one to step outside. He is the master explorer; he is the captain of this little ship; this is his show, from first to last. He is eager to get outside, too, to clamber down that ladder and sink his boots into this extrasolar turf and utter whatever the first words of the first human visitor to a world of another star are going to be. But he is too canny an explorer to rush right out there, however eager he may be. There are housekeeping details to look after first. Determination and recording of their exact position, external temperature readings to take, geophysical soundings to make sure that the ship has not been set down in some precarious unstable place and will fall over the moment he starts to climb out of it, and so forth and so forth. All of that takes close to an hour.

While this is going on Huw notices, after a time, that he has started to feel a little odd.

Uneasy. Queasy. Even a little creepy, maybe.

These are unusual feelings for him. Huw is a robust and ebullient man, to whom such sensations as dismay and apprehension and disquietude and agitation are utterly foreign. He is generally prudent and circumspect, useful traits in one who finds his greatest pleasure in entering unfamiliar and dangerous places, but a tendency toward anxiety is not part of his psychological makeup.

He feels a good deal of anxiety now. He knows that what he feels can be called anxiety, because there is a strange knot in the pit of his stomach, and a curious lump has appeared in his throat that makes swallowing difficult, and he has read that these feelings are symptoms of anxiety, which is a species of fear. Up until now he has never experienced these symptoms, not that he can recall, nor has he experienced very much in the way of any other sort of fear, either.

How very peculiar, he thinks. This place is far less threatening than Venus, where the temperature at its mildest was as hot as an oven and one whiff of the atmosphere would have killed him in an instant, and he hadn't felt a bit of this stuff there. The worst that could have happened to him on Venus was that he would die, after all, and though he was far from ready for dying, Huw quite clearly had understood ahead of time that he might be putting himself in harm's way by going there. Likewise when he had visited Mercury, and Ganymede, and roaring volcanic Io, and all the rest of the uncongenial but fascinating worlds and worldlets that his ventures had taken him to. So why these sensations of —*fear!*—as he sits here, fully space-suited, inside the sealed snug-as-a-bug environment of this elegantly designed and sturdily constructed little spaceship?

It is almost time for extravehicular now. Huw steals a glance at Giovanna, cradled in the acceleration chair to his right, and at Marcus, on his other side. He can see only their faces. Neither one looks very cheerful. Marcus is frowning a little, but then, Marcus almost always frowns. Giovanna's expression, too, might be a bit on the apprehensive side, and yet it might just be a look of deep concentration; no doubt she is contemplating the experiments she intends to carry out here.

Huw remains mystified at his own attack of edginess. Is that a droplet of sweat running down the tip of his nose? Yes, yes, that is what it seems to be. And another one trickling across his forehead. He appears to be doing quite a bit of perspiring. He is actually beginning to feel very poorly indeed.

Something I ate, maybe, he tells himself. My digestion is fundamentally sound but there is always the odd apple in the barrel, isn't there?

"Well, now," he says to Giovanna and to Marcus, and to everyone listening aboard the *Wotan*. "The moment has arrived for me to go out and claim this land in the name of Henry Tudor."

He makes sure that his tone is a ringing, hearty one. His little private joke stirs no laughter among his companions. He doesn't like that. And how curious, he thinks, that he needs to *work* at sounding hearty! He runs through one final suit-check and begins to set up the hatch-opening commands.

"When I go out," he says, "you stay put right where you are until I call for you, all right? Let's make sure I'm okay before anybody tries to join me. I'll give the signal and you come out next, Giovanna. We check how that goes and then I'll call for you, Marcus. Is that clear?"

They confirm that it is quite clear.

The hatch is open. Huw crawls through the lock, pauses for a moment, begins to descend the ladder in slow stately strides, trying to remember those lines of poetry about stout Cortez silent on that peak in Darien—feeling like some watcher of the skies, was it, when a new planet swims into his ken?

His left boot touches the surface of Planet A.

"Jesus Goddamn Christ!" Huw cries, a piercing anachronistic yawp that rips not only into the earphones of his fellow explorers but also, alas, into the annals of exploration as the first recorded statement of the first human visitor to an extrasolar planet.

"Huw, are you all right?" Giovanna asks from within, and he can hear the year-captain's voice coming over the line from the *Wotan,* asking the same thing. It must have been one devil of a yell, Huw thinks.

"I'm fine," he says, trying not to sound too shaky. "Turned my ankle a little when I put my foot down, that's all."

He completes the descent and steps away from the drone probe.

He is lying about his ankle and he is lying about feeling fine. He is, as a matter of fact, not feeling fine at all.

He is experiencing some sort of descent into the jaws of Hell.

The—uneasiness, anxiety, whatever it was—that he was feeling a few minutes ago on board the probe is nothing at all in comparison to this. The intensity of the discomfort has risen by several orders of magnitude—rose, actually, in the very instant that his boot touched the ground. It was the psychic equivalent of stepping on a fiery-hot metal griddle. And now he has passed beyond anxiety into some other kind of fear that is, perhaps, bordering on real terror. Panic, even.

These feelings are all completely new to him. He finds it almost as terrifying to realize that he is capable of being afraid as it is to be experiencing this intense fear.

Nor does Huw have any idea what it is that he might be afraid of. The fear is simply *there,* a fact of existence, like his

chin, like his left kneecap. It seems to be bubbling up out of the ground into him through his feet, passing up into his calves, his shins, his thighs, his groin, his gut.

What the hell, what the hell, what the hell, what the hell—

Huw knows he needs to regain control of himself. The last thing he wants is for any of the others to suspect what is going on inside him. No more than a few seconds have passed since his emergence from the probe, and his initial anguished screech is the only sign he has given thus far that anything is amiss.

Now the strength gained through a lifetime of self-confident high achievement asserts itself. This can't be happening to him, he tells himself, because he is not the sort of man to whom things like this happen: Q.E.D. The initial feeling of shock at that first touch of boot against ground has given way to a kind of steady low-level discomfort: he seems to be getting used to the effect. Does not like it, does not like it at all, but is already learning how to tolerate it, perhaps.

He walks five or six paces farther away from the probe, stops, takes a deep breath, another, another. Squares his shoulders, stands as erect as is possible to stand. Pushes the welling tide of terror back down his body millimeter by millimeter, down through his legs, his ankles, his toes.

There.

It's still there, trying to get back up into his chest to seize his heart and then move on beyond that to his lungs, his throat, his brain. But he has it, whatever the hell it is, in check. More or less. Its presence baffles him but he is holding it at bay, at the expense of considerable mental and moral energy. It requires from him a constant struggle against the profound desire to scream and weep and fling his arms around wildly. But it is a struggle that he appears to be winning, and now he

can proceed with the business of taking a little look around this place.

Now he hears a moaning sound just to his left, which calls to his attention the fact that someone else is out here with him. One of the others has left the probe without waiting for the go-ahead signal; the moan is probably an initial response to the hot-griddle effect of making direct contact with this planet's surface.

"*Hey!*" he yells. "Didn't I say to stay in there until I called you out?"

It is Marcus, Huw realizes. Which is even worse: Giovanna was the one whom he had chosen to be the second one out of the probe. Marcus has exited the ship on his own authority and out of turn, and now, moving in what seems like an oddly dazed and disoriented way, he is wandering around in irregular circles near the base of the ladder, scuffing his boot against the soil and stirring up little clouds of dust.

"I'm coming out too," Giovanna says over the phones. "I don't feel so happy being cooped up in here."

"No, wait—" Huw says, but it is too late. Already he sees her poking out of the hatch and starting to climb down. The year-captain is saying something over the phones, apparently asking what's taking place down there, but Huw can't take the time to reply just now. He is still fighting the bursts of seemingly unmotivated terror that feel as though they are pulsing up through the ground at him, and he needs to get his crew back under control too. He jogs over toward Marcus, who has stopped scuffing at the ground and now is walking, or, to put it more accurately, staggering, in a zigzag path heading away from the probe on the far side.

"Marcus!" Huw calls sharply. "Halt where you are, Marcus! That's an order!"

ROBERT SILVERBERG

Marcus shambles to a stop. But then after a couple of seconds he starts moving again in an aimless, drifting, stumbling way, traveling along a wide curving trajectory that soon begins to carry him once more away from the probe.

Giovanna is out of the ship now. She comes up alongside Huw, running awkwardly in this light-gravity environment. He peers through the faceplate of her suit and sees that her forehead is shiny with bright beads of sweat and her eyes look wild. Marcus is continuing to put distance between himself and the probe.

"I don't know," Giovanna says, as though replying to a question that Huw has not asked. "I feel—weird, Huw."

"Weird how?" He tries to make his voice sound completely normal.

"Scared. Strange." A look of shame flickers across her face. "Like I'm having some sort of a nightmare. But I know that I'm awake. I *am* awake, right, Huw?"

"Wide awake," he says. So he is not the only one, then. Both of them are feeling it too. Interesting. Interesting. And oddly reassuring, after a fashion, at least so far as he is concerned personally. But it sounds like bad news for the expedition. Huw clamps his gloved hand over Giovanna's wrist. "Come on. Let's go after Marcus before he roams too far."

Marcus is perhaps thirty meters away now. Still maintaining his grip on Giovanna's wrist—Huw isn't certain how much in command of herself she is just now, and he wants to keep the group together—Huw trots over the flat dusty ground toward him, half dragging Giovanna along at his side. After a moment she seems to get into the rhythm of it, coping with the slightly lessened gravity and all, and they start to move with some commonality of purpose. It takes them a minute or so to catch up with Marcus, who halts, wheeling around to face them like a trapped fox, and then lurches toward them, holding out both his hands to them in a gesture of desperate appeal.

"Oh, Jesus, Jesus, Jesus," he begins to mutter, in a kind of whining sob. Invoking the archaic name, a name having no real meaning for him or any of them, but somehow bringing comfort. "I'm so afraid, Huw!"

"Are you, now, boy?" Huw asks. He takes the proffered hand and indicates to Giovanna that she should take the other one. And then the three of them are holding hands like children standing in a ring, staring at each other bewilderedly, while the year-captain in orbit high overhead continues to assail Huw's ears with questions that Huw still is unable to answer. The rough sound of sobbing comes over the phones from Marcus. Giovanna is showing better self-control, but her face is still rigid with fright.

Huw checks his own internal weather. It's still stormy. For as much time as he is in motion, taking charge of things and behaving like the strong, efficient leader that he is, he seems able to fight the panic away. But the moment he stops moving, it threatens to break through his defenses again.

Being close to the other two helps, a little. Each one now is aware that the disturbance is a general one, that all three of them are affected in the same basic way. So long as they stand here holding hands, some kind of current of reassurance is passing between them, providing a little extra measure of strength that can be used in resisting the sweeping waves of pure unmotivated fear that continue relentlessly to attack them.

"What's it like for you?" Huw asks.

Marcus can't seem to utter articulate speech. He makes

ROBERT SILVERBERG

a ghastly little stammering sound and trails off into silence. But Giovanna is in better shape, apparently. "It's like everything I was ever afraid of when I was a girl, all rolled into one big horror. The nightmares that won't stop even after they wake me up. The eye that opens in the wall and stares at me. The insects with huge snapping jaws coming out of the closet. The snakes at the bottom of my bed."

"It started to hit you inside the drone?"

"As soon as we landed, yes. But it's worse out here. A lot worse. Are you getting hit with the same stuff?"

"Yes," Huw says distantly. "Pretty much the same."

Pretty much, yes. Teeth itching, tingling, seemingly expanding until they fill his mouth. A throbbing in his groin, and not the good kind of throbbing. Jagged blocks of ice moving about in his belly. And always that steady pounding of dread, dread, dread. A relentless neural discharge activating the terror-synapses that he had not even known he owned.

No wonder there don't seem to be any higher life-forms on this planet. Animal evolution has met its match here. Any nervous system complicated enough to operate the various homeostatic processes that are involved in upper-phylum life is too complicated to withstand this constant barrage of fear and trembling. No neural hookup more elaborate than those of bugs and worms can put up with it for long without giving way.

"What do you think it is?" Giovanna asks. "And what are we going to do?"

"I don't know and I don't know," he tells her.

Then, addressing himself to the *Wotan,* he says, "We're having a little problem down here. We've all come out of the probe ship and we find that we seem to be suffering from some sort of a collective psychological breakdown. No reason for it apparent. It's just happening. Has been since the moment of touchdown. As though this place is—"

From Marcus, suddenly, comes a dismal retching sound.

"—haunted in some way," Huw finishes.

Marcus has pulled free of them and is clawing at the helmet of his suit. Before Huw can do anything, Marcus has his faceplate open and he is breathing the unfiltered air of this alien world, the first human being ever to do such a thing. He is, in fact, vomiting into the air of this alien world, which is why he has opened his faceplate in the first place. Huw watches helplessly as Marcus doubles over in the most violent attack of nausea Huw has ever seen. Marcus falls to his knees, quivering convulsively. Hugs his belly, spews up spurts of thin fluid in what seems like an endless racking process.

Marcus is not a pretty sight as he does this, but he is, at the very least, providing a useful test of the effects of the atmosphere of Planet A on human lungs, which is something that they would have had to carry out sooner or later during the course of this landing anyway. And the effect so far is neutral, which is to say that Marcus does not appear to be suffering any obvious damage from breathing the stuff. Of course, he may be in such a state of desperate psychic disarray by now that a little lung corrosion would seem like only an incidental distraction.

Eventually Marcus straightens up. He looks numbed and addled but fractionally calmer than before, as though that wild eruption of regurgitation has steadied him a little.

"Well?" Huw says, perhaps too roughly. "Feel better now?"

Marcus does not reply.

"Give us a report on the atmosphere, at least. Now that you're breathing the stuff, tell us what it's like."

Marcus stares at him, glassy-eyed. Lips moving after a moment. Speech centers not quite in gear.

"I — I —"

No good. He's all but unhinged.

Huw, strangely, finds that he has grown almost accustomed to the panic effect by this time. He doesn't like it — he hates it, actually — but now that he has come to understand that it is not a function of some sudden character disintegration of his own, but seems, rather, to be endemic to this miserable place, he is able to encapsulate and negate the worst of its effects. His flesh continues to crawl, yes, and cold bony fingers are still playing along the stem of his medulla oblongata, and unhappy intestinal maneuvers seem distressingly close to occurring. But there is work to do here, tests to be carried out, things to investigate, and Huw focuses on that with beneficial effect.

He says, speaking as much to his listeners aboard the *Wotan* as to Giovanna and the hapless Marcus, "There are a lot of possibilities. One is that this place is inhabited by sentient life-forms that we aren't able to detect, and they're beaming some kind of mind-scrambling ray at us that's doing this to us. Pretty far-fetched, but at this point we can't rule anything out. Another thought is that it's the planet itself, radiating psychic garbage at us right out of the ground, a kind of mental radioactivity. Which is likewise on the improbable side, I admit. But both of those ideas, crazy as they sound, seem more acceptable to me than my third notion, which is that human beings come equipped with some kind of inherent terror syndrome that goes into operation when we arrive at a habitable planet that isn't Earth, almost a sort of wizard's spell, but one that was hard-wired into our nervous systems somewhere during the evolutionary process to prevent us, God only knows why, from settling on some other— Marcus! Damn you, Marcus, come back!"

Marcus has fled right in the middle of Huw's windy hypothesizing, and is running now—not lurching, not staggering, but *running*, as fast as his legs will take him—across the rough parched landscape of the landing zone.

"Shit," Huw mutters, and sets out after him.

Marcus is heading up the sloping side of the basin in which they have landed. He moves with lunatic fastidiousness around the borders of the elliptical groves of yellow-headed bushes, running in figure-eight patterns past them, up one and down the next, as he ascends the shallow rise. Huw ponderously gives pursuit. Marcus is young, long-limbed, and slender; Huw is fifteen years older and constructed in quite the opposite way, and high-speed running has never been one of his pastimes. Running seems to intensify the disagreeable quality of this place too: each pounding step sends a jolt of electric despair up the side of Huw's leg on a direct route to his brain. He has never experienced such raggedness of spirit before. It is a great temptation to give over the chase and drop down in a fetal crouch and sob like a baby.

But Huw runs onward anyway. He knows that he needs to get a grip on Marcus, since Marcus seems incapable of getting a grip on himself, and put him back on board the probe before he does some real harm to himself as he sprints around this desert.

Marcus is moving, though, as if he plans to cover half a continent or so before pausing for breath, and Huw very quickly finds himself winded and dizzy, with a savage stitch in his side and a sensation of growing lameness in his left leg. And the terror quotient has begun to rise again, back to the levels he was experiencing right after leaving the probe. He can force himself to run, or he can fight off the demonic psychic radiation of this place, but it seems that he can't do both at once.

He pulls up short, midway up the slope, gasping in hoarse noisy spasms and close to tears for the first time in his adult life. Marcus has vanished over the rim of the basin, losing himself among the black corona of fiercely fanged lunar-looking rocks that forms its upper boundary.

Giovanna, bless her, comes jogging up next to him as he stands there swaying and quivering.

"Did you see which way he went?" she asks.

Huw, pulling himself together with one more huge expenditure of effort, points toward the rim above them. "Somewhere up there. Into that tangle of pointy formations."

She nods. "And are you all right?"

"I'm fine. I'm absolutely wonderful. Let's go up there and find him."

They hold hands as they scramble up the rise. There is, once again, some benefit conferred by actual physical contact, even through their heavy gloves. Huw sets a slower pace than before: he is getting troublesome messages from his chest now that indicate it would be a smart idea not to try to do any more running for the time being. The slope of the basin is not quite as shallow as it had seemed from the landing site. And the ground is rough, very rough, unexpected little sandy pits everywhere and nasty tangles of flat, wiry vines and a tiresome number of sharp, loose rocks in just the places where you would prefer to place your foot.

But eventually they get to the top. On the far side there is a fairly steep descent to a sprawling valley pockmarked with more of the yellow bushes, which grow in the same elliptical grove. Here, too, each grove is bizarrely set with mathematical precision at identical distances from all of its neighbors. Some tall, ugly, sparse-leaved trees are visible beyond them, and in the hazy region farther out there seems to be a completely flat savannah that runs clear to the horizon.

At first there is no sign of Marcus.

Then Giovanna sucks in her breath sharply and points. Huw follows the line of her arm down the hill. Marcus. Yes.

Marcus is lying about a hundred meters downslope from them, facedown, his arms wrapped around a flat-faced rectangular boulder as though he is hugging it. From the angle that Marcus's head makes against his shoulders, Huw knows that the news is not going to be good, but all the same he feels obliged to get himself down to him just as fast as his aching legs and overtaxed heart will permit. The anxiety that he feels now is of an entirely different quality from the one with which this planet has been filling his mind for the past couple of hours.

He kneels at Marcus's side. Marcus is not, Huw sees now, actually hugging the boulder; he is simply sprawled loosely against it with his arms splayed out over it and his cheek pressed to the flat surface of the rock that he must have hit when he tripped and fell. There is a deep cut, virtually an indentation, along one side of his head. A trickle of blood is coming from the corner of Marcus's mouth, and another from one of his nostrils. His lips are parted and slack. His eyes are open, but not functioning. He is not breathing. His neck, Huw assumes, is broken.

Huw is hard pressed to remember the last time he saw a dead person. Twenty years ago, perhaps; thirty, even. Death is not a common event in Huw's world, certainly not death at Marcus's age. There are occasional unfortunate accidents, yes, few and far between, but in general death is not considered a normal option for people less than a century old. The idiotic, meaningless death of this young man on this alien world strikes Huw with massive impact. Above and beyond the special things that Planet A has been doing to his mind since the moment of landing, completely separate from all of that, Huw feels a pure hot shaft of grief and shock and utter despondency run through the core of his soul. He sags for a moment, and has to steady himself against this unexpected weakness. This planet is teaching him things about the limits of his resilience, which he once had thought was boundless.

"What can we do?" Giovanna asks. "Is there something in the medical kit that will—"

Huw laughs. It is such a harsh laugh that she flinches from him, and he feels almost like apologizing, but doesn't. "What we have to do," he says, as gently as he can, "is pick him up and carry him back to the ship, I suppose. That's all. The other option, the practical thing to do, would be to leave him right here, with a cairn to mark the place, but we really can't do that, you know. Not without permission. The one thing we can't do is bring him back to life, Giovanna."

The year-captain cuts in once more, wanting to know what's going on.

"We have a casualty here," Huw says somberly. He is furious with himself, though he knows that none of this is his fault. "There's something about this goddamned place that drives you crazy. Marcus panicked and bolted and ran. Up the hill, down the other side. And tripped and fell headlong against a rock and broke his stupid neck."

Silence, for a moment, at the other end.

"Are you saying that he's dead, Huw?" the year-captain finally asks.

"I'm saying that, yes."

"Do you want to talk to Leon?"

"About what?" Huw asks savagely. "Mouth-to-mouth resuscitation? Marcus is really dead and he's going to stay that way. He can't be fixed, not by me, not by Leon if I bring him back up there, not by Jesus Christ himself. Believe me." There's Jesus Christ again, Huw thinks. The old myths keep surfacing. Something about this planet makes you want to invoke divine aid, it would seem. "Or Zeus, for that matter," Huw says, still angry, angry at the year-captain, at Marcus, at himself, at the universe.

Once again the year-captain is slow to respond.

"I think what we have here is an uninhabitable planet," Huw says, as the silence from above stretches intolerably. "That's not a final conclusion but it looks pretty overwhelming. There's something very peculiar here, some kind of a psychic field, that starts operating on you the moment you make surface contact with the planet, and it doesn't let up. You just go on and on, feeling horrible, every minute you're here. Some minutes are worse than others, but none of them is ever any good. Do you understand what I'm saying, year-captain?"

"We've been following your ground conversations. We have some idea of what it's been like."

"You have *no* idea, none. You only think you do. What shall I do with Marcus? Bury him here?"

"No. Bring him back with you."

"You think he isn't really dead?"

"I think salvaging what we can of him for the ship's organ bank makes more sense than putting him in a hole in the ground," the year-captain says, sounding brusque. "You're going to start back up here right away, aren't you?"

"No."

"No?"

"That would be aborting the mission, captain. Do you want me to do that?"

"You said the place is uninhabitable."

"I said *I think* it's uninhabitable. We've only experienced one small patch of it. Suppose this psychic field, if that's what it is, is a factor only in this one region? The least I can do is check out some other area before we write the mission off as a complete failure."

"It's cost us one life already, Huw."

"Exactly. That's why I want to make absolutely sure that we can't use this planet before we give up on it. Marcus will really have died in vain if we let one bad experience spook us away from a planet that might have worked out for us had we only bothered to take a little more time for a good look at the rest of it."

Still another spell of nonresponse now from on high. Huw wonders what effect Marcus's death is having on the year-captain and the rest of them up there. He himself is growing almost numb to it, he realizes. Marcus's twisted form, lying right at his feet, seems to him to be nothing more than a badly constructed doll now.

Once more Huw is compelled to break the silence himself. "Are you ordering me to abort the mission, captain?"

"No. I'm not doing that. What's your actual plan, Huw?"

"I was originally going to make a trek to the seashore near here, but there's no sense in that now. What we're going to do is make a landing on a second continent, a brief reconnaissance. If we get the same kind of negative results there too, we'll head for home right away. Bringing Marcus with us, as you request. What do you say?"

"Go ahead," says the year-captain. "Check out a second continent, if that's what you want to do."

Huw closes Marcus's faceplate and signals to Giovanna, and together they carry the dead man up the slope, down the far side, and across the basin to the ship. It is not an easy task, despite Marcus's slenderness and the slightly lessened gravitational pull. The dispiriting emanations of this planet claw at their souls, robbing them of will and strength. But somehow they manage. They load Marcus into his acceleration chair and slide into their own.

Giovanna says, "You're really going to investigate some other site before we go back?"

"I really am, yes. Don't you think you can handle it?"

"I think it's a waste of time."

"So do I," Huw says. "But we've worked very hard to get ourselves here. If I don't make one more attempt at seeing if we can cope with this world, I'm going to wonder for the rest of my life whether I was too hasty in leaving. Humor me, Giovanna. I can't turn back this fast."

"Even with Marcus sitting here next to us and—"

ROBERT SILVERBERG

"Even with," he says. As he speaks, he is busy requesting lift-off assistance from the drive intelligence. The drone probe works its way through its sealing maneuvers, the hatch swings closed, and the usual array of readouts begins to announce the little ship's readiness for going airborne. Huw does not attempt to take direct command of the vessel himself; he is too drained by what has occurred here, and he wants simply to sink back in his acceleration chair and let things happen around him, at least for a little while.

They are in the air now. Heading eastward, flying at an altitude of a thousand kilometers, crossing a calm gray-green ocean with an almost waveless surface that has a curiously greasy look. Night begins to descend around them, and very quickly they are in darkness. This planet has no moon. The stars, against that pure black backdrop, are nearly as intense in their gleaming as they would be in space. Huw, studying the sky, tries to arrange the unfamiliar patterns into constellations. That one, he thinks, is something like a tree with huge feathery branches, and he traces another outline that strikes him as reminiscent of a dog's head, and another that seems to be a warrior about to throw a spear. He tries to point these figures out to Giovanna, but she is unable to see them no matter how carefully he directs her to the key stars, and gradually Huw loses them himself in the general confusion of the bright cosmic clutter.

The probe is over land again. A greenish dawn is breaking. Huw assumes manual control and searches for a good place to bring them down.

This continent is one big desert, a sea of orange dunes. Perhaps it doesn't radiate nightmare waves like the continent in the western hemisphere, but it doesn't look like a very good bet for settlement all the same. From the air Huw sees nothing that might be a river, a lake, even a stream—just sand and more sand, and squat flattopped hills separating one cluster of dunes from another, and some isolated patches of dismal scrubby vegetation. Still, he has come here for the purpose of finding out something particular about this side of the planet, and he intends to follow through on that intention.

Huw sets the probe down carefully in a windswept area where the dunes have been pushed aside, and begins the hatch-opening procedure. But already the wrongness of this world is manifesting itself once more upon them, here in the first instants of their second landfall. He can feel the icy, invisible skeletal fingers scrabbling at his brainstem again, the queasiness expanding in his gut, the conviction that a web of some constricting fabric is being woven around his heart.

There is a curse on this filthy place, he tells himself.

He glances over at Giovanna. She nods. She's feeling it too.

"Let's go outside anyway," Huw says.

"What for?"

"To say that we did. Come on."

Giovanna shrugs and releases herself from her acceleration chair and follows him out. As before, the waves of fear intensify as they make actual contact with the surface of the ground. Huw looks upward at the brightening morning sky. An unreasoning conviction begins to grow in him that there are winged creatures circling around up there, though he has not seen any form of animal life at all, airborne or otherwise, since their arrival on this world: huge gliding monsters overhead with sharp teeth and great curving black wings, he is sure of it, batlike beasts that even now are making ready to swoop down on them and wrap those dreadful wings around their faces.

There is nothing in the sky. No monsters. Not even a cloud.

He fears them, even so. He imagines that he can hear the slashing sound of their swift descent, the heavy rustling of those immense wings as they enfold him. He feels the dry, rough, rasping texture of them. Smells the parched, burned odor of them. His breath shortens and his heart pounds. He puts his hand to his throat. He is choking. He is definitely choking.

He takes it for a moment more. Then, suddenly, Huw pulls his faceplate open and fills his lungs with the air of this terrible planet.

It is cold, harsh, thin air, the kind of air that Mars would have, perhaps, if Mars had any air at all. There is a disagreeable medicinal undertaste to it, bitter stuff: some unfamiliar trace element, no doubt, present in a quantity larger than Huw is accustomed to getting in his air. But he sucks it in anyway in great sighing gusting intakes of breath.

Giovanna is looking at him worriedly. "Why are you doing that?" she asks.

Huw doesn't want to say anything to her about airborne monsters, about huge rough-skinned wings clamping remorselessly down over his head to cut off his intake of air. He simply says, "I've come a long distance to get here. I want to breathe the air of another world before I leave."

"And if breathing it is dangerous?"

"Marcus was breathing it," Huw says. "It's just air. Oxygen and nitrogen and CO_2 and some other things. What danger can there be in that?"

"Marcus is dead now."

"Not from breathing the air," says Huw. But after a couple of further inhalations he fastens his faceplate again.

His sampling of the atmosphere of Planet A leaves an unpleasant chemical aftertaste in his nostrils and throat, but he suspects that there's little significance to that, if any: for all he knows, it's mere imagination, just another of Planet A's cheery psychic tricks, one more turn of the screw.

They are here to explore. So they dutifully walk around a little, fifty meters this way, thirty the other. Giovanna prods at the sandy soil and discovers a colony of shining, metallic-looking insects just below the surface, and they occupy her scientific curiosity for a minute or two.

But it is only too obvious that the same malaise of soul is afflicting them here as on the other continent. Huw keeps watching the sky for monsters; Giovanna is unable to focus her concentration very long on her investigations. The same fidgety fitfulness is afflicting them both, though neither has admitted it to the other yet. Whatever the effect is, it doesn't seem to be a phenomenon confined to a single locality, not if two random landings have produced the same results, but must emanate from the core of this world to its entire surface.

Huw looks toward Giovanna. She is outwardly calm, but her face is pale, sweat-shiny. Evidently she, like him, has already learned some techniques for holding Planet A's terrors at bay; but clearly it is as much of a full-time struggle for her as it is for him. A planet where you are always thirty seconds away from a wild shriek of horrible baseless fear is not a wise place to choose for mankind's second home.

"It's no good," he says. "We might as well clear out of here."

"Yes. We might as well."

They return to the ship. Marcus, unsurprisingly, is right where they left him in his acceleration chair. To find him anywhere else would have been real occasion for shock, and

ROBERT SILVERBERG

yet Huw is unable to avoid wincing as he sees the strapped-in corpse lying there. Giovanna, coming in behind him, appears to avert her eyes from the sight of Marcus as she enters her chair.

"Well?" she asks, as Huw starts setting up flight instructions. "Do we try one more time somewhere else?"

"No," says Huw. "Enough is enough."

The year-captain says, "You think it's absolutely hopeless, then? That we wouldn't ever get used to the mental effects?"

Huw spreads his thick-fingered hands out before him, studying their fleshy tips rather than looking up at the other man. This is the third day since Huw's return to the starship. He and Giovanna have just emerged from postmission quarantine, after a thorough checkout to ascertain whether they have picked up potentially troublesome alien microorganisms down below.

"I can't say that we wouldn't *ever* get used to them," he tells the year-captain. "How could I know that? In five hundred years, a thousand, we might come to love them. We might miss all that stomach-turning disorientation if it were suddenly taken away. But I don't think it's very likely."

"It's hard for me to understand how a planet could possibly put forth a psychic effect so powerful that—"

"It's hard for me to understand it too, old brother. But I felt it, and it was real, and like nothing I had ever felt in my life. A force, a power, acting on my mind. As though there's some physical feature down there that has the property of working as a giant amplifier, maybe, and setting up feedback loops within the nervous system of any complex organism. I'm not saying that that's what it actually is, you understand. I'm simply telling you that the effect is *there,* for whatever reason, and it makes your flesh crawl. Made *my* flesh crawl. Made Giovanna's flesh crawl. Sent Marcus into such wild panic that he lost his mind completely. Of course, as I say, there's always a chance that we could learn to live with it after a while. The human species is very adaptable that way. But would you *want* to live with it? What sort of price would we have to pay for living with it, eh, captain?"

The year-captain, monitoring Huw's facial expressions and vocal inflections with great care, is grateful that he had had someone like Huw available to send on this mission. Huw is probably the most stable man on board, and certainly the most fearless, though it has crossed the year-captain's mind that noisy, blustering Paco runs him a close second. Huw has been shaken deeply by the landing on Planet A: no question of that. And it isn't simply Marcus's death that has affected Huw so deeply. The planet itself seems to be the problem. The planet must be intolerable.

It is a matter of some regret to the year-captain that Planet A isn't going to be suitable. He wants the expedition quickly to find a place where it can settle, before their long confinement aboard the *Wotan* starts creating debilitating psychological effects. And he is sorry that he will not get a chance to explore Planet A's surface himself, awful though the place seems to be. But the intense negativity of Huw's report leaves him no choice but to write Planet A off and get the starship heading out on the next leg of its quest.

He has said none of this aloud, though. Huw, left waiting for the year-captain to reply to his last statement, eventually speaks up again himself. "It's a lousy world for us in any case, you know. Parts of it are dry and other parts are even drier. We'd have a tough time with agriculture, and there doesn't seem to be any native livestock at all. We—"

"Yes. All right, Huw. We aren't going to settle there."

Huw's taut face seems to break up in relief, as though he had privately feared that the year-captain was going to insist on a colonizing landing despite everything. "Damn right we aren't," he says. "I'm glad you agree with me on that." The two men stand. They are of about the same height, the year-captain maybe a centimeter or two taller, but Huw is twice as sturdy, a good forty kilos heavier. He catches the year-captain in a fierce bear-hug. "I had a very shitty time down there, old brother," Huw says softly into the year-captain's ear.

"I know you did," says the year-captain. "Come. We're going to hold a memorial service for Marcus now."

The year-captain isn't looking forward to this. He had never expected such a thing to be part of his captainly responsibilities, and he has no very clear idea of what he is going to say. But it seems to be necessary to say something. The people of the *Wotan* have taken Marcus's death very heavily indeed.

It isn't that Marcus was such a central member of the society that the members of the expedition have constructed. He was quiet, maybe a little shy, generally uncommunicative. At no time had he been part of the contingent of *Go* players, nor had he sought to establish any sort of regular mating relationship aboard the ship. He had had brief unstructured liaisons, the captain knows, with Celeste and Imogen and Natasha, and possibly some others, but he had, so it seemed, always preferred to remain in the little pool of a dozen or so voyagers who avoided any kind of formal extended sexual involvement with one particular person.

No, it is simply the fact that Marcus is dead, rather than that he figured in any large way in the social life of the ship, that has stirred them all so deeply. They had been fifty; now they are forty-nine; their very first venture outside the sealed enclosure that is the starship had afflicted them with a subtraction. That is a grievous wound. And then, too, there is the unbalance to reckon with. There will not now be twenty-five neatly deployed couples when the engendering of children begins. Whether the voyagers would indeed have clung to the old bipolar traditions of marriage on the new Earth is not something that the year-captain or anyone else knows at this time, of course. Those traditions have long been in disarray on Earth, and there is no necessary reason for reviving them in their ancient strict formality out among the stars. But now it is quite certain that some variation from tradition is going to be required eventually, because ideally everyone will be expected to play an active role in populating the new world, or so the general assumption goes at this point, and now it will be impossible to match every woman of the expedition with one and only one man. That may be a problem, eventually. But the real problem is that the people of the *Wotan* had come to feel that they were living a life outside all mortality, here within this machine that floats silently across space at unthinkable velocities, and that sweet illusion had been shattered the very first time a few of them had emerged from their ark.

It was Julia who suggested to the year-captain that a memorial service would be a good idea. A general catharsis, a public act of healing—that was what was needed. Everyone is stunned at the death, but some—Elizabeth, Althea, Jean-Claude, one or two others—seem altogether devastated. Bodies are self-healing these days, up to a point; minds, less so. Since the return of the landing party Leon has been dispensing psychoactive drugs to those in need of chemical therapy; Edmund, Alberto, Maria, and Noori, all of whom have some gift for counseling, are making their help available to the sorely troubled; the year-captain has even, to his great surprise, seen the usually uninvolved Noelle embracing a weeping, shaky Elizabeth in the baths, tenderly stroking Elizabeth's shoulders as she sobs. Some communal acknowledgment of their general bereavement may be the best way of putting the matter to rest, Julia thought, and the year-captain agrees.

Everyone gathers at the usual place for a general assembly, and the year-captain puts his back against the usual bulkhead, facing them all.

He finds it difficult, at first, to locate the proper words. It is not a matter of stage fright—he of all people wouldn't worry about that—but rather of a sense of inadequacy, of fundamental awkwardness. The year-captain's dispassionate nature is perhaps not the one best suited, aboard this ship, for the task at hand. But he is the captain, chosen overwhelmingly by their vote at the time of departure, and ratified again a year after that. He is the one who must speak to this issue.

"Friends—" he begins, as his hesitation begins to pass from him. Every face is turned toward him. "Friends, we are all greatly wounded by the loss of Marcus, and now we must all pray for healing. But where do we turn when we go to pray? To whom do we address our prayers? We are a race that has outlived its gods. We are proud, I think, that we are beyond all superstition, that we live in a realm of the altogether tangible, the accurately measurable. But yet—yet—at a time like this—"

They are staring at him intently. Wondering where he's heading, perhaps.

"Marcus is dead, and no words will bring him back. Prayer itself, even if there were gods and the gods were listening to us, would not be capable of doing that. If there are gods, then it was the will of the gods that Marcus be gathered to them, and we would have no choice but to bend to that will. And if, as we are all so confident, there are no gods—"

He pauses. He looks from one to another to another, from Heinz to Huw to Paco, from Elizabeth to Noelle to Celeste, looks at Leila, looks at Roy, Zena, seeking for signs of restlessness, puzzlement, irritation. But no. No. He has their attention completely.

"In ancient times," he goes on, "this might have been easier for us. We would have said it was the will of the gods, or the will of some particular god, perhaps, that Marcus should die young in a strange and hostile place, and then we would have gone on about our work, secure in the knowledge that the workings of the gods are so mysterious that we need not seek explanations for them beyond the circular one that says that what has happened was fated to be. That was in a simpler era. We modern folk have dispensed with gods; we are left with the problem of finding our own explanations, or of living without explanations entirely. I urge the latter choice on you.

"Marcus's death was an accident. It needs no explanation. There have always been risks in any venture of exploration, and even though most of the human race has forgotten that, we of all people should keep it constantly in mind. Courageously Marcus came out here to the stars with us to help in the task of finding a new home for the human race. Courageously he went down with Giovanna and Huw to the surface of the world we see out there; and there he encountered a force too strong for him to understand or handle, and it destroyed him. So be it. The simplest explanation is the best one here. Humanity is no longer, in general, a risk-taking race. But we are the exceptions. We fifty human beings have chosen to revive the willingness to take risks that most of us have lost. Marcus is only the first victim of that willingness. He is gone, and we mourn his loss. We mourn that loss because he was young, someone who had great contributions to make in the world we will someday build and who will not now make those contributions; and because he has been deprived of knowing the joy that the fulfillment of our mission ultimately will bring us; and because he was one of us. Mainly, I think, we mourn him because he was one of us.

"But is that a reason to mourn, really? He *still* is one of us. He always will be. As we go onward among the stars, to Planet B and Planet C and, if necessary, Planets X and Y and Z and beyond, we will carry Marcus with us—the memory of Marcus—the first of our martyrs, the first to give his life in this great quest on which we all are bound. It was *necessary* for some of us to go down to the surface of that planet. Marcus went. Marcus died. He was performing his function as one of us, and he died because of it. Others of us, I very much suspect, will meet with similar fates as this voyage goes along. So be it. We willingly embraced all risks when we left home and friends and family and world behind to undertake this voyage across the universe. We gave up the assurance of a long and safe and comfortable life on Earth in return for the rewards—and perils—of a venture such as no human beings have ever undertaken before. And as our work unfolds, we are not likely, any of us, to find it altogether comfortable, and certainly not very safe.

"So Marcus is dead, much too soon. So be it. So be it. He is beyond all pain now, beyond all uncertainties and insufficiencies, all knowledge of failure and defeat now. In that we should find comfort. But also we must see to it, friends—for our own sakes, not his—that Marcus's death was not without purpose. We must go on, and on and on and on if need be, from one end of the cosmos to the other, if we must, to find the world that we are to settle. And when we get there—and we *will* get there—we must see to it that our children and our children's children remember always the name of Marcus, the first of the martyrs of our enterprise, who gave his life so that their world could be. When we write the histories of our voyage, the name of Marcus will be written in letters of fire. We will make Marcus immortal that way. As all of us will be immortal—glorious figures of myth, demigods, even gods, perhaps—in the minds of the people of that new world. We who are without gods to pray to ourselves will become gods, I think, to the settlers of the new Earth of the years to come. Immortal gods, all of us. And Marcus has simply entered his immortality earlier than the rest of us, that's all."

Again he pauses. Looks from face to face. Too grand? he wonders. Too high-flown?

But everyone is utterly silent and still; everyone's eyes are on him, even the blind eyes of Noelle. He has captured them. As in the old days, the Hamlet days, the Oedipus days. Yes. A successful performance, one of his best. Perhaps even accomplishing something useful.

Good. Quit while you're ahead, he thinks.

He says in a different tone of voice, a sudden downward shift of rhetorical intensity, "One thing more, and then we'll break this up. This afternoon we'll begin calculating the course for our next shunt, which will take us—what is it, Hesper, eighty light-years? ninety?—to another possible colony-world. Actual departure time will be announced later. Naturally, I have no idea whether this second destination is going to work out any better than the first one did. We're simply going to go out there and have a look, just as we did here. At this point we have no particular expectations, one way or the other. Of course, I hope that it's the world we're seeking, and I know you all feel the same way. But there are others waiting to be explored beyond that one, if need be, and, if need be, we will go onward until we find what we want. I thank you all for listening. Meeting dismissed."

Paco, Hesper, Julia, Sieglinde, Roy, and Heinz begin the process of working out the course that will take the *Wotan* to Planet B. The year-captain goes off with Noelle to send the communiqué to Earth that will report on the failure of the mission to Planet A and the death of Marcus.

He is worried about the effect that such news will have on the people of Earth. The people of Earth are accustomed to success. For them, he thinks, this voyage is a sort of fairy-tale adventure, and fairy tales are supposed to have benign outcomes, even though the occasional wicked witch may be met with along the way. The fact that one of the adventurers has actually *died* from his encounter with some dark magical force may not fit the pattern that they expect to be enacted out here. They may insulate themselves from further jolts, he fears, by retreating from their interest in the *Wotan*'s voyage, by decoupling themselves entirely from their involvement in the enterprise.

Still, they have to be told. It would be wrong to withhold the truth from them. They know that a planetary landing has been made; they must be allowed to know the outcome of it.

"How is transmission quality today?" he asks Noelle.

"Some interference. Not too serious."

"All right, then. Are you ready to go?"

"Whenever you are."

He begins to dictate the message that he has drafted a little while before. Glancing at his text now, he sees that it amounts to a litany of unbroken gloom. *Abortive mission . . . severe and inexplicable zones of psychic disturbance everywhere . . . violent irrational reactions by landing personnel . . . deplorable fatal accident . . . immediate withdrawal from planetary surface . . . abandonment of exploration effort . . .* It's all true, but it sounds terrible. He tries to soften it a little, improvising as he reads, inserting little phrases like "hopeful first attempt" and "encouraging to have found so Earthlike a planet, whatever its drawbacks, so quickly." He speaks of their coming departure for Planet B and his optimistic sense that the galaxy is so replete with worlds of the appropriate size, temperature range, and atmosphere that there can be hardly any doubt at all of the forthcoming discovery of an adequate planet for settlement.

There. Let them chew on that for a while.

Noelle tires quickly as she pumps his words across the

universe to Yvonne. The strain on her is all too obvious. Her shoulders sag, her head slumps forward, there is a tense flickering of the musculature of her face. There is more interference with the transmission today, apparently, than Noelle has indicated to him. And yet she goes gamely onward, until at last she looks up at him with a seraphic smile of relief, sighs wearily, and announces, "That's it. I think she's got it all."

"What does she say?"

"That she's very sorry about Marcus. That she wishes us all better luck on Planet B."

Is Noelle telling him the truth? For one wild moment the year-captain finds himself thinking that this whole business of instantaneous mental contact between two sisters scores of light-years apart is nothing more than a fantasy and a fraud, that Noelle has merely been pretending to be sending his communiqués to Earth and is inventing all of Yvonne's responses.

No. No. No. No.

An idiotic thought. He banishes it angrily from his mind. Noelle is incapable of such duplicity. And even if she were, she simply could not have managed to invent—to improvise, yet—all of Yvonne's bulletins from Earth, the little details of ongoing daily life there, the occasional messages from relatives of the members of the expedition. For example, the year-captain's father, who is a painter. He works in archaic modes—angels, demons, saints, all rendered with meticulous realism. He lives near the southern tip of Africa, on a dry rocky promontory eternally bathed in hot sunlight and planted with grotesque succulent things native to the region. In the past thirty years the two of them have met only twice. They have never had much fondness for each other. And yet the year-captain's father, who is 130 years old, has quite sur-

prisingly sent birthday greetings recently via the Yvonne-
Noelle loop to his son, who is less than half his age. He has
spoken of his recent paintings, his garden, the inroads time is
beginning to make on his stamina. How could Noelle have
known any of that? The year-captain wonders what upwelling
of stress within himself has led him to these absurd and un-
worthy suspicions of the blameless Noelle. The failure of the
planetary landing, he supposes. The death of Marcus. No
doubt that's it. He's been under great pressure. They all have.
He resolves to get some extra rest once they have returned to
nospace travel.

Assuming Noelle will want her usual nap after this de-
manding transmission, he starts to leave her cabin. "Wait," she
says. "Where are you going?"

"The baths, I think." Spur of the moment: he hadn't
been planning on it.

"I'll go with you, all right? And then afterward, perhaps, we could go to the gaming lounge."

He is puzzled by this. "You don't want to get some
sleep now?"

"Not this time, no." Indeed, despite her show of fatigue
a few minutes before, she seems strangely full of energy now,
not at all depleted as she normally is when she has finished
transmitting to Yvonne. This despite the problem of the
static—or because of it, maybe? He will never understand her.

But a good soak in the baths right now strikes him as a
welcome notion, and if Noelle doesn't feel like napping today,
that's entirely her own affair. She drops her clothing quite
casually, with seeming innocence. As though she is completely
unaware how provocative that might seem to be, with just the
two of them here in her cabin like this. But in her eternal
darkness she probably gives no thought to the effect that the

ROBERT SILVERBERG

sight of her nakedness might have on others. Or perhaps she does.

He waits just a moment, an oddly tense one, to see what she will do next. Take him by the hand, lead him to the bed? No. Nothing at all like that. She really *is* an innocent. Calmly she opens the cabin door and gestures for him to precede her into the hall.

They go down the corridor to the baths together.

Sieglinde, Huw, and Imogen are there when they arrive. The brawny Sieglinde is in the tepid tub by herself; beefy Huw and petite, golden-haired Imogen are sharing the hot tank. Huw and Imogen are a couple these days, apparently, at least some of the time, and this seems to be one of the times. She is stretched full length in the tub, all but submerged, her head against Huw's shoulder, her shining hair outspread in the water, the pink tips of her small breasts rising above the surface. He is so much more massive than she is that she seems like a doll beside him.

Huw lifts an eyebrow as Noelle and the year-captain enter, one naked, one not. Public nudity is not an extraordinary thing aboard the starship, and people sometimes come to the baths already undressed, but it is not a widespread custom. The year-captain wonders whether Huw is assuming an intimacy between him and Noelle that does not at all exist. The thought annoys him. He is aware that there is much ignorant conjecture aboard ship about his sexual habits, and he finds the furtive gossip more amusing than bothersome; but he isn't eager to enmesh Noelle, who might be disturbed at finding herself the subject of such rumors, in these lascivious whisperings.

"May we join you?" the year-captain asks, sliding out of his clothes. The question is routine politeness. Huw ges-

tures grandly, and the year-captain and Noelle slip into the
tub on the side opposite from Imogen and Huw. There's no
need for helping Noelle; she makes her way over the side of
the tub as easily as if she were sighted. As they settle into the
warm water the side of Noelle's thigh presses up against the
year-captain's, though, which he assumes is accidental, the tub
being as small and as crowded as it is, and Noelle's sense of
spatial perception not as accurate in water as it is where sound
waves travel unimpeded. The year-captain automatically
moves a couple of centimeters to his left; but a few moments
later, as further positional adjustments are made by the occupants of the tub, he feels Noelle coming in contact with him
again. It is hard now not to believe that this is deliberate, that
all of this is, the suggestion that they go to the baths together,
the casual stripping in her cabin, the nude promenade through
the corridor. But why? Noelle is a beautiful woman, yes;
highly attractive, even, and fascinating in her enigmatic cool
dignity; but after all this time she still has played no role that
he knows of in the pattern of sexual entanglements aboard the
starship, and though she certainly seems to be offering herself
to him now, the year-captain finds it difficult to accept the
belief that she actually is. He prefers to look upon her as
guileless and her present behavior as innocent. He continues
to think of her as an asexual being, given over wholly to the
bond with her distant sister and needing no other. Possibly
she's just in a playful mood just now, without any genuine
erotic subtext; or perhaps she is experimenting with a new
way of unwinding from the tensions of her message-sending.
In any case he has no intention of responding to the invitation
she seems to be extending, whether or not it's real. As always,
a sexual involvement with Noelle strikes him as a potentially
explosive thing. He doesn't think it could ever be the kind of

coolly recreational coupling that his affair with Julia is. There were bound to be immense messy complications, somehow. Noelle is of vital importance to the voyage; so is he; he will not risk involving them in something that carries with it such a high probability of diverting their energies into troublesome areas.

Nevertheless, this time the year-captain allows his thigh to remain in contact with hers. It would be rude to pull away a second time.

"You spoke very well," Imogen says to him, "about Marcus the other day. I was extremely moved. I think we all were."

"Thank you." It seems like a mindless kind of reply to make, but he can't think of any other response.

"He was so difficult to get to know," Imogen says. She and Marcus had been lovers for a brief time early in the voyage. Imogen is one of the ship's metallurgists; she is also assistant medical officer. Everyone has odd combinations of specialties. "Even in bed, you know?" she says. "Right here in the baths is where it happened, the first time. We were just sitting side by side, the way I am with Huw now, neither of us saying very much, and then Marcus turned to me and smiled and touched my wrist and gestured with his head toward one of the side rooms. Didn't say a word. And we got right up and went in there. Not a word out of him the whole time."

Huw is smiling benignly, as though Imogen is merely speaking of having gone off with Marcus to play a few games of *Go*. But quite possibly he doesn't see much difference between the one recreation and the other, except that *Go* requires heavier thinking.

Imogen says, "It was like that every time, the whole week that we were together. He was good, very good, in fact, but he never said a personal thing about himself, never asked anything about me. Friendly but distant: a mystery man. I liked him, though, I admired him, I respected his intelligence, his seriousness. I believed that sooner or later he'd open up a little. And then one afternoon we were sitting in here together and Natasha was here too, and he turned to her just the way he had turned to me the week before, and that was that for Marcus and me. It was over, as simply as that. But I always thought that Marcus and I would have a chance to get to know each other eventually, later on, maybe much later on. And now we never will."

"Such a waste," Sieglinde says, from the other tub.

"A fine young man," says Huw. "It ripped me apart, watching him crack up down there. It ripped me apart."

The year-captain nods abstractedly. This conversation is a necessary one, he supposes, part of the healing process for them, but it is making him uncomfortable. And the pressure of Noelle's bare thigh against his in the tub is having an unsettling effect on him.

"They are very sad for us, the people on Earth," Noelle says. "You know, they love us very much, they follow everything that we are doing with the greatest interest. The expedition to Planet A—it was the only thing they talked about on Earth all week, my sister says. And then—to learn that Marcus had died—" She shakes her head. "They are having memorial services for him today everywhere on Earth, do you know?"

"How wonderful," Imogen says. "How good that will be for them. And for us as well."

The year-captain looks at Noelle in surprise. That little detail, the thing about the memorial services, comes as news to him. Noelle had said nothing about that during the transmis-

ROBERT SILVERBERG

sion meeting. Is she still in contact with Yvonne at this moment, receiving a steady flow of reports of Earth's reactions to the death of Marcus? Or—he hates the idea, but it will not stay buried—is she simply inventing things as she goes along?

"You didn't tell me that," he says, a little reproachfully. "About the services."

"Oh. Yes. Everywhere on Earth."

"We are the big news," Sieglinde says, with her usual coarse guffaw. "We fly around the universe, we live, we die, we find nasty planets, it is the great event for them. The only event. We astonish them, and they are unaccustomed to astonishment. Sheep, is what they are! Lazy as sheep! We should make up deaths every now and then, even if there aren't any more, just to keep them excited. To keep them interested in us. Also to remind them that there is such a thing as death."

Everyone turns to look at her. Sieglinde's face is red with anger, fiery. She has a capacity for stirring herself up mightily. But then she grins—smirks, really—and the high color fades as swiftly as it had come.

More gently she says, "It was very bad, the thing about Marcus. I am greatly troubled by it, still. Such a quiet boy. Such a good mind he had. We must have no more losses of that kind, year-captain, do you hear me?"

"I wish we hadn't had even that one," he replies.

There is a dark moment of silence in the room.

"Well," Huw says finally. He heaves his bulky body out of the water. He is reddened from the heat, looking at least half boiled. "We should be moving along, I think." Reaching down with one hand, he lifts little Imogen out of the tub as easily as though she were a child, pulling her up over the tiled rim and letting her feet dangle in the air a moment before

S T A R B O R N E

setting her down. They go off to the cold showers, and then dress and leave.

"I will be going also," Sieglinde announces. "There is work I should be doing in the control cabin."

Noelle and the year-captain are left alone in the baths. They sit facing the same way, thighs still touching. It is suddenly a highly awkward situation, with the other three gone. The tension of the moment in her cabin when Noelle had removed her clothes now returns to the year-captain, if indeed it has ever left. The nearest of the three lovemaking chambers next to the baths is just a few meters away. They could very easily stroll over to it right now. But the year-captain has no idea what Noelle wants him to do. He has no very clear idea what he himself wants to do. Again he waits, resolved to take his cue from her.

And again Noelle offers him nothing more than the usual simple innocence, the usual sweet indifference to the possibilities of the situation.

"Shall we go to the gaming lounge now, year-captain?"

"Of course. Whatever you say, Noelle."

They return to her cabin first. He remains outside while she dresses; then they go up to the gaming lounge, where they find Paco and Roy playing, and also Sylvia and Heinz. The year-captain sets up the third board for himself and Noelle.

It is several weeks since he has played. The expedition to the surface of Planet A has kept him sufficiently distracted lately. He sinks quickly into the game now, but for all his skill, he doesn't stand a chance. Noelle, playing black, greets him with an aggressive strategy that he has never seen before, and her swarming warriors devour his white stones with appalling swiftness, hollowing out his forces and setting up elliptical

ROBERT SILVERBERG

rings of conquered territory all over the board. It's a complete rout. The game is over so quickly that Roy and Heinz, glancing over simultaneously from their own boards in the moment of Noelle's triumph, both grunt in amazement as they realize that it has ended.

Everything has been calculated, and checked and rechecked, and today is the day of our departure for the world that at this point we call, with such drab unpoetic simplicity, Planet B. Let us hope that we have reason to give it some more colorful and memorable name later on: let us hope that it is to be our new home. Hope costs us nothing. It does no harm and perhaps accomplishes some good.

I found myself, as the hour of the new shunt approached, standing in front of the viewplate, looking out at the solar system we were about to leave. Down over there, the broad brown breast of Planet A itself, turning indifferently on its axis, giving us not an iota of its attention. We are like gnats to it. Less than gnats: we are nothing. In the most offhand of ways it has claimed one of our lives, and now it swings onward around its golden sun as it always has, ignoring the unwanted and unwelcomed visitors who briefly disturbed its solitude and now soon will be gone. What folly, to think that this heartless place could ever have been our home! But Marcus's life was the price we had to pay for learning that.

It isn't an evil world, of course. There isn't any such thing as an evil world. Worlds are indifferent things. This one simply is not a world we can use.

And now—Planet B—Planet C, perhaps—Planet Z—

I stood by the viewplate, watching this alien sky, this strange repellent planet that we had come here to explore, its yellow sun, its neighbor worlds wandering the dark sky all about us, and the hint of other stars in the sky behind them, mere bright specks, betokening the vastness of the universe in which we are soon once more to be wandering; and then, in a twinkling, the whole scene was gone, wiped from my sight in a single abolishing stroke, and I was looking once again at the rippling, eddying, shimmering blankness that is nospace. We had successfully made our shunt. How I had missed that dazzling gray emptiness! How I rejoiced now at seeing it once more!

So again we are outside space and time, crossing through unfathomable nowhere on our route from somewhere to somewhere, and I realize that I have in some fashion begun to become a denizen of nospace: I am happiest, it seems, when we have ripped ourselves loose of the fabric of normal space and time and are floating in this quiet featureless other reality, this void within the void, this inexplicable strangeness, this mathematical construct, that we call nospace. Nospace travel is only a means to an end; why, then, do I take such pleasure in returning to it? Can it be that my secret preference, unknown even to me, is that we never find any suitable world at all, that we roam the galaxy forever like the crew of the accursed Flying Dutchman? *Surely not. Surely I want us to discover that Planet B is a warm and friendly land, where we will settle and thrive and live happily ever after.*

Surely.

The journey, Paco tells me, will take five or six months, or perhaps as many as eight — he can't be entirely certain, the mathematics of nospace travel being the paradoxical business that is. No less than five, no more than eight, anyway. And then we do the whole survey-mission thing all over again, with better luck, let us hope, than this time.

The chances are, of course, that B won't work out any better than A did. Our requirements are too fastidious: a place with our kind of atmosphere, a place with actual H_2O water, one that isn't too hot or too cold, that doesn't already belong to some intelligent species, et cetera, et cetera. But Hesper has more worlds up his sleeve, eight or ten of them by now that strike him as promising prospects. And there will be others beyond those. The galaxy is unthinkably huge, and we are, after all, still essentially in Earth's own backyard, bouncing around a sphere no more than a hundred light-years in diameter, out here in one small arm of the galaxy, 30,000 light-years from the center. The galaxy in its entirety has — how many stars? two hundred billion? four hundred billion? — and if only one out of a thousand of those has planets, and one planet out of a thousand falls within the criteria for habitability that we must impose, then there are more potential worlds for us out there than we could ever reach in our lifetimes, or in those of the children that may be born aboard this starship as our voyage proceeds. Surely one of those will work out for us.

Surely.

They are well along now in this leg of their journey, and interference problems have developed again for Noelle. The static, the fuzziness of transmission quality, that first had begun to set in in the fifth month of the voyage, and that had at some points become severe and at others had almost vanished, has returned again in much greater force than before. There are some days when Noelle can barely make contact with her sister at all.

Though the voyage is uneventful now, one serene day
following another, the year-captain insists on making the daily
transmissions to Earth. He continues to believe that that is an
important, even essential, activity for them: that the people of
Earth are vicariously living the greatest adventure of their
languid lives through the men and women of the *Wotan,* and
derive immense psychological value from their daily dose of
news from those intrepid travelers who fearlessly roam the
distant stars. It does his crew some good, too, to get word
from Earth regularly of the things that are taking place there,
such as they are.

But now, day by day, the transmission problems are
becoming more extreme, and Noelle must struggle with ever-
greater outlay of effort to maintain her weakening connection
with far-off Yvonne. She is working at it so hard that the year-
captain has begun to fear for her. He is feeling the strain
himself.

"I have the new communiqué ready to send," he tells
her edgily. "Do you feel up to it?"

"Of course I do." She gives him a ferocious smile.
"Don't even hint at giving up, year-captain. There absolutely
has to be some way around this interference."

"Absolutely," he says. He rustles his papers restlessly.
"Okay, then, Noelle. Let's go. This is shipday number—"

"Wait," she says. "Give me just another moment to get
ready, all right?"

He pauses. She closes her eyes and begins to enter the
transmitting state. She is conscious, as ever, of Yvonne's presence. Even when no specific information is flowing between
them, there is perpetual low-level contact, there is the sense
that the other is near, that warm proprioceptive awareness

such as one has of one's own arm or leg or hip. But between that impalpable subliminal contact and the actual transmission of specific content lie several key steps. Yvonne and Noelle are human biopsychic resonators constituting a long-range communications network; there is a tuning procedure for them as for any other transmitters and receivers. Noelle opens herself to the radiant energy spectrum, vibratory, pulsating, that will carry her message to her Earthbound sister. As the transmitting circuit in this interchange she must be the one to attain maximum energy flow. Quickly, intuitively, she activates her own energy centers, the one in the spine, the one in the solar plexus, the one at the top of the skull; a stream of energy pours from her and instantaneously spans the galaxy.

But today there is an odd and troublesome splashback effect: Noelle, monitoring the circuit, is immediately aware that the signal has failed to reach Yvonne. Yvonne is there, Yvonne is tuned and expectant, yet something is jamming the channel and nothing gets through, not a single syllable.

"The interference is worse than ever," she tells the year-captain. "I feel as if I could put my hand out and *touch* Yvonne. But she's not reading me and nothing's coming back from her."

With a little shake of her shoulders Noelle alters the sending frequency; she feels a corresponding adjustment at Yvonne's end of the connection; but again they are thwarted, again there is total blockage. Her signal is going forth and is being soaked up by—what? How can such a thing happen?

Now she makes a determined effort to boost the output of the system. She addresses herself to the neural center in her spine, exciting its energies, using them to drive the next center to a more intense vibrational tone, harnessing that to push the highest center of all to its greatest harmonic capacity. Up and down the energy bands she roves. Nothing. Nothing. She shivers; she huddles; she is visibly depleted by the strain, pale, struggling for breath. "I can't get through," she murmurs. "Yvonne's there, I can feel her there, I know she's working to read me. But I can't transmit any sort of intelligible coherent message."

A hundred, two hundred, however many light-years from Earth it is that they are, and the only communication channel is blocked. The year-captain finds himself unexpectedly beleaguered by frosty terrors. They can report nothing to the mother world; they can receive nothing. It should not matter, really, but it does. It matters terribly, somehow. The ship, the self-sufficient autonomous ship, has become a mere gnat blowing in a hurricane. There is darkness on all sides of them. The voyagers now hurtle blindly onward into the depths of an unknown universe, alone, alone, alone.

He sits by himself in the control cabin, brooding. He has failed Noelle, he knows, fleeing helplessly from her in the moment of her need, overwhelmed by the immensity of her loss, for it is her loss even more than it is theirs. All about him meaningless readout lights flash and wink. He is dumbfounded by the depth of the sudden despair that has engulfed him.

He had been so smug about not needing any link to Earth, but now that the link is gone he shivers and cowers. He

barely can recognize himself in this new unraveled man that
he has become. Everything has been made new. There are no
rules. Human beings have never been this far from home, and
the tenuous, invisible bond between the sisters had been their
lifeline, he realizes now, and now the sisters are sundered and
that lifeline is gone. It is gone. The water is wide and their ship
is very small. He walks out into the corridor and presses
himself against the viewplate; and the famous grayness of the
Intermundium just beyond, swirling and eddying, the grayness that had been so beautiful to him and so full of revelations, mocks him now with its unbearable immensity. Mocks
and seduces all at once. Leap into me, it calls. Leap, leap, lose
yourself in me, drown in me.

Behind him, the sound of soft footsteps. Noelle. She
touches his hunched, knotted shoulders. "It's all right," she
whispers. "You're overreacting. Don't make such a tragedy
out of it." But it is. Her tragedy in particular, hers and
Yvonne's. He is amazed that she can even think of giving
comfort to him in this moment, when it is he who should be
comforting her. Noelle and Yvonne have spent their lives in
the deepest of unions, a union fundamentally incomprehensible to everyone but them, and that is lost to them now. How
brave she is, he thinks. How strong in the face of this, her
great disaster.

But also, he knows, it is his disaster, his tragedy, theirs,
everybody's. They are all cut off. Lost forever in a foggy silence. Whatever triumphs they may achieve out here, if ever
any triumphs there are to be, they will never be able to share
them with the mother world. Or at least will not be able to
share them for a century or more, until the news of their
accomplishments creeps finally back to Earth on whatever

conventional carrier wave they use to send it. None of the fifty who sailed the stars aboard the *Wotan* can hope still to be alive by then.

From the gaming lounge, far down the corridor, comes the sound of singing. Boisterous voices, Elliot, Chang, Leon. They know nothing, yet, of what has happened.

> *Well, Travelin' Dan was a spacefarin' man*
> *Who jumped in the nospace tube —*

The year-captain still has not turned. Something that might have been a sigh or might perhaps have been a sob escapes from Noelle, behind him. He whirls, seizes her, pulls her against him. Feels her trembling. Comforts her, where a moment before she had been comforting him. "Yes, yes, yes, yes," he murmurs. With his arm around her shoulders he swings around, pivoting so that they both are facing the viewplate. As if she could see. Nospace dances and churns a couple of centimeters from his nose, just beyond that transparent shield. That shimmering grayness, that deep infinite well of nothingness, his great Intermundium. It frightens him now. He feels a fierce wind blowing out of the viewplate and through the ship, the khamsin, the sirocco, the simoom, the leveche, a sultry wind, a killing wind coming out of the gray strangeness, all the grim, dry deadly winds that rove the Earth bringing fire and madness, hot winds and cold ones, the mistral, the tramontana. No, he thinks. No. He forces himself not to fear that wind. He tells himself that it is a wind of joy, a cool sweet wind, a wind of life. Why should he think there is anything to fear in the realm beyond the viewplate? Until today he has always loved to stand here and stare into it: how

ROBERT SILVERBERG

beautiful it is out there, how ecstatically beautiful, that is what he has always thought! And it is. It is. Noelle is quivering against him as if she sees what he sees, and he begins to grow calm, begins to find beauty in the sight of the nospace realm again. How sad, the year-captain thinks, that we can never tell anyone about it now, except one another.

A strange peace unexpectedly descends on him. He has found once more that zone of calm that he had learned, in his monastery days, the secret of attaining. Everything is going to be all right, he insists. No harm will come of what has happened. And perhaps some good. And perhaps some good. Benefits lurk in the darkest places.

Noelle plays *Go* obsessively, beating everyone. She seems to live in the lounge twenty hours a day. Sometimes she takes on two opponents at once—an incredible feat, considering that she must hold the constantly changing intricacies of both boards in her memory—and defeats them both: two days after losing verbal-level contact with Yvonne, she simultaneously triumphs over Roy and Heinz before an astounded audience of fifteen or twenty of her shipmates. She looks animated and buoyant; they all have been told by now what has happened, but whatever sorrow she must feel over the snapping of the link she takes care to conceal. She expresses it, the others suspect, only by her manic *Go*-playing. The year-captain is one of her most frequent adversaries now, taking his turn at the board in the time he would have devoted to composing and dictating the communiqués for Earth. He had thought *Go* was over for him years ago, but he, too, is playing obsessively these days, building walls and the unassailable fortresses known as eyes. There is satisfaction and reassurance in the rhythmic clacking march of the black and white stones. But Noelle wins every game she plays against him. She covers the board with eyes.

The quest for Planet B serves, to a considerable degree, to distract the voyagers from the problems that the disruption of contact with Earth has created. Expectations quickly begin to rise. Suddenly there is great optimism about Planet B among the members of the expedition. If there are no more cozy messages from home, there is, at least, the counterbalancing pleasure of contemplating the possibility that a wonderful new Earthlike home lies at the end of this stretch of their voyage.

Hesper has refined his correlation techniques and is able to provide them with a plethora of data of high-order reliability, so he claims, about the world toward which they go. It is, he says, the second of five planets that surround a medium-size K-type star. Whether a star of that spectral type can be hot enough to sustain temperatures in the range agreeable for protoplasmic life is something that arouses some debate aboard ship, but Hesper assures everybody that the star that is their destination is a K of better-than-median luminosity, and that Planet B is close enough to it so that there should be ample warmth, perhaps even a little too much for complete comfort.

ROBERT SILVERBERG

How can Hesper know all this stuff? No one can figure it out: it is a perpetual mystery aboard the ship. He doesn't have access to direct astronomical observation of the target system, not out here in nospace; they all are aware that he is simply playing around with a bunch of cryptic reality-analogs, a set of data-equivalents that he decodes by means of methods that nobody else can comprehend. Still, he was right enough about Planet A, so far as the question of its size, temperature range, atmospheric makeup, and other salient points was concerned. Hesper had indeed missed one small detail about Planet A that made it notably unsuitable for human settlement, but that was one that no instrument yet devised could have detected in advance of an actual manned landing.

What Hesper says about Planet B is even more encouraging than his preliminary reports on its unhappy predecessor. Planet B, Hesper asserts, is a planet of goodly size, with a diameter that is something like 15 percent greater than that of Earth, but it must be made up largely of the lighter elements, because its mass is no bigger than Earth's and its gravitational pull, presumably, is about the same. It definitely has an atmosphere, according to Hesper, and here the news is very good indeed, the good old oxygen-nitrogen-and-a-smattering-of-CO_2, mixed pretty much the way human lungs prefer to have it, except that there's a tad more CO_2 than is found on Earth. Possibly a tad more than a tad, in truth—a bit of a greenhouse effect, Hesper admits, probably giving rise to a sort of steamy Mesozoic texture for the place. But the Mesozoic on Earth was a life-friendly era, a time of gloriously flourishing fauna and flora, and there should be nothing to worry about, Hesper tells them. Think tropical, he says; and, child of the sun-blasted tropics that he is himself, his eyes light up with the thrill of anticipation. All will be well. It will be a planet-size

Hawaii, he indicates. Or a planet-size Madagascar. Warm, warm, warm, lots of moisture where moisture does the most good, a shining, humid paradise, a sweet lush leafy Eden.

Well, maybe so. Some of the older members of the crew remember that the Mesozoic was the dinosaur era, and they don't see anything particularly enticing about setting up a colony in the midst of a lot of dinosaurs. But there isn't any logical necessity to the analogy, which others promptly point out. Evolution doesn't have to follow the same track on every world. High humidity and tropical temperatures from pole to pole and an extra dollop of CO_2 in the air may have given rise to a dominant race of giant reptiles on Earth, sure, but on Planet B the same circumstances may have brought forth nothing more complex than a tribe of happy jellyfish dreamily adrift in the balmy oceans.

Oh, the oceans. A bit of a puzzle there, Hesper has to concede. His long-distance proxy-equivalent hocus-pocus has, at least so far, failed to turn up evidence that there *are* any oceans on Planet B. That doesn't make a lot of sense, considering the apparent prevalence of water molecules in the atmosphere and the generally high global mean temperatures, which might reasonably have been expected to induce a lot of rainfall. But Planet B's surface, as manifested in the surrogate form of Hesper's long-range data, seems to have the same even texture everywhere, no inequalities of albedo or temperature or anything else significant, so either there is a single vast planetary ocean or none at all. The latter is by far the more probable hypothesis. So a little mystery exists in that quarter—one that will have to await resolution for a while, until they are much closer and can carry out some direct optical inspection of the place itself.

And then, one would assume, once there has been a

good look-see from low orbit and the place is found worthy of further checking out, there will be the whole thing of sending down a drone probe again, followed, if everything looks good, by a manned ship, an exploratory party. Everyone has started to assume that things *will* look good down there, in fact that things will be downright ideal, and therefore that an exploratory party is ultimately in the cards. Which brings up some questions that have already arisen once before in the course of the voyage—the makeup of the landing party that will go down to confirm the usefulness and beauty of Planet B, and the concomitant issue of the expiration of the year-captain's second year in office.

That second year is almost up now. And he will want to be part of any exploration team that goes down to visit Planet B, of course. So they have the troublesome business of an election to deal with, once again.

It is dealt with, quietly and quickly, in a caucus consisting of the dozen members of the expedition who care most about these matters.

"He is essential and indispensable," Heinz says. "There's no other plausible possibility for the job, is there? Is there?"

"Well, is there?" Paco asks. "You tell us."

"Obviously there's no one," says Elizabeth. "He'll have to be reelected."

"You three have it very neatly worked out, don't you?" Julia says.

Heinz gives her a quick look. "You don't like it? Does that mean you're volunteering to run again yourself?"

"You know I would, if I thought it would do any good. But I have to agree with you that if we took another vote, I wouldn't be elected. He would."

"And he will be," says Heinz. "Just as he was last year."

Huw says, "He'll erupt. He'll absolutely explode."

"If we hand him a *fait accompli*?" Sylvia says. "Simply tell him that he's been reelected again by acclamation, and appeal to his sense of duty?"

"His sense of duty," says Huw, "is directed entirely toward the exploration of the planets we discover. He didn't sign on to be captain for life. It's a job that's supposed to rotate from year to year, isn't it? So why would he let himself be stuck with it forever if it permanently disqualifies him from doing the one thing that he signed on to do?"

They consider that for a while. It's a valid enough point; but in the end they agree that there's no one else on board who can rally the necessary support. The year-captain has established himself in everyone's mind as the captain-for-life; replacing him now with somebody else would have something of the quality of an insurrection. And who would they choose, anyway? Roy, Giovanna, Julia, Huw, Leon? Those who are qualified, even remotely, for the captaincy are either unwilling to take the job or else unsuitable by virtue of their existing responsibilities.

In the end, they decide quietly to canvass the ship's entire complement and present the year-captain with the results of the tally. This is done; and the vote confirming his reelection is unanimous. Huw, Heinz, Julia, and Leon agree to be the members of the delegation that will bring this news to the year-captain. At the last moment Noelle, who has been present in the gaming lounge while this part of the operation is under discussion, asks to be included in the group.

"No," says the year-captain instantly when he is apprised of what has been going on. "Forget it. Don't waste your

R O B E R T   S I L V E R B E R G

time even thinking about it. My term is coming to its end, thank God, and you have to start finding somebody else to be captain."

"The vote, you know, was unanim—" Leon begins.

"So? What of it?" the year-captain demands, speaking over him. "Did anyone consult me? Did anyone take the trouble to ask me whether I was going to be a candidate for reelection? Which I most emphatically do not intend to be. I took this second term with the greatest reluctance and I'm not going to take a third term under any circumstances whatsoever. Is that clear?"

Of course it's clear; it's been clear to everybody for a long time. But they can't accept his refusal, because the ship must have a captain, and no other satisfactory and electible prospect for that job is on the horizon. They tell him this, and he tells them once again how adamant he intends to be about his desire to give up his office, and for a time everyone is speaking at once. A great deal of heat is generated, but not much light.

In a moment of sudden stillness that pops with almost comic predictability into the general hubbub, Noelle's quiet voice abruptly is heard for the first time: "Is the rule about not being able to be part of the landing expedition the thing that makes you not want to go on being captain?"

"Of course it is."

"And that's the only reason? There's nothing else?"

He considers that for a moment. "Nothing of any real significance, I suppose."

"Then why don't we change the rule?" Noelle asks.

They all look thunderstruck by the sheer simplicity of her suggestion, even the year-captain. Leon is the first to speak, finally. "The rule isn't just an arbitrary nuisance. Planetary landings are risky things, and we are under orders not to risk the life of the year-captain in adventures of that sort."

"But if there isn't going to be any year-captain at all unless we allow the one we have to take that risk," Julia says, "then what good is the—"

"Besides," Leon continues implacably, "we have all agreed *a priori* to abide by the terms of the Articles of the Voyage. We have no right to abrogate or modify any of those terms unilaterally. Without consultation with Earth, and the permission of—"

Now it is Noelle who cuts in. "There's no way we can consult with Earth," she points out. "The contact has been severed. You know that."

"Even so," says Leon, "we have an obligation to maintain and uphold—"

"What obligation? To whom?" Heinz says. And Huw calls out boomingly, "Hear, hear! Hear, hear!"

There is another round of hubbub. This time the year-captain restores order by rapping on the cabin wall with the flat of his hand until they are all silent.

Then he says, in a chilly take-no-prisoners voice, "We have here the seeds of a compromise, I think. I'll agree to accept the captaincy for another year provided we amend the Articles of the Voyage to permit me to take part, at my sole discretion, in any future missions of planetary exploration that may occur during my term in office."

"It can't be done," Leon cries. "Earth will have a fit!"

"Earth won't ever know a thing," says Heinz. "We're permanently out of touch with Earth. Isn't that so, Noelle? No contact with your sister any more, and no hope of restoring it?"

ROBERT SILVERBERG

"That's so," Noelle says, in a tone that barely rises above a whisper.

"Well, then. We're on our own from now on, right?" declares Heinz triumphantly. "Sorry, Leon. We can't let ourselves worry about what positions Earth may take about decisions that we choose to make. We just have to make the best possible decisions for ourselves in the light of changing circumstances that Earth couldn't begin to understand anyway." He turns toward the year-captain. "Let's hear it once more, captain, just to be sure that we have it right. You'll take the job for another year, under the condition that we change the rules so that you can go off for a look at Planet B, is that it?"

"Yes."

"And if we don't change the present rules about planetary landings, there's nothing else that could induce you to stay on in office?"

"Nothing."

Now Heinz faces the others again. "So it's a take-it-or-leave-it situation, friends. We can have the year-captain on his terms or not at all. Under the cirumstances, considering that Earth's wishes in this matter are not only unknown but are unknowable and irrelevant as a result of the unfortunate breakdown in communications with Earth, I propose that we regard ourselves as free agents from this point onward, and that we call a general asembly and put the matter of amending the Articles to a vote."

"Seconded," Huw and Julia say at the same time.

Leon sputters but says nothing.

So there is an agreement of sorts. The delegates leave, and later in the day the proposal is put to a vote of the entire voyage, and it is passed handily, with Leon the only voice in opposition. The year-captain accepts the outcome with reasonably good grace. Despite it all, he is almost as uneasy as Leon about amending the Articles; there is something disturbingly nihilistic about doing that, a kind of blithe lawless willfulness that offends his sense of the proper order of things. They *have*, after all, promised most solemnly to govern themselves by the terms of the Articles, and here they are tinkering with those terms behind Earth's back, so to speak, without the slightest sort of by-your-leave.

But Heinz is right. With contact apparently lost for good — Noelle continues to have no luck in reaching Yvonne — Earth has ceased to be a major factor in their calculations: has ceased to be a factor at all, really. Where an Article proves itself to be unworkable, they themselves must be the only judges of whether it is to be amended. Besides, the Articles call for a change in the captaincy every year, and that rule has been, if not amended, then simply ignored. And so, in consequence of that, they must now dispense with the one about penning up the year-captain aboard the ship. Once again some new planet is about to swim into their ken, as Huw likes to say, and this time the year-captain does not intend to be left behind when they go down to look at it. That's the essential thing now. He does not intend to be left behind.

So my third term as year-captain now begins. I think I should perhaps get used to the idea of holding this job for the rest of my life.

The election was a grubby thing, of course, a lot of shameless political bargaining. But the deal is done: they have their quid, *I have*

ROBERT SILVERBERG

my quo, and that's that. I'm used to being captain by now. Ironic, considering how elaborately I always used to go out of my way to spare myself from taking on the responsibilities of society; but what I used to do can't be allowed to control my sense of what must be done now.

The ship has to have a captain. I seem to be the right person for the job. What I need is to continue traveling the course I chose for myself long ago, which means continued exploration of one kind or another. What Earth needs —

Yes, what Earth needs. I must never forget about that.

Poor old Earth! All the ancient squalor is gone, most of the pain — and yet something is wrong. Disease and hunger are conquered. Life is just about eternal if you want it to be that way. War is something we read about in history texts, something anthropological and remote, an odd obsolete practice of our ancestors, like cannibalism or bloodletting. And yet! Something wrong! I think back through all that I know of human history, and I know a great deal, really — the plagues, the massacres, all the episodes of torture for the sheer fun of it, the great and petty vilenesses, the whole catalog of sins that Sophocles and Shakespeare and Strindberg understood so well — and I wonder why we aren't more jubilant about what we have attained in our own time. What I have to conclude is that we are a driven race, never satisfied with anything, even with utter blissful contentedness. There's always something missing, even in perfection. And our awareness of that missing something is what drives us on and on and on, forever looking for it.

Which is what caused the massacres and all of that — a sense even among our primitive forebears that something needs to be fixed, by whatever ham-fisted methods happen to be available at the moment. Our methods have become more humane and also more efficient as we grow more — well, civilized — but that need, that hunger, still operates on us. And now has pushed us out among the stars to grapple with unknown worlds.

Or am I projecting my own needs and hungers and awareness of inadequacies onto the whole human race? Are most of us quite happy with our lives in this glorious modern age, and do those happy ones feel sorry for the pitiful maladjusted few who were willing to go off on this wild voyage into the dark?

I don't believe that. I don't want to believe that, at any rate. And we will go onward, we fifty, until we find what we are seeking. (We forty-nine, I should say now, but the old phrase is ingrained so deeply!) And when we find it, which I am certain we will, I want to think that for a moment, at least, we will know a little peace.

I wish we were still in touch with Earth.

I worry about Noelle. She seems to be all right, even in the absence of the contact with her sister that has nourished and sustained her all her life. But is she, really? Is she?

The breakdown in the communication link with Earth has been the subject of much discussion, naturally. Whether it is a total and irreversible breakdown is not entirely certain yet. Yes, Noelle had said, at the meeting between the year-captain and the delegation that had come to apprise him of the election results, that there was no way of restoring contact with her sister; but—as she admitted privately to the year-captain the next day—she had simply been saying that by way of bolstering Heinz's arguments in favor of amending the Articles of the Voyage. In truth Noelle has no idea whether contact can be restored, and she feels just a little guilty for having given everyone the notion that it can't be. "I did it because I wanted everyone to go along with the deal that was taking shape," she confesses, but only to the year-captain. "If we can't speak with Earth any more, we don't need to worry what they'll think about our changing the Articles, isn't that so? But it's always possible that I'll regain Yvonne's signal sooner or later. It's happened before that the signal has weakened and then become strong again."

She does, she says, still feel Yvonne's mental presence somewhere within her. But, as has been true for days now, she is unable to pick up any verbal content in what Yvonne is sending, and she suspects—it is only a guess, but she thinks there's real probability to it—that nothing she's sending Earthward is reaching Yvonne, either. She still makes daily attempts at reopening the link, but to no avail. For all intents and purposes they are cut off from Earth and very likely will remain cut off forever.

No one believes that the problem is a function of anything so obvious as distance. Noelle has been quite convincing on that score: a signal that propagates perfectly for the first sixteen light-years of a journey ought not abruptly to deteriorate a couple of light-minutes farther along the road. There should at least have been prior sign of attenuation, and there was no attenuation, only noise suddenly cutting in, noise that interfered with and ultimately destroyed the signal.

"It's some kind of a force," Roy suggests, "that has reached in here and messed up the connection."

A force? What kind of force?

Noelle's old idea that what is intervening between her and her sister is some physical effect analogous to sunspot static—that it is the product of radiation emitted by this or that giant star into whose vicinity they have come during the course of their travels—is brought up again, and is in the end rejected again. There is, both Roy and Sieglinde point out, no energy interface between realspace and nospace, no opportunity for any kind of electromagnetic intrusion. That much had been amply demonstrated long before any manned voyages were undertaken. Hesper's scanning instruments, yes, are able to pick up information of a nonelectromagnetic kind out of the realspace continuum, information that can be translated into comprehensible data about that continuum; but no material thing belonging to realspace can penetrate here. The nospace tube is an impermeable wall separating them from the continuum of phenomena. They are effectively outside the universe. They could in theory pass, and perhaps they already have, right through the heart of a star in the course of their journey without causing any disruption either to the star or to themselves. Nothing that has mass or charge can leap the barrier between the universe of real-world phenomena and the cocoon of nothingness that the ship's drive mechanism has woven about them; nor can a photon get across, nor even a slippery neutrino.

But something, it seems, *is* getting through, and is doing damage. Many speculations excite the voyagers. The one force that *can* cross the barrier, Roy observes, is thought. Thought is intangible, unmeasurable, limitless. The ease with which Noelle and Yvonne maintained contact on an instantaneous basis throughout the first five months of the voyage has demonstrated that.

"But let us suppose," Roy says—it is clear from his lofty tone that this is merely some hypothesis he is putting forth, an airy *gedankenexperiment*—"that the interference Noelle is experiencing is caused by beings of powerful telepathic capacity that live in the space between the stars."

"Beings that live between the stars," Paco repeats in wonderment. Plainly he thinks that Roy has launched into something crazy, but he has enough respect for the power of Roy's intellect to hold off on his scorn until the mathematician has finished putting forth his idea.

"Yes, between the stars," Roy goes on. "Or *in* the stars, or surrounding them. Who can say? Let us suppose that each of these beings is capable of emitting mental transmissions, just as Noelle is, but that their sending capacity is far more powerful than hers. As these transmissions go flooding outward, perhaps each one sweeping out a sphere with a radius of many light-years, the trajectory of the *Wotan* carries them in and out of these spheres and the telepathic impulses cross the nospace barrier just as readily as the thoughts of Noelle and Yvonne do. And it is these alien mental emanations, let us suppose, that are smothering the signal coming from Earth."

Paco is ready to jump in now with objections; but Heinz is already speaking, extending Roy's suggestion into a different area of possibility.

"What if," Heinz says, "these beings that Roy has suggested are denizens not of the space between the stars but of nospace itself? Living right here in the tube, let us say, and as we travel along we keep running into their domains."

"The nospace tube must be matter-free except for the ship that moves through it," Sieglinde observes acidly. "Otherwise a body moving at speeds faster than light, as we are, would generate destructive resonances, since in conventional physical terms our mass is equal to infinity, and a body with infinite mass leaves no room in its universe for anything else."

"Indeed true," Heinz replies, unruffled as always. "But I don't remember speaking of these beings as material objects. What I imagine are gigantic incorporeal beings as big as asteroids, as big as planets, maybe, that have no mass at all, no essence, only *existence* — great convergences of pure mental force that drift freely through the tube. They are the native life-forms of nospace. They are not made up of anything that we can regard as matter. They are something of a nature absolutely unknown to us, occupying this otherworldy zone that we call nospace, living out there the way angels live in Heaven."

"Angels," Paco snorts.

"Angels, yes!" cries Elizabeth, as though inspired, and claps her hands in a sort of rapture of fantasy.

"Of course, I don't mean that literally," says Heinz, a little sourly. He casts an annoyed look in Elizabeth's direction. "But let's postulate that they are there, whatever they are, these alien beings, these strange gigantic things. And as we pass through them, they give off biopsychic transmissions that disrupt the Yvonne–Noelle circuit—"

"Biopsychic transmissions," Paco repeats mockingly.

"Yes, biopsychic transmissions, causing accidental interference—or maybe it's deliberate, maybe they are actually *feeding* on the sisters' mental output, soaking it up, reveling in the energy flow that comes their way—"

" 'So in a voice, so in a shapeless flame, angels affect us oft, and worshipped be,' " says Elizabeth.

"What?" Huw asks, mystified as usual by her.

"She's quoting poetry again," Heinz once more explains to him. "Shakespeare, I think."

"John Donne," says Elizabeth. "Why do you always think it's Shakespeare?"

"Shakespeare is the only poet he's ever heard of," Paco says.

" 'Hear, all ye angels, progeny of light,' " says Elizabeth. " 'Thrones, Dominations, Princedoms, Virtues, Powers, hear my decree, which unrevoked shall stand.' "

"Now, *that's* Shakespeare for sure," Heinz says.

"Milton," Elizabeth tells him sweetly. Heinz only shrugs. "Shakespeare is 'Angels and ministers of grace defend us,'" she continues. "Shakespeare is 'Good night, sweet prince, and flights of angels sing thee to thy rest!'"

Elizabeth is an inexhaustible reservoir. She is capable of going on indefinitely quoting scraps of verse about angels, and is certainly willing to do so, but Heinz's improbable little burst of poetic fancy, which Heinz plainly has come to regret almost immediately, has excited everyone in the room and no one cares to listen to her further recitations, because they all have things of their own to say. Paco, unsurprisingly, wants to bury the whole idea beneath a mound of manly contempt, and stolid Huw is having a great deal of trouble grasping the idea of noncorporeal life-forms at all, let alone angels, and Heinz keeps insisting that he was simply reaching for a figure of speech, not making a serious suggestion; but nearly everyone else finds it a striking concept, if a trifle implausible, and those others who have serious reservations about it are too abashed by the general enthusiasm to speak up openly against it. And in any case the term "angels" seems a convenient shorthand for whatever may be out there causing the problem.

Almost everybody is fascinated by the idea and they all want to provide individual embellishments of the general theme, speculating about whether the "angels" are benign or malevolent, whether they are supremely intelligent or mindless, immortal or evanescent, and so on and so on. Giovanna suggests that they could even be responsible for the sinister effects that she and Huw and Marcus had experienced during their visit to Planet A. Why not? Perhaps these space beings, these "angels," are troubled by humanity's incursion into interstellar space and are taking steps to thrust it back. But

Huw, practical as ever, suggests that they wait to see if the same things happen to those who make the landing on Planet B before coming to any conclusions of that sort.

Where the space beings might live is discussed too, but not with any clarity. It is generally agreed that whether the "angels" live within the tube as proposed by Heinz, or in some sector of realspace just outside it as pictured by Roy, is unimportant to decide at the moment; the basic concept is what needs exploration. And a consensus has definitely emerged in the group this afternoon that the interference Noelle is experiencing is in all likelihood the work of some kind of alien intelligence into whose vicinity they keep moving from time to time. That idea arouses wonder in all, even Huw. Even — however much he tries to conceal the fact — in Paco.

The year-captain, who has not been present for any of this, arrives at the lounge now, and stands perplexed by the entrance for a few moments as the talk of angels and bio-psychic transmissions swirls about him.

"What angels?" he asks after a while. "Where?"

They try to explain, two or three talking at once. Heinz is silent, arms folded, looking smug. He has overcome his initial annoyance at the excitement his casual choice of words has caused, and now he likes the idea of having stirred everyone up over so ethereal a theory. Sly worldly Heinz, postulating angels in the nospace tube! He isn't really serious, at least not about the angel part of it, the year-captain sees. But should any part of his wild idea be taken seriously? The year-captain, when he has heard them out and managed to grasp something of what they are babbling at him, seems to think so. "Angels," he says, looking pensive and grave. "Well, why shouldn't that be so? As good a metaphor as any other. It's certainly worth investigating."

They turn, all of them, and stare at him. They are all more or less aware of his background in monasticism—in mysticism, even: those years at that odd monkish retreat near the Arctic Circle, that strange interlude in his life between his time as an explorer of the moons of Jupiter and Saturn and his enrollment in the crew of the *Wotan*. He never speaks of that period to anyone on board, nor do any of them really understand why he chose to withdraw from the world at the peak of a great scientific career and enter a monastery, any more than they understand why, much earlier, after training to be a scientist, he chose to go on the stage. He has always been a complete mystery to them, which is one reason they prefer him to remain as their captain. But they are all agreed that he is a serious person, a deep thinker—unlike Paco, say, or Heinz—and if he, the true philosopher of their group, finds something of interest in this "angels" hypothesis, then very likely there must be something in it.

What to do now, though? If they are indeed in the presence of alien beings of extraordinary nature and power, can some way be found of opening a dialog with them?

Innelda suggests asking Hesper to put his scanning devices to work in an attempt to determine their location. Roy proposes an all-out campaign to find them by conventional radio means after the voyagers have emerged from the nospace tube to investigate Planet B. Huw, gamely trying to enter into the spirit of a thing that is basically uncongenial to his pragmatic nature, puts forth the idea that they ought to aim radio transmissions at the things while still *within* the nospace tube, since if the "angels" are in it with them they might well have the capacity to detect electromagnetic energy as well as thought waves.

Then Heinz says, "There's one other thing we can try.

Regardless of where these creatures actually live, it would seem that their energy-wave, their thought-manifestations, whatever it is, can come inside the tube here with us, since Noelle's thought-beam is being affected by them. Very well. We should be able to reach them the same way, by mental transmission. Noelle could try to speak directly to them. Ask them who they are, where they live, why they're suppressing her contact with Earth."

"Yes!" someone shouts—it is Elliot—and Maria echoes her, and then Jean-Claude. "Of course! Noelle should try! Noelle! Noelle!"

All eyes are on Noelle.

She looks flustered, even a little frightened, but to some degree amenable nonetheless. Softly she says, smiling shyly, "I've never *tried* to talk with angels before, you know. If that's what they are. But if you all want me to try—"

"Yes," the year-captain breaks in, saying the word in a tone of voice that often is better understood aboard the ship as meaning *No.* "We should definitely consider the project, a little later on. But this isn't the moment for it, really. We're coming within range of the solar system of Planet B. We have that to deal with first; we can worry about speaking with angels afterwards."

An end has been made, then, at least for the time being, to the excitement over Heinz's angel theory. Heinz and Roy's theory, really, though Roy's crucial role in propounding it has quickly been overshadowed in the general consciousness by Heinz's quickness with a lively metaphor. Nobody on board is religious in the way that term once had been understood, but the long months of isolation aboard the starship, perhaps, may have conjured a streak of irrationality in some of the voyagers, and of fierce playfulness in others. "Angels" is what everybody now calls the hypothetical alien beings that hypothetically surround the ship. Even hard-core skeptics like Paco and Huw use the term for lack of any better one.

But there will be no immediate attempt at a telepathic foray by Noelle for the purpose of making contact with supposed incorporeal creatures of extraterrestrial origin that may be lurking in their vicinity of nospace or realspace. As the year-captain has pointed out, the impending arrival of the *Wotan* at Planet B is a matter of higher priority just now.

The year-captain wonders what the Abbot would have

said about his suppression of the angel discussion. He thinks about the Abbot's disapproval whenever he does something that is blatantly manipulative or selfish; and that is certainly what he has done just now, something both manipulative *and* selfish, though he hopes he is the only one aboard who fully understands that.

His ostensible reason for derailing the conversation—that they need to concentrate instead on the challenge of Planet B—is legitimate enough. But behind it lies something else entirely, a matter of compassion, of concern for the most delicate member of the ship's community. He could see, even if none of the others could, the look of fear on Noelle's face, and he could hear the little quaver in her voice. Suppose these angels, or whatever they are, *did* exist, and suppose she *could* in some fashion open her mind to them, how did anyone know what would become of her? His mind had gone at once to all those Greek myths of women who had wanted to be embraced by this or that god in all his might, and had been granted their wish, and had been consumed unto ashes by the full glory of the deity. They needed to consider, very carefully indeed, all the consequences of a mental union between Noelle and one of these supposed creatures of the void, before shoving her into the attempt.

So the desire to protect Noelle lurks beneath his stated reason for tabling the project. And because—he isn't sure why—he is reluctant to reveal that underlying desire to the others, he has chosen to hide it behind an acceptable but secondary explanation that would achieve the same goal. That was a manipulative act, he feels.

The selfishness is hidden one further layer down. What if Noelle tries to speak with these creatures, and succeeds, and

actually strikes some détente with them under which the communications channel linking her to her sister could be re-
opened? What, then, would become of his own hard-won deal
giving him the right to participate in the Planet B landing
expedition in return for accepting a third year as captain?
Many of them, he suspects, had voted for the change in the
Articles of the Voyage only because they believed that contact
with Earth had been forever lost and they were under no
obligation now to obey inconvenient regulations that Earth
had imposed upon them. But if that contact were to be restored—

He has put the "angel" thing aside, therefore, for three
good and proper reasons, one that is simply sensible, one that
is tenderhearted, and one that is out-and-out selfish.

But the year-captain knows that the Abbot, if only he
could be consulted in these matters, would focus on the third
of those reasons, and would ask him whether it was likely that
the other two would have had much force in his mind if the
third one had not been driving him; and there would be no
good answer to that. There never were any good answers to
the Abbot's questions. He never condemned; he left that job to
you yourself; but he could never be fooled, either.

Alone in his cabin now, the year-captain closes his eyes
and the formidable figure of the Abbot rises vividly in his
mind: a small, compactly constructed man, a fleshless man,
bone and muscle only, ageless, indefatigable. He was probably
about a hundred years old, but no one would have been
greatly astonished had it been demonstrated that he was twice
that age, or three times it, or that he had come into the world
in the latter days of the Pleistocene. He seemed indestructible.
An unforgettable face: broad forehead, dense mat of curling

dark hair, piercing violet eyes, firmly jutting nose, practically lipless mouth. No one knew his name. He was simply the Abbot. Had he founded the monastery? No one knew that, either. The residents of the monastery did not indulge in historical research. They were there; so was he; he was the Abbot. Beyond that, very little mattered.

The year-captain revered him. In the hour before dawn, when he would arise and go down to the icy shore for the first of the day's rituals of discipline, he would always find the Abbot already there, kneeling by the water's edge, holding his hands beneath the surface. Not to mortify the flesh, not to incur the sin of pride by demonstrating how much self-inflicted damage he could tolerate, but simply to focus his concentration, to clarify the operations of his mind. All of the Lofoten exercises were like that. One performed them for their own sake, and not to convince others or even oneself of one's great holiness. Holiness was beside the point here; the monastery, in this entirely secular age, was entirely secular in its orientation.

The year-captain relives, for the moment, those Lofoten days. The jagged chain of bleak rocky islands, rising like the spines of some submerged dinosaur's enormous back from the sea off Norway's fjord-sundered northwest coast. A stark landscape here. The dark, stormy Vestfjord that separated them from the mainland. The white-covered alpine peaks towering steeply in the background, a wall of wrinkled granite. The sparse grassy patches; the sodden cranberry moors; the broad ominous breast of the Atlantic curving off toward the west. Once these had been fishing islands, but the swarms of silvery cod were long extinct, and so were the fishing villages that had harvested the abundant catch. Mostly the islands were empty now, except

ROBERT SILVERBERG

for the one where the monastery sat, a neat row of stone buildings a short way inland from the sea.

The Gulf Stream flows here; the climate is harsh but not as extreme as the Arctic location might suggest. After Ganymede and Io and Callisto and Titan, these Lofoten islands might seem almost like paradise. There are no cranberry bogs on Ganymede. There are no grassy patches. One would derive no spiritual benefit from thrusting one's bare hands into the waters of one of Titan's hydrocarbon lakes, only a quick death. It was after his final excursion to the moons of Saturn that he had entered the monastery, leaving Huw to reap the glory of their exploit all alone. Returning from Saturn, he had felt a need to—was it to flee the society of his fellow humans? No, not flee, exactly, but certainly to withdraw from it, to go to some quiet place where he could reflect on the things he had seen and learned, the prevalence of living things in places like Titan and Io, the stubbornness of the life-force in the face of the most hostile of surroundings. What, if anything, did that stubbornness mean? What kind of ticking mechanism was this universe, and what forces had set it going? He didn't really expect answers to those questions; he wasn't entirely sure that answers were what he was really looking for. He wanted simply to ask the questions over and over again, and to discover, perhaps, some pattern of meaning that *connected*, rather than "answered," them. Lofoten was there and available to him; Lofoten was suddenly irresistible. So it was to Lofoten he went—he was Scandinavian himself, and had always known of the place; going there was like coming home, only more so—and it was on Lofoten that he stayed, going down to the icy sea to clarify his mind by numbing his hands, until at last the enterprise of the starship beckoned to him and he knew he had to move on.

The Abbot had known it even before he had. "I have come to request permission to leave," he had said, and the Abbot, smiling a smile as cool and remote as the light of the farthest galaxies, had said, "Yes, it is the time when you must carry us to the stars, is that not so?"

H uw says, "We'll go down and take a look at it, won't we?" And then, when the year-captain remains silent: "Won't we?"

The *Wotan* has made the shunt out of nospace successfully once again, and Julia has executed the appropriate braking maneuvers, and now the starship hangs in orbit a couple of million kilometers above the surface of the second world of this nameless K-type sun's solar system. For three days they have been studying the characteristics of that world via the ship's instruments. Huw and the year-captain are looking at it now, a furry gray-white sphere centered perfectly in the viewplate. A planet-shaped blanket of thick cloud, with a planet hiding behind it.

What kind of planet, though?

"We have to go down and give it the old once-over, don't you think?" Huw asks. There is something of a touch of desperation in his voice. The year-captain has been at his most opaque today, his inner feelings as thoroughly shrouded as the surface of that planet in the viewplate.

Once again Hesper's long-range calculations have been miraculously confirmed by direct instrument scan. It has turned out to be the case that Planet B is somewhat larger in diameter than Earth but has very similar gravitation, and that its atmospheric composition is 22 percent oxygen and 70.5 percent nitrogen and 4.5 percent water vapor, which is a lot, along with a hefty, though not unmanageable, 1.75 percent CO_2 and assorted minor quantities of methane and various inert gases. That suggests a steamy tropical climate, and indeed the instrument scan has revealed that the mean temperature of this Planet B varies scarcely a degree from pole to pole: it is uniformly hot, a sweaty 45 degrees Celsius everywhere. A jungle world. Plenty of vegetation, photosynthesizing that lofty tonnage of CO_2 like crazy. The good old Mesozoic, waiting for them down there.

No visual evidence of cities or towns. No electromagnetic output anywhere along the spectrum from gammas up to the longest radio waves and beyond. Nobody home, apparently.

No oceans, no lakes, no rivers, either. A solid landmass from pole to pole. That's odd, in view of the startlingly high proportion of water vapor in the atmosphere. All that H_2O must condense and precipitate out occasionally, right? There should, in fact, be almost constant rainfall on such a world. Where does that enormous quantity of rain go? Does it all evaporate right back into the cloud layer? Doesn't it collect anywhere on the surface in the form of large bodies of water?

The sonar probe shows something even odder. The planet is a big ball of rock, extremely skimpy on heavy metals, maybe on metals of any sort. Most of it is just basalt. But the sonar indicates that this world is swaddled in a huge layer of something relatively soft that covers the entire surface, the *entire* surface, not a break in it anywhere. Vegetable matter, evidently. A planetary jungle. Well, that's congruent with the climatic and atmospheric figures. But this worldwide layer of vegetable stuff seems to be two or three hundred kilometers thick. That's quite a thickness. The tallest mountain on Earth is only about nine kilometers high. The idea that this planet is covered by a wrapping of jungle that has roots going down twenty times as deep as Mount Everest is tall is pretty hard to accept.

The people of the *Wotan*, in the main, are still basking in the warmth of their own expectations about Planet B, which they have been nourishing all during the journey across no-space from the other solar system. For many months now they have been convinced that Planet B is the pot of gold at the end of their rainbow, and until they learn otherwise that is the attitude they are determined to maintain. But those few who have actually been looking at the direct data from Planet B have already understood that those expectations are doomed to be dashed, and they are starting to wonder how their fellow voyagers are going to react to the extreme disappointment that they have set up for themselves.

The year-captain says to Huw, finally, "Do you think the damned place can possibly be of any use to us?"

"Who can tell, unless we go down for a look?"

"I can tell from here. So can you. You know you can."

Huw acknowledges the point with the most minute of nods. "It seems definitely unusual, I admit."

"Too hot for us. No useful metals. No free water. Some kind of probably impenetrable jungle covering the whole thing."

"We've come a long way to find it. Are we just going to move along without even sending out a drone probe?" Huw asks.

Once again the year-captain falls into unresponsiveness.

Huw says, "And, truth to tell, a drone probe isn't what I have in mind. We need to get someone down there and check out Giovanna's theory about the angels."

"What theory is that?"

"You don't remember? That the angels want us to get out of their territory altogether, and so they've not only fouled up Noelle's transmissions but also did that job on Marcus and Giovanna and me when we landed on Planet B."

The year-captain has locked himself behind some sort of wall and will not come out. "The very existence of these so-called angels is an unproven concept at this point," he says.

"So it is, old brother. But by landing a couple of people on this planet in front of us, we can at least begin to get some determination of whether it's going to be possible for us to occupy any planet at all without somehow first obtaining the blessing of these troublesome beings. If they exist, that is. What I'm saying is that if some of us go down there and we *don't* happen to hit the same problems that were encountered on—"

"I know what you're saying, Huw."

"We need to go and find out, wouldn't you agree?"

The year-captain shuts his eyes for a moment. "Who do you propose for such a mission, then?"

"You, of course. Now that you have the legal right to go. And yet you don't seem to want to, which I confess I can't understand at all, old brother. You ought to be climbing all over yourself in your hurry to get down there."

"I want to go, yes. If anyone goes. But the planet is probably useless for our purposes. Is it not a waste of time and perhaps lives to bother looking at it at close range? —Who else would you want to suggest for the mission?"

"Myself."

"Yes. That goes without saying, Huw. Who else?"

"Nobody else."

"Just you and me?"

"That's right, old brother."

"You argued for the necessity of a three-person expedition to Planet A's surface," the year-captain says.

"So I did. But just the two of us was enough for Titan and Ganymede and Callisto," Huw replies. "We should be able to manage things pretty well by ourselves here too. We don't need to put anyone else at risk. Look here, old brother, let's send a probe down today and take some samples. And then you and I will descend and expose ourselves to whatever spooks may be in charge of things down there, unless there are no spooks, in which case we can begin to assume that even though Planet A flamed out for us, there is no reason to expect the same effects everyplace we happen to wander. What do you say, captain-sir, old brother?"

"Let me think about it," the year-captain says.

In fact the year-captain most passionately wants to visit the surface of Planet B, and has been in the grip of that passion since long before the *Wotan*'s latest emergence from nospace. He has been fighting against the idea, though, because he knows that his desire is a purely selfish one, and he feels that he's had his quota of selfishness for the time being.

Obviously the planet is useless for the purposes of colonization. The year-captain knows that already, even if most of his fellow voyagers don't. It has some bare possibility of being suitable for human habitation, yes, but the year-captain is certain even without first-hand on-site data that life down there would be endlessly difficult, uncomfortable, and challenging for them. A certain degree of challenge is a valuable stimulus to the growth of civilization, he realizes, but there is a point beyond that at which the human spirit is simply crushed by overwhelming struggle. That is what probably would happen here, the year-captain thinks. Better to write the place off without bothering with it further, and go in search of some other, less difficult, world.

And yet—and yet—

A planet, a unique unknown planet right out there within his grasp, a planet that beyond much doubt has given rise to *some sort of life-form* completely beyond human experience—

He wants it. He can't deny it to himself, not after the battle to win the right to take part in reconnaissance missions outside the ship. And, in the end, he allows Huw's use of Giovanna's variant on the angel theory to sway his decision. They do need to find out whether some omnipotent external force has decided to block their access to the worlds of space, and a landing on Planet B would shed a little light on that. Might shed some, anyway. A positive finding in that area might help to compensate for the letdown that people are going to feel when Planet B fizzles out, as the year-captain is sure it will, as a potential settlement site. So he authorizes the sending of one of the drone probes to collect a little more direct information about conditions down there, and lets it be known that a follow-up manned expedition will be the next step, if warranted by the drone's findings.

Huw, operating the drone by remote control, puts it in

an orbit a thousand kilometers outside Planet B's murky atmosphere and does some infrared eyeballing to get a clue to what's underneath the cloud layer. His cameras are capable of peeling away thicker fog than that, and they pierce right through, providing him with new mystifications.

"Look there," he tells the year-captain. "Those hot lines everywhere. It's like a big ball of twine down there. Or a lot of rubber bands wound round and round the whole place."

"Vines, I think," the year-captain says.

"A planet entirely tied up in a wrapping of vines? Vines two hundred kilometers thick?"

"We'll need to take a closer look at it," the year-captain says.

"I already have." Huw kicks the imaging magnification up a couple of levels and cuts in an ultraviolet filter. "Now we're looking just below the surface. You see the dark lines between the hot ones?"

"Tunnels?" the year-captain suggests.

"Tunnels, yes, I'd say." Huw indicates the infrared readings. "And things moving in the tunnels, no?"

The year-captain peers closely at the screen's blue-green surface. Dots of hot purple light, the purple indicating a temperature different from the temperature of the tightly wound lines, are slowly traversing the long darknesses that they have identified as tunnels.

"How big, would you guess?" he asks.

Huw shrugs. "Twenty meters long? Fifty? Big things, anyway. Very big. I don't think we have a civilization down there, old brother, but I think we do have something."

"Which requires investigation."

"Absolutely."

Huw grins. The year-captain does not. They understand each other, though. They will be shameless. Irresponsible, even. This is a useless world. But they want to see what's down there; and so they will. They have earned the right. Curiosities must be satisfied. And—who knows?—they may even be able to answer some questions that very much need to be answered before the expedition can proceed to its next destination.

So the word goes forth to the ship's community that it has been determined that a landing is desirable—no details about *why* that might be felt to be a good idea—and therefore a landing will be made, and that Huw and the year-captain will be the landing party, and Huw sets about once more readying one of the probes for a manned voyage. And if anyone aboard the *Wotan* thinks that the year-captain is needlessly exposing two of the most valuable members of the expedition to great risk, that person does not share those thoughts with anyone else.

Huw winks broadly and does a thumbs-up as he and the year-captain secure themselves in their acceleration chairs. It's a long time since these two have undertaken a mission of exploration together.

"Well, old brother, shall we shove off?" Huw asks.

"Whenever you're ready, Huw. You're the captain aboard this ship, you know. You make the decisions."

"Right. Right." Huw puts the little vessel under the control of the *Wotan*'s drive intelligence and the mother ship's main computer takes charge, easing the drone out of the bay. When they are a safe distance from the *Wotan* the drone goes into powered flight and begins its descent from orbit.

The spider-armed lopsided awkwardness of the *Wotan* quickly gets smaller behind them. The cloud-swaddled face of Planet B expands with breathtaking swiftness.

Then they are inside the cloud layer, which the probe has previously determined to be nothing at all like the ghastly sulfuric-acid wrapper that covers Venus, but just a lot of plain H_2O and some CO_2, your basic veil of ordinary clouds, very, very dense but chemically harmless. They drop down through it and find themselves in the mother of all rainstorms, a planetary deluge of extraordinary intensity. It falls in green loops all around them, thick, viscous-looking rain. Now they understand where this world's oceans are. They are in constant transit through the atmosphere, going up in the form of evaporation and coming down in the form of rain, and never once pausing to accumulate on the ground.

"It is a bitch of a place for certain, old brother," Huw declares, as he takes over from the drive intelligence and begins to seek a decent landing place.

They are close enough to the ground now to see, even through the driving rain, that their guesses from on high were correct, that this planet is completely engulfed by an enormous webwork of gigantic woody vines, seemingly endless vines whose trunks have a diameter of at least ten meters and probably more, vines like horizontal trees that crisscross and overlap and entangle, leaving no free spaces between them anywhere.

Sonar shows the underground tunnels they had noticed from above, weaving through the vines beginning at a depth of perhaps forty meters and running both laterally and downward, in some places descending for a kilometer or more. Below the tunnel zone lies something that appears to be one great solid spongy mass, hundreds of kilometers thick, out of which all the vines seem to be sprouting. It is the mother substance, apparently, the living substructure of the entire giant organism—for it is rapidly becoming clear to them now that Planet B is occupied by one immense vegetable entity, which is this spongy subterranean mass, from which all else springs. And beneath that is the stone understructure of the planet, the hidden basalt core.

Where to land? There are no open places, no meadows, no plains.

Huw expends a little reaction mass to create one, tipping the probe up on end and flaming the upper edges of a few vines until there is a satisfactorily flat landing zone below them. There is no reaction from the vines adjacent. They do not writhe, nor do they even stir; they give no indication of any sort that Huw's assault on this very small sector of the planetary flora has caused the slightest resentment, let alone set in motion some kind of retaliatory action.

He sets the probe down nicely. Waits a moment for it to finish rocking. The landing zone he has improvised is a little on the uneven side.

"Tests, now," Huw tells the year-captain, unnecessarily.

They run through all the prescribed extravehicular testing routines, checking this thing and that, the acid content of the rain and the possibility of atmospheric toxins and such. Not that they have any intention of exposing themselves to direct unshielded intake of the atmosphere out there, not on an alien world that they are already almost certain will be of no avail as a place where human beings might settle happily. But they are aware that extraterrestrial chemistries might provide nasty surprises even for explorers protected by spacesuits. So they take the proper precautions.

The rain is unrelenting. It works the skin of the little spaceship over like a trillion tiny hammers.

"At this point on the last planet," Huw says, "I was

already beginning to feel strange. The queasies had started to strike before I was even out of the probe."

"And now?"

"Nothing. You?"

"Nothing at all."

"But let's see how it goes for us when we're outside, shall we?"

A little comedy surrounds their going outside the ship. The year-captain, having previously made it clear that he looks upon Huw as the leader of the party, indicates with a nod that he will defer to Huw in the matter of being the first to set foot on this planet. But Huw, who has been the first to set foot on one extrasolar planet already, is quite willing to let the year-captain have the honor on this one, and defers right back to him. Of course, there is the possibility that the first one outside the ship will be the recipient of some sort of disagreeable jolt, but each man, in his deference to the other, goes to some length to make it clear that such fear is definitely not an item in his considerations, not at all. Courtesy is the only issue.

"Go *on*," the year-captain says irritably in the end.

"Well, then. Yes, if so you say."

Huw shimmies through the hatch and cautiously steps down onto the charred, still faintly sizzling surface of the landing area that he has fashioned. There is a slight resilience, a little give, beneath his weight. He can detect no untoward psychological effects.

"Everything all right so far," he announces.

The year-captain joins him. Together they walk toward the edge of the clearing; and then, after just a moment of hesitation, they step out together onto the upper surface of one of the unburned vines.

It is an unappealing surface. Big scrofulous leaves,

blue-black and stemless, pocked with ugly blister-shaped air bladders, sprout directly from the wood at sparse intervals. Dull red streamers hang from their edges like bursts of entrails. In the bare places between the leaves the trunks of the vine have a disagreeably gluey texture.

"Well?" Huw asks.

"A little sticky, isn't it?"

"I mean your mind."

"Still functioning, thank you. And yours?"

"I was ready to scream by this point on Planet A. Already *was* screaming a little, as a matter of fact. Things are different here, it seems. So much for Giovanna's theory, let's hope."

"Vile place even so, isn't it?" the year-captain says.

"Utterly repugnant. Absolute trumps, as repugnant goes. Shall we move a little farther onward, old brother?"

It is almost like being under water. By their calculations it's the midday hour, with a medium-size sun hovering right above them just a few dozens of millions of kilometers away, and yet they are shrouded in a deep twilight gloom. There is one place in the sky where a somewhat lighter blurry patch stands out against the thick gray mantle of clouds: that's the sun lurking back there, no doubt. The rain, falling as it does in dense sheets, is dispiriting in the extreme. It must not have stopped raining here in millions of years. The water hits the corrugated woody surfaces of the huge vines and goes slithering off into the narrow crevices between them. Perhaps some of it trickles downward from the planetary surface for hundreds of kilometers until it comes to rest in pockets of unimaginable darkness along the flat face of the rocky core; but most of the deluge simply bounces right back up in instant evaporation. All about them they can see heavy clouds of vapor climbing stubbornly through the furious vertical scything of the downpour.

The vines themselves form a virtually impenetrable covering. They lie side by side like the threads in some colossal tapestry, occasionally overlapping, each one stretching on and on for what may well be kilometers; there is not so much as a fingersbreadth of room between each one and its neighbor. Their greenish-purplish bark is sturdy and yet rubbery, yielding a little beneath the feet of the two explorers. It bears not just leaves but pulpy fungoid masses that sprout in random patches all over it, and also scabrous gray coatings of the local equivalent of lichen. These are soft as cheese, these parasites or saprophytes or symbiotes, whatever the case may be, creating a treacherously slippery surface, but it is difficult to avoid walking on them. Between these various excrescent outgrowths it is possible to see numerous large oval bodies, greenish in color and smooth in texture, set in the bark of the vines four or five meters apart from one another like a host of unblinking eyes: they appear to have a significant function for the vines, perhaps supplementary instruments that aid the strange leaves in conducting some kind of photosynthetic process in this dismal subaqueous light.

Everything here seems to be rotting, decaying, decomposing, and reconstituting itself all in the same process. This world would have made a good penal colony, maybe, in the fine old days when cruel and unusual punishment was a popular human pastime. But it doesn't seem good for very much else.

"Have we seen enough, do you think?" Huw says.

The year-captain points straight ahead. There is a round dark place up there, like the mouth of a cave, set between two vine trunks. The entrance, it seems, to one of those long underground tunnels that had shown up on the sonar images. "Shall we take a look inside?" he asks.

"Ah. You want to go in there."

"I want to go in there, yes," says the year-captain in a quiet tone.

"Well, then, why not?" says Huw, not very enthusiastically. "Why not, indeed?"

The year-captain leads the way, without discussion of issues of precedence. The tunnel is wide and low-roofed, ten or twelve meters broad but scarcely higher than the tops of their heads in some places. It runs at a gently sloping downward angle right through the corpus of the vines, slicing casually from one to the next; its walls, which are the substance of the vines, are moist and pink, like intestines, and a kind of sickly phosphorescent illumination comes from them, a feeble glow that breaks the dense darkness but is of little help to vision. Huw and the year-captain activate their helmet lamps and step a little farther within, and then a little farther yet.

Huw says, "I wonder what could have constructed these—"

"Hush," says the year-captain, pointing ahead once again. "Look."

He walks forward another dozen meters or so and steps up the intensity of his beam. The tunnel appears to be blocked up ahead by a plug of some sort; but as they get closer to the blockage they can see that the "plug" is slowly retreating from them—that it is, in fact, some enormous sluggish, elongated flattopped creature that not only is moving in wormlike fashion along the floor of the tunnel but is evidently *creating* the tunnel, or at least expanding it, by devouring the fabric of the vine through which the tunnel runs.

"Fabulous," Huw murmurs. "What do you know,

we've found extraterrestrial animal life at last, old brother! And what a beauty it is!"

There is no way for them to tell how long the tunnel worm is. Its front end is lost in the darkness far down the way. But they are able to see that its body is three times the width of a man's, and rises nearly to their height. Its flesh is translucent and pink in color, a deeper pink than that of the tunnel itself, more in the direction of scarlet, and has a soft, buttery look about it. Black hairy fist-size pores are set low along the creature's sides, every fifty centimeters or thereabouts, going forward on it as far as they can see. From these orifices comes a steady trickle of thin whitish slime that runs down the curving sides of the thing and lies puddled in rivulets and pools along the tunnel floor around it. An excretion product, no doubt. The worm seems to be nothing more than an eating machine, mindless, implacable. It is steadily munching its way through the vine and turning what it eats into a stream of slime.

Indeed they can hear the sounds of feeding coming from the other end of the creature: a snuffling noise and a harsh chomping noise, both above a constant sixty-cycle drone. All these sounds, which seem to be related, go on without letup. An eating machine, yes.

The two men creep a little nearer, taking care not to let their boots come in contact with the deposits of slime that the great worm has left in their path. When they are as close to the creature as they dare to get, it becomes possible for them to perceive curious glowing cystlike structures, dark and round and solid and about the size of a man's head, distributed with seeming randomness within the flesh of the thing, scattered here and there at depths of a third of a meter or more. These cysts make their presence known by a bright gleam like yellow fire that emanates from them and rises up through the flesh of the worm to its pink puckered skin.

"Internal organs?" Huw asks. "Elements of its nervous system, could they be?"

"I don't think so," the year-captain says. "I think they may belong to *this.*"

Once more he points, jabbing his finger urgently forward two or three times into the pinkish gloom, and turns the beam of his helmet lamp up to its highest level.

Another creature has appeared from somewhere, a creature far smaller than the worm, and has taken up a perch atop the worm's back just about at the farthest distance where they are able to see anything. It is a thing about the size of a large dog, vaguely insectoidal in form, with jointed pipe-stem legs, eight or maybe ten of them, and a narrow body made up of several segments. It has a savage-looking beak and a pair of huge glittering golden-green eyes like great jewels, which it turns on them for a moment in a long, baleful stare as the light of the year-captain's lamp comes to rest on it. Then it returns to its work.

Its work consists of digging a hole deep down in the worm's flesh and laying an egg in it.

The egg is waiting, glued to the creature's underbelly: a many-faceted bluish-purple sphere of goodly size. The hole, it seems, is nearly finished. The insectoid-thing, standing upright and bracing itself by spreading its lowest pair of limbs, bends forward at a sharp angle until its head and the upper half of its thorax disappear within the worm. Rapid drilling movements are apparent, the visible half of the creature rocking in quick rhythms, the hidden head no doubt bobbing furiously below to send that terrible beak deeper and deeper into the soft vulnerable material that makes up the worm. The process goes on for an unpleasantly long time.

Then the creature straightens up. It appears to be satisfied with its labors. Once again it glowers warningly at the two watching humans; then it does an odd little strutting dance atop the worm, which, after a moment, can be seen not to be a dance at all, but simply a procedure by which the thing is pulling its huge egg free of its underbelly and laboriously shoving it downward, moving it from one pair of limbs to another, until the next-to-last pair is holding it. At that point the creature flops forward over its excavation, spearing the point of its beak into the skin of the worm as though to anchor itself, and the legs that grasp the egg plunge fiercely downward, jamming the egg deep into the hole that awaits it.

That is all. The creature extricates itself, throws one more huge-eyed glare at Huw and the year-captain, and goes scuttling off into the darkness beyond.

The worm has not reacted in any visible way to the entire event. The snuffling and chomping sounds, and the accompanying sixty-cycle drone, have continued unabated.

"The worm's flesh will heal around the egg, I suppose," the year-captain says. "A cyst will form, and there the egg will stay until it hatches, giving off that lovely yellow light. Then, I would imagine, a cheery little thing much like its mother will come forth and will find all the food it needs close at hand. And the worm will never notice a thing."

"Lovely. Very lovely," says Huw.

The year-captain moves forward another couple of paces to have a closer look at the opening in which the insectoid-thing has inserted its egg. Huw does not accompany him. It is necessary, the year-captain finds, to clamber up onto the worm's back for a proper view of what he wants to see. The year-captain's heavy boots sink a few millimeters into the worm's yielding flesh as he mounts, but the worm does not react to the year-captain's presence. The year-captain stares into the aperture, carefully pulling its edges apart so that he can peer into its interior.

"Watch it!" Huw yells. "Mommy is coming back!"

The year-captain looks up. Indeed the insectoid-thing has reappeared, as though its egg has sounded some sort of alarm that has summoned it back from the darker depths of the tunnel. By the light of his helmet lamp the year-captain can see the creature advancing at a startling pace, mandibles clacking, front claws waving ferociously, eyes bright with rage, clouds of what looks like venom emerging from vents along its thorax.

Hastily the year-captain jumps down from the worm and backs away. But the insectoid-thing keeps coming, and swiftly. It seems quite clear to the year-captain that the infuriated creature intends to hurl itself on him and bite him in half, and it appears quite capable of doing just that.

Both men are armed with energy guns, purely as a precautionary thing. The year-captain draws his now, raises it almost without aiming, and fires one quick bolt.

The insectoid-thing explodes in a burst of yellow flame.

"A damned close thing," Huw says softly as he comes up beside him. "Hell hath no fury like a giant alien bug whose egg is in danger."

"It wasn't in any danger," the year-captain murmurs.

"The bug didn't know that."

"No. No. The bug didn't know." The year-captain, shaken, nudges the fragments of the thing with the boot of one toe. "I've never killed anything before," he says. "A mosquito, maybe. A spider. But not something like this."

"You had no choice," Huw says. "Two seconds more and it would have been going for your throat."

The year-captain acknowledges that.

"Anyway, it was very damned ugly, old brother."

"It may have been an intelligent life-form," says the year-captain. "At the very least, a highly developed one. In any case, it belongs here and we don't." His voice is thick with anger and disgust.

He pauses beside the dead creature a little while longer. Then he turns and walks slowly from the tunnel.

Huw follows him out. For a little while they stand together outside the entrance, saying nothing, watching the viscous rain come down in thick looping sheets.

"Would you like to collect a couple of those eggs to take back to the ship for study?" Huw asks finally, goading just a little, but in what he wants to think is a pleasant way, trying to ease the tension of the moment.

The year-captain does not answer immediately.

"No," he says at last. "I think not."

"But the eternal quest of science, old brother, does it not require us to —"

"Let the eternal quest of science be damned just this once," the year-captain tells him sharply. There is a sudden explosive note of anger just barely under control in his voice. "I don't want to talk about this. Let's just get ourselves back to the ship."

This heat, this tone of fury being held in check with great difficulty, is altogether out of character for him. Huw gives him a quick look of surprise verging on alarm. Then, by way of defusing the situation, he lets out a long comic exhalation of relief. "And are we truly going from here, then? Oh, praises be to all the gods! I thought you would keep us poking about in this filthy place forever, my friend."

Zed Hesper, of course, has the tempting Planet C to propose to them, and plenty of others beyond that. The sky is full of worlds, Hesper's instruments indicate, and he is as eager as ever for them to go zooming off in quest of them.

But the first two adventures in planetary exploration have been less than rewarding, in fact have been a bit on the crushing side—one world sending out a broadcast in the psychotic part of the spectrum and the next one populated entirely by loathsome monsters—and in the aftermath of the most recent landing a strange dark mood of negativity is emerging for the first time aboard the *Wotan*. The loss of contact with Earth—those chatty little bulletins from home, those trifling reminders that they once had *had* a home other than this wandering starship—has had something to do with that. And the voyagers have seen Huw and Giovanna come back pale and shaken from one planet, and Huw and the year-captain equally shaken from another. The effect on the year-captain in particular of the visit to the appalling Planet B is only too apparent even several days after his return, and it disturbs everyone to see that normally impassive man looking so rattled.

The horror that Planet B has turned out to be, after the great expectations that they had all allowed themselves to foster for it, has indeed taken a terrible toll, and not just on the two men who experienced that horror at close range.

It is suddenly occurring to those on the *Wotan*—many of them, at any rate—that after having left the predictability and comfort of Earth behind for the sake of undertaking a great exploit, they are faced now with the possibility of touring the galaxy forever without finding a world that can become a tolerable home for them. And the wildness of the thing they have volunteered to do, the utter fantastic gamble that it is, has begun to oppress their souls. They are afraid now, many of them, that they have simply thrown away their lives.

The year-captain struggles to transcend this bleak mood in himself, so that he will be better able to purge it from the others. But the sights and sounds of Planet B haunt him day and night, and they engulf him in a dire morass of melancholy. An entire world so hopelessly dismal: it is enough to make one deny the existence of the Creator, assuming one believed in Him in the first place. What divine purpose could have been served by the creation of a planet of endless rain, of titanic vines that constrict and strangle every hectare of the place, colossal brainless worms that feed on the vines, diabolic parasitic bugs that feed on the worms? No doubt it is the best of all possible worlds for the vines and the worms and the jewel-eyed bugs. But such objectivity is beyond him just now. He feels as though he has made a little excursion into some hitherto unrecorded subsidiary circle of Dante's own Hell.

He yearns to speak with the Abbot about Planet B, if only he could. He hungers for the few quick acerbic sentences that would demolish all the darkness that clings to him now. But the Abbot is beyond his reach. And so, very gradually, over a period of days, the year-captain manages to pull himself up out of the slough of despond without the aid of the Abbot's direct intervention. There is no other course that he can allow himself to take.

Some of the others, primarily Hesper and Paco and Julia and Huw and even Sieglinde, have been able to retain their optimistic outlook toward the expedition despite the sobering outcome of the Planet B event. "The remarkable thing isn't that the first two landings failed," Julia says. "The remarkable thing is that we found two worlds that were worth checking out within the first couple of years of the voyage."

"Hear, hear," Huw bellows, as Huw likes to do. Huw knows that much depends now on his show of hearty high spirits and indomitable will, and he makes sure that he is never seen to be anything but his usual stalwart self, even after all that he has observed and felt on Planet A and the very different but equally oppressive Planet B. There is a price for this. He is willing to pay it.

But there are some aboard who have become deeply bemired in funk. These are the ones who had chosen, for whatever reason, to put a great many emotional chips down on the success of the Planet B mission, and were devastated by the spectacular failure of their wagers. Elizabeth is part of this group, and Imogen, and Sylvia, and several of the men: Roy, Elliot, Chang, Jean-Claude. Among these, who now spend most of their time at *Go* in the gaming lounge, there has begun to be some talk of giving up the voyage entirely, of swinging around and heading back to Earth.

"Don't be idiots," Paco says. "I can't even imagine creeping back there."

"You can't imagine it," says Elliot. "But I can."

Elliot's specialty is urban planning; it is Elliot who will

design the future extraterrestrial settlements that the *Wotan* people hope to found. Since the Planet B fiasco he has convinced himself that he will never get a chance to practice his profession among these alien worlds, that the enterprise on which they all are bound is quixotic and foolish. Marcus's death has affected Elliot deeply; so has the loss of contact with Earth.

Paco says to him, "If you want to go back, Elliot, why don't you go? Maybe Huw will let you have one of the drone probes, and you can ride back to Earth in that. You and whoever else wants to go home. It'll take you about three hundred years, give or take five or six, but if you're as homesick as all that you won't mind waiting a—"

"Stop it, Paco," Elizabeth says.

Paco turns to her. "You'd like to go with him, wouldn't you? Well, that's fine with me. I'll even calculate the course for you, if you like." The Paco-Heinz-Elizabeth triad has just about collapsed in recent weeks; Heinz has been sleeping in a random, intermittent way with Jean-Claude and sometimes with Leila; and Paco, though he still spends some of his nights with Elizabeth and the occasional one with Heinz, has drifted off into a collateral entanglement with Giovanna. "Here," Paco says, grabbing Elizabeth roughly and shoving her against Elliot. "She's all yours. My blessings."

Elliot is so annoyed that he pushes her back. Heinz gathers Elizabeth up as she rebounds from Elliot and tucks her against the side of his chest. To Paco he says quietly, "Can you try to calm down a little?"

"I hate all this talk of giving up and going back to Earth. It's completely insane."

"Is it, now?" Roy asks, looking up from the game of *Go* he is playing with Noelle. He is another who has let it be known that he may have already had a sufficiency of nospace travel.

"Of course it is. We're here to do a job, and we're going to do it. Julia's right—one or two bad planets, that doesn't mean a thing. We've only begun to search. Besides, do you think anyone could ever talk the captain into turning back? Has that man ever turned back from anything in his life?"

"He doesn't necessarily have to go on being captain forever," Elliot says, a little sullenly. "The job was supposed to be for one year. We gave him three. We could replace him."

"With someone who wants to bring the voyage to an end?" Paco asks. "Somebody willing to turn back, you mean?"

"Absolutely."

Huw says, from the corner where he is playing a languorous game of *Go* with Chang, "He would never step down in favor of anyone who would take that position. He may not have wanted to keep the job this long, but he'll keep it forever rather than hand it over to someone who—"

"I'm not talking of asking him voluntarily to step down," says Elliot. "I'm talking of replacing him."

"Mutiny?" Huw asks. "Is that the word you're looking for?"

"A new captain," says Elliot doggedly. "That's what I'm looking for. And a new direction for the voyage."

"You're talking mutiny," Huw says, lost in wonderment. "You're talking a coup d'état aboard the ship, overthrowing the captain by force, abandoning the Articles of the Voyage completely—"

"He's talking idiocy," Paco says. "He's talking like a lunatic. He ought to be sedated. Where's Leon?" Leon is playing *Go* with Sylvia. He looks up, scowling. "Leon, we've got a crazy man here for you to take care of! Give him an injection of something, will you?"

"Please," Noelle says, very softly.

She has been silent up until now, concentrating entirely on her game, bending over her *Go* board as though it were the entire universe. As it so often does, the very softness of her tone succeeds in drawing the attention of everyone in the room, and they all look in her direction.

"Please," she says again. "We mustn't fight like this. The voyage is going to continue. You know it will, Elliot. It *has* to. So why even talk about these things?"

"We have to talk about them, Noelle," says Elliot, sounding a little abashed at persisting. No one wants to be on the wrong side of a discussion with Noelle, because she is widely believed to possess a kind of innate incontrovertible wisdom. And also they all have a horror of involving her in any kind of confrontation, so fragile does she seem to them. "Ever since we lost contact with Earth," Elliot goes on, "can it really be said that the expedition still has a purpose?"

"Its purpose is to find another world where people can live," says Noelle. "And we haven't lost contact with Earth."

There is a general gasp of amazement in the room.

"We haven't?" several of them ask at once.

Noelle smiles. "Not forever. I'm sure of that. It's just a temporary thing, this interference, these 'angels' that Heinz was talking about—" Every one of them is staring intently in her direction now. "I'm going to try to speak with them," she says. "You know that I promised to do that. To speak with them, to ask them to let me make contact with my sister again. If I can do that—and if they agree—"

So the project of making contact with the angels is alive once again, at Noelle's own instigation, after having been in suspension the whole time of the Planet B event. The hope of regaining contact with Earth inspires them all; the mood of despair that has enshrouded so many of them since the return of Huw and the year-captain from Planet B begins to lift.

The project is alive, yes, but nothing actually is attempted just yet. The days go by—they are heading now toward Planet C, a hundred fifteen light-years from Earth in some entirely different part of the galaxy from the one they have just visited—and it is assumed by everyone that Noelle is preparing herself to reach out in some telepathic fashion toward the extraterrestrial beings that supposedly have interrupted the contact between her and her sister. But the two people who are most closely concerned with the project—the year-captain, who must give Noelle the order to make the attempt, and Noelle herself—are both in their separate ways uneasy about the enterprise to which Noelle has so publicly committed herself. And so both of them in their separate ways have hesitated to move forward with it.

Noelle has never so much as experimented with opening her mind to anyone but her sister, and the idea is a little troublesome to her. It seems almost like an act of infidelity. But, on the other hand, doing it might very well restore the contact with Yvonne that has been the most precious thing in her life. Therefore Noelle remains willing to try it, if uncertain about how the task is actually going to be accomplished, when and if. But she is waiting for the year-captain to tell her to initiate the maneuver.

The year-captain is holding back, though, as he has from the moment any of this first surfaced, because he is afraid that Noelle will somehow be damaged in the attempt.

He has had a classical education. The myth of Semele is very much on his mind.

"Who was she?" Noelle asks him when he allows some of his concern to slip into view.

"Semele was the daughter of an ancient Greek king," he tells her. They are in the ship's recreation area, where they have just been swimming in the long, narrow lap-pool, and now they are sitting along the edge of the pool with their legs dangling in the water. "Zeus had taken her as one of his lovers." Noelle has turned toward him, and she seems to be listening carefully, but her face is completely expressionless. "You know who Zeus was? The chief of the Greek gods, the ruler of the universe."

"Yes. Yes."

"And quite a ladies' man. Zeus was completely infatuated with beautiful young Semele, and had a child with her, who was destined to grow up to be the god Dionysus; and Hera, Zeus's wife, who had had to put up with much too much of this stuff during the course of her marriage and didn't care for it, decides to take action. She dons human disguise and goes to visit Semele and asks her if she knows who it is that she's been sleeping with. Yes, says Semele proudly, he is Zeus, the father of the gods. And have you ever seen him in all his glory? Hera asks. No, says Semele, never, he always comes to me in the form of a man. Well, then, says sly Hera, you should ask him to reveal himself to you in his full majesty. Now, *that* would be something to see!"

"I think I know this story," Noelle says.

Nevertheless the year-captain does not halt in his telling of the tale. "The next time Zeus comes to her, Semele says to him, 'You never show yourself to me as you really are.' And Zeus says, 'No, no, that would be too much for you, the sight would be overwhelming.' But Semele insists. She reminds Zeus that he had promised her, long ago, to grant any wish that she might make. To refuse her nothing. Zeus is trapped. He can't go back on his promise, though he knows what's going to happen. So, reluctantly, he gives Semele what she's asking for. There is a tremendous clap of thunder and Zeus appears before her in his chariot in a great aurora of light. No human being can look upon the true form of Zeus and survive. Semele is destroyed by the heat that emanates from the god. She is burned utterly to ashes by it; and so Hera has had her revenge."

Noelle has drawn back into herself during this part of the story. She has wrapped her arms tightly around her body, and it seems to the year-captain that she is trembling a little.

"But something good came forth out of that, didn't it?" she asks. "There was Dionysus the god. Semele's son. He survived the flames, didn't he?"

"Yes. He survived. Zeus spared him, and scooped him

up in the moment of Semele's destruction, carrying him off and hiding him from Hera's wrath until he was grown."

"So, then. That's the point of the story. The miraculous birth of the god Dionysus."

She is definitely trembling, he sees. Shivering, even. They are still naked after their swim, but it is, as always, quite warm here in the recreation area.

"The point of the story is that Semele overreached herself and died," the year-captain says. "Dionysus is just an incidental part of the myth. The point is that ordinary mortals can't hope to have unrestricted contact with gods."

"The birth of a new god can't just be an incidental part of anything," Noelle says. The year-captain thinks he hears her teeth chattering.

"Are you feeling all right, Noelle?"

"Just a little chilly."

"It isn't chilly in here, though."

"But I feel that way. Maybe we should go on across into the baths."

"Yes. Yes. A little time in the hot tub will get you feeling better in no time."

The baths are just on the other side of the corridor from the lap pool. They collect their towels and discarded clothing and go across. The room is empty when they get there.

"Why did you tell me that story?" Noelle asks him.

"You know the answer to that, don't you?"

"Yes. Yes, I do."

"I can't help feeling worried about what will happen when you try to—"

"It isn't the same in any way. I'm not Semele. The angels aren't Zeus."

"How do you know what they are?"

ROBERT SILVERBERG

"I don't," she says. "Not really. How could I? But I just don't think—I'm quite confident that I—that they—that when I—" She is really shaking now. They are at the edge of the hot tank. The usual procedure is to step quickly into the cold tub, then go on to the hot one, and finish by returning to the tepid tank or even the cold one. But instead of going into any of them now Noelle stands trembling at the brink of the hot tub for a long moment; and then she turns, suddenly, and presses herself into his arms.

He enfolds her and holds her tightly and gently strokes her back, trying to soothe her, trying to comfort her and ease whatever terror it is that has taken possession of her. All of it very manly and paternal, and then a moment later not paternal in the least, for the year-captain is trembling too, and they stand there for a long while in a close embrace.

Then she breaks free of him and steps a few paces back. She is smiling, and her eyes, those mysterious sightless eyes that are nevertheless often so expressive, have taken on a strange mischievous light. She reaches out a hand toward him.

The year-captain is amazed at how her body, which he has seen on so many other occasions here in the baths and in the pool, now suddenly seems unfamiliar—different, transformed. The same full round breasts, yes, the same flat belly, the same deeply indented navel. But it is all different. There is an inner light emanating from her. She is gleaming, radiant. He is powerfully drawn to her. He wonders how he had ever managed to fail to find her attractive—why she had never seemed to him, really, like a sexual being at all. Certainly she seems like one now.

"Come," she whispers, and tugs at his hand, and leads him deftly and unhesitatingly over the tiled floor into one of the little lovemaking rooms that adjoin the baths.

They sink down together onto the hard narrow bed. It is entirely obvious to him now that he has wanted this since the beginning of the voyage, that he has always been drawn to her, that he has hedged himself around with a host of caveats and uncertainties and self-imposed prohibitions precisely because he has desired her all along with such frightening intensity.

He covers her lips, her throat, her closed eyelids with kisses. She clings to him, murmuring, thrusting herself against him. At the last moment before he could possibly turn back he remembers that odd thought he once had had, more than a year before, that she might actually be a virgin, and even that her telepathic powers might somehow depend on the preservation of that virginity and would be forever lost at the first touch of a man's insistent body.

No. No. That's idiocy. She isn't a creature out of some fantastic myth. Her telepathy is not a magical power that can be lost through the violation of an oath of chastity.

And in any case there's no longer any possibility that he can hold back, not now, nor is Noelle willing to allow it. Her legs part and he enters her quickly, almost roughly, and in that moment Noelle throws back her head and lets out a cry that is surely one of ecstasy and not of pain, and in almost the same moment he comes. He is completely unable to prevent that from happening. It erupts from him with a force that he has not felt since he was eighteen. And he hears her ecstatic hissing gasp, feels her bucking almost convulsively beneath him.

He wonders, in the first bewildered and almost distraught moment afterward, whether Yvonne has experienced their pleasure too, somewhere far away. Whether Yvonne has come with them, even, perhaps.

They lie still for a little while. Neither of them speaks.

He is faintly stunned by what has happened; and also relieved, enormously relieved, that the long half-conscious courtship is over, that they have at last put an end to all the games of attraction and repulsion that they have been playing with each other almost since the beginning of the voyage, and finally have allowed themselves to come crashing together in the union—a union of opposites, is it?—that had been ordained for them all along. He is pleased, pleased and happy, and a little amazed, and just a bit frightened, also.

Then very shortly he feels his strength returning, coming back to him with unexpected and almost improbable quickness, and they begin to move once again, less hastily this time, less wildly. It is as though they have traveled in just these first few moments beyond the initial stage of breathless heedless frenzy and are already beginning to become experienced lovers.

This time when it is over she grins up at him and says, "I waited and waited. I thought you never would."

"I was afraid."

"Of me?"

"Of damaging your powers, somehow."

"What?"

"As though the magic would go away if you—if I—if you and I—"

"Silly. You've read too many old fables."

"Maybe I have."

"Yes. I definitely think you have."

But now, even now, even after all that, another week goes by and still nothing is done about reaching out to the angels. This time the excuse is that Noelle and the year-captain want to explore their newfound bliss; the effort of the angel experiment will certainly be an immense drain on her energies, and so it is better to postpone it a little while longer, they tell themselves, while the two of them devote their energies to endeavors of a more familiar kind.

The truth is that they are both still afraid to make the attempt. He continues to have Semele's fate on his mind, troubling him all the more now that a new dimension has been added to their relationship; and she has hesitations of her own, a complex mixture of things—the natural fear of the unknown, and that curious feeling that she would somehow be unfaithful to Yvonne if she were to speak with the angels, and also a certain sense that she was simply inadequate to the task, incapable of fulfilling the high hopes that her shipmates are investing in her.

But it has to be attempted. Of that much the year-

ROBERT SILVERBERG

captain is certain. Whatever the risks, it has to be attempted. They all placed themselves permanently at risk the moment they first affiliated themselves with this project. If there is a possibility that Noelle can extricate them from their predicament, then that possibility must be explored. He sees no choice. He can't allow himself so great an evasion.

They have had no contact with Earth for many shipweeks, for months, even, and the psychological effects are beginning to manifest themselves in a host of troublesome ways. It has started to seem almost as though Earth has been destroyed in some great cataclysm, that they are the sole surviving representatives of humanity, an ark, unfettered by any ties to the past whatsoever and permitted to reshape the rules of their lives whichever way they please. The year-captain's conservative nature rebels at such anarchy. Earth still is there. The voyagers are beholden to Earth for their presence here. This mission is being executed at the behest of Earth, to fulfill certain needs of Earth.

But with Earth lost to them forever in the vast whirlpool of the skies —

He bides his time. He waits for his moment.

He and Noelle are recognized now aboard ship as lovers. Hiding it would be difficult, perhaps impossible, anyway: he has no desire to impose on her the sort of hole-and-corner relationship that he had carried on for so long with Julia. *Let* them see. *Let* them know. They were all expecting it to happen anyway; he understands that now. Some, like Heinz, evidently had seen the whole thing coming a couple of years before he did. Julia too: she smiles knowingly at him, as if to acknowledge that the long-awaited inevitable has at last occurred. Julia doesn't seem to be hurt by it. Quite the contrary.

So he and Noelle are seen together in the baths, in the

Go lounge, in the corridors. He spends nights in her cabin, or she in his—the first time since the beginning of the voyage that he has known anything but solitary sleep. She is a marvelous mixture of passion and innocence, or at least the semblance of innocence; there is unexpected skill and fire in her lovemaking, but also an eagerness to be led into unfamiliar paths, to be taught previously unknown ways. It reminds him, after a fashion, of the way Noelle had approached learning *Go* once upon a time: the attentiveness, the seriousness, the concern with understanding the fundamentals of the game—and, ultimately, the revelation of enormous mastery.

The *Go* obsession has never diminished aboard ship, and the year-captain, who has been only an occasional player since his reawakening of interest in the game, now goes to the lounge whenever his official duties permit. His superior skills make it difficult for most of the others to enjoy playing with him, and he plays almost exclusively with Roy and Leon and Noelle, most often with Noelle.

She is a merciless player. He wins against her no more often than once out of every four or five games.

Today, playing black, the year-captain has been able to remain on the offensive through the 89th move. But Noelle then breaks through his north stones, which are weakly deployed, and closes a major center territory. The year-captain finds himself unable to mount a satisfactory reply. Before he can get very much going, Noelle has run a chain of stones across the 19th line, boxing him in, in an embarrassing way. He manages to fend off further calamity for a while, but he knows that all he is doing is playing for time as he heads toward inevitable defeat. At Move 141 he launches what he suspects is a hopeless attack, and his forces are easily crushed by Noelle within her own territory. A little while later he finds himself confronted with the classic cat-in-a-basket trap, by which he will lose a large group in the process of capturing one stone, and at Move 196 he concedes that he has been beaten. She has taken 81 stones to his 62.

As they clear the board for a rematch he says, trying to be casual about it, "Have you been giving any thought to the business of the angels, Noelle?"

"Of course. I think about them a great deal."

"And?"

"And what?" she asks.

"Do you have any idea how you'd go about it? Making the contact, I mean."

"I have some theories, yes. But naturally they're only theories. I won't really know anything until I make the actual attempt."

The year-captain waits just a beat. "And when do you think that will be?"

She gives him one of those special looks of hers, those baffling sightless focusings of her eyes that somehow manage to convey an expression. The expression that she conveys this time is one of disingenuousness.

"Whenever you'd like it to be," she says.

"What about today, then?"

What about today? Yes. What about today. There is no way that it can be postponed any longer. He knows that; she knows that; they are in agreement. This is the moment. Today. Now.

In her cabin. Alone, among her familiar things. She has insisted on that. She grants herself a few moments of delay first, a little self-indulgence, moving about the room, picking up things and handling them, the sea-urchin shell, the polished piece of jade, the small bronze statuettes, the furry stuffed animal. In her former life these things had been hers and Yvonne's jointly; neither of them had ever had any sense of "mine" or "yours," not while they were together, but Yvonne had insisted, as the time for the launch of the *Wotan* drew near, that Noelle take all these with her, these beloved objects, the talismans of their shared life. "After all," she had said, "I'll be able to feel them through your hands." Yes. But not any longer.

Perhaps what Noelle is about to do will restore Yvonne's access to these little things, the things that once had been *theirs* and now were merely *hers*. Perhaps. Perhaps.

R O B E R T   S I L V E R B E R G

She lies down. Takes deep breaths. Closes her eyes. Something about having them closed seems to enhance the force of her power, she often thinks.

Extends a tenuous tendril of thought now that probes warily outward like a rivulet of quicksilver. Through the metal wall of the ship, into the surrounding grayness, upward, outward, toward, toward—

Angels?

Who knows what they are? But she has been conscious of their presence all along, ever since the interference first began, cloudy presences, huge, heavy masses of mentation hovering around her, somewhere out there in—what does he call it? The Intermundium? Yes, the Intermundium, the great gray space between the worlds. She has felt them out there, not as individual entities but only as presences, or perhaps *one* presence having many parts.

Now she seeks them.

Angels! Angels! Angels!

She is well beyond the ship and keeps moving outward and outward into the undifferentiated void of the nospace tube, extending herself to what she thinks is the limit of her reach and then reaching even farther yet. She envisions herself now as a line of bright light stretched out across the cosmos, a line that has neither beginning nor end but has no substance, either—an infinitely extended point of radiant energy, a dazzling immaterial streak, a mere beam.

Reaching. Reaching.

Angels!

Oh. She feels the presence now. So they are real, yes. Whatever they are, they are really there. They may not be actual angels, but they are there, not far away. They *exist.* Brightness. Strength. Magnetism. Yes. Awareness now of a fierce roiling mass of concentrated energy close by her. A gigantic mass in motion, laying a terrible stress on the fabric of the cosmos.

How strange! The angel has angular momentum! It tumbles ponderously on its colossal axis. Who could have thought that angels would be so huge? But they are angels; they can be whatever they please to be.

Noelle is oppressed by the shifting weight of the angel as it makes its slow, heavy axial swing. She moves closer.

Oh.

She is dazzled by it.

Oh. Oh.

She hears it roaring, the way a furnace might roar. But what a deafening furnace-roar this is! *Oh. Oh. Oh. Oh.* She hears a crackling too, a hissing, a sizzling: the sounds of inexorable power unremittingly unleashed.

Too much light! Too much power!

She is fascinated as much as she is frightened. But she must be cautious. This is a great monster lurking here. Noelle draws back a little, and then a little more, overwhelmed by the intensity of the other being's output. Such a mighty mind: she feels dwarfed. If she touches it even glancingly with her own mind she is certain that she will be destroyed. She must step down the aperture and establish some kind of transformer in the circuit that will shield her against the full bellowing blast of power that comes from the thing.

So she withdraws, pulling herself back and back and back until she is once again inside the ship, and rests, and studies the problem. It will require time and discipline to do what has to be done. She must make adjustments, master new techniques, discover capacities she had not known she possessed. All that requires time and discipline. Minutes, hours, days? She doesn't know. She will do what is necessary. And does it, patiently, cautiously.

And now. She's ready once more.

Yes.

Try again, now. Slowly, slowly, slowly, with utmost care. Outward goes the questing tendril.

Yes.

Approaching the angel.

See? Here am I. Noelle. Noelle. Noelle. I come to you in love and fear. Touch me lightly. Just touch me—

Just a touch—

Touch—

Oh. Oh.

I see you. The light—eye of crystal—fountains of lava—oh, the light—your light—I see—I see—

Oh, like a god—

She had looked up the story in the ship's archives of literature just after the time the year-captain had told it to her, the story of Semele, the myth. And it was just as he had said that day, the day that they first became lovers.

—and Semele wished to behold Zeus in all his brightness, and Zeus would have discouraged her; but Semele insisted and Zeus, who loved her, could not refuse her; so Zeus came upon her in full majesty and Semele was consumed by his glory, so that only the ashes of her remained, but the son she had conceived by Zeus, the boy Dionysus, was not destroyed, and Zeus saved Dionysus and took him away sealed in his thigh, bringing him forth afterward and bestowing godhood upon him—

—oh God I am Semele—

Now she is terrified. This is too much to face. She will be consumed; she will be obliterated. Noelle withdraws again, hastily. Back within the sanctuary of the ship. Rests, regroups.

Tries to regenerate her powers, but they are badly depleted. Exhausted, at least for the time being. Rest, then. Rest. This is very difficult, very dangerous. She knows it's unwise to continue right now. She will not attempt to go out into the Intermundium a third time that day.

They're really and truly there," she says. She is pale, weary, still badly off balance. It is two hours since her return from her adventure. The entire excursion had taken no more than a few minutes, apparently. It seemed like years to her. And to those waiting for her to emerge from her trance.

They are with her in the control cabin for the debriefing: Heinz, Huw, Leon, Elizabeth, Imogen, Julia. The year-captain is there too, of course. "I could feel them hovering somewhere outside the ship. Angels."

"Angels?" Heinz asks, sounding startled. He seems uncharacteristically subdued. "Actually, literally?"

"You mean, divine beings with human form, only with wings, like in the old paintings?" Noelle says.

"And names and identities," says Elizabeth. "Gabriel, Michael, Raphael, Azrael. God's lieutenants."

"I don't know that they're really angels," Noelle says. "That was just the word we all started to use for them."

"And surely you must know that I was just using the word lightly," Heinz says. "It was only a hypothesis, a thought-experiment, when I talked about angels. I never seri-

ROBERT SILVERBERG

ously believed there was any kind of intelligence out there, let alone angels. You say you saw *something*, though."

There are frowns. It is strange to speak of Noelle as "seeing" anything. But who knows what sort of sense-equivalents she experiences through her mind-powers?

"Felt," says Noelle. "Didn't see."

"And were they really angels or weren't they?" Heinz asks.

Noelle smiles faintly, shakes her head. "How would I know? But I don't think they were, not literal angels. I told you, I didn't see anything. But I felt them. *Forces.* Immense nodes of power, each one revolving on its own axis. If that's what angels are, then the presence of angels is what I felt."

"Forces," Elizabeth says. "I wonder, is that one of the categories of angels?" She counts on her fingers. "Choirs, Thrones, Dominations, Princedoms, Virtues, Powers — Powers, that would be just about the same as Forces — "

The year-captain leans forward and says quietly to Noelle, "Are you able to give us any kind of description in words of what you experienced?"

"No."

"How far from the ship were you when you began to perceive them?"

"I can't tell you that, either. Nothing makes sense out there. Certainly not distance. It's all just one infinite feature-less gray blur, just like what you say you see through the viewplate, but going on and on and on."

"Did they seem relatively close, at least?" he asks.

Noelle turns the palms of her hands upward and outward, a gesture signifying helplessness. "I can't say. There's nothing like 'close' or 'far' out there. Everything is the same distance from everything else. I don't know whether I was in the tube or out of it when I saw them."

"And yet you could distinguish relative sizes, at least. These things were *big*."

"Bigger than me, yes. Much bigger. Immense. That was easy enough to tell. I felt enormous power. It was like standing at the edge of a gigantic furnace. I could hear it roaring."

"One furnace, or many?" Huw asks.

"I don't know. I just don't know. Sometimes it felt like just one, sometimes I thought there were thousands of them all around me." Noelle gives them a faint, ashen-faced smile. "You're all trying to get me to put what I felt into concrete, understandable terms, but that just isn't possible. All I can tell you is that I went out there and after a little while I felt something, *something*, very large, very powerful, a huge radiant source of energy. If that's what angels are like, then I encountered an angel. I don't know what meeting an angel is supposed to be like. Or how important it is to call what I met by any sort of name. I only know that there was *something* out there and I think that it's the something that's interfering with the transmissions."

"Will you want to try contacting it again?" the year-captain asks gently.

"Not right now."

"I understand. Later on, though?"

"Of course. I'm not going to stop here. I can't. But not now—not—now—"

Leon says, "We should let her rest."

The year-captain nods. "Yes. Absolutely." He signals to the others, and they begin to leave. "Come," he says to Noelle. "I'll take you back to your cabin."

Ordinarily she bridles at being offered help in getting

around the ship. Not today, though. She gets slowly to her feet and he slips his arm around her shoulders, and they walk together down the corridor, slowly, very slowly.

He halts at the door of the cabin. He does not attempt to go in with her, nor does she invite him to.

Softly he says, "Was it very scary?"

"Scary and wonderful, both. I'll go out there and do it again when I've had a chance to rest."

"I don't want you to harm yourself, Noelle."

"As long as I rest enough between each attempt, I'll be all right."

"And if you should make contact, real contact, and the power turns out to be too strong for you to handle—?"

"Semele?"

"Semele, yes."

"I looked the story up, you know. It's in the myth section of the archives, exactly the way you told it to me, except that you left out the part about Zeus hiding the baby in his thigh. But that isn't important. Semele dies, yes. But first she gets to be the lover of a god. And the mother of another one. And she lives forever in the myth."

"That's all well and good. But you mustn't take any unnecessary risks."

"These are necessary risks. It has to be done."

"Yes," the year-captain says. "It does have to be done, doesn't it? I should let you rest now, Noelle."

She goes inside. He closes the cabin door behind her and walks slowly up the corridor to his own room.

There is great general excitement and no little bewilderment over Noelle's discovery outside the ship; but then a few days go by, and a few more, and she does not make a new attempt at reaching the angels. She is not ready yet, she says. She must find ways of insulating herself against the immense magnitude of the force that she will encounter.

And so they wait, and discuss, and speculate, and wonder. What else can they do?

During this time the ship continues to head toward Hesper's Planet C, and Hesper continues to fill them with his usual torrent of optimistic details about their upcoming destination's great potential as a settlement world. It is, he says, the large and impressive sixth planet of a large and impressive golden-red sun. It has, he declares, all the right properties of atmosphere and gravitation and temperature and such, and a crust that he is completely certain will yield a richly rewarding abundance of every useful element known to the universe. He believes that Planet C has oceans and rivers and lakes, and a

R O B E R T   S I L V E R B E R G

fine-looking moon just about as large as the moon of Earth, and a great many other outstanding features that will afford much comfort and pleasure to the lonely wanderers from Earth.

In Hesper's mind, it would seem, the *Wotan* has already reached Planet C and a successful surveillance mission has been carried out, and now they have all shuttled down to its richly rewarding surface and are busily constructing the crude but charming buildings that will house the colony in its developmental stages. No one else, though, pays much attention to Hesper's rapturous forecasts. The minds of the others are focused almost entirely on the angels that lurk somewhere all about them in the mysterious void outside the ship. "Angels" is still what everybody calls them, for lack of any better term.

But nothing more will be learned about the angels until Noelle is ready to make another try at speaking with them. And Noelle is not ready yet. She spends her time apart from everyone else, emerging from her cabin only for meals, saying little when she does.

So they wait. What else, after all, can they do? They play *Go* and visit the baths and swim laps in the pool, and draw books and plays and music from the almost infinitely capacious resources of the ship's archives, and indulge, as most of them always have indulged, in couplings and triplings and other sexual entertainments. And the time passes.

She keeps her distance even from the year-captain, which he finds very painful. Now that he has broken through his ascetic forbearance, finally, he has no further interest in living a monastic life. He longs for her as intensely as he has ever longed for anyone or anything. But she has retreated into herself; and so does he. Julia lets it be known that she is still available to him, and he thanks her warmly, but he doesn't avail himself of her availability. Time passes. Like everyone else, the year-captain waits for Noelle.

At last she announces, with a show of outward confidence, that she is ready to try again.

She is alone when she does, in her cabin, everything as before. Closes her eyes. Lets herself drift upward, outward.

The grayness.

She is in the tube. The infinite void of nospace. She extends herself across it until she has no beginning, no end; she has become infinite herself, an infinite being in a universe of infinities. A streak of pure light. Which reaches out. Reaches. Reaches.

Angels? Are you there today, angels?

Yes. She feels one almost at once, the immensity of it, the power. Goes toward it. Spreads her arms wide, lifts up her face to it, feels the warmth. The heat. That burning fiery furnace, roaring and hissing and sizzling and crackling.

She thinks—hopes—that she has insulated herself this time against destruction, that she has found a way of channeling the overflow of energy so that it will run down past her and dissipate itself harmlessly. She thinks so. Hopes so.

She is very frightened.

But she realizes that this must be done. And she is aware that she stands at the brink of wonders.

Now. Now. The questing mind reaches forth.

Touches.

Or almost touches. There is still a barrier, and Noelle is afraid to cross it. She waits there, looking outward, *seeing* the angel, actually *seeing* it. Its vast cosmos-filling surface. An ocean of fire. The angel's face is awash with hurricanes of unthinkable activity. Wild tongues of flame rise from it like bristling curls. The broad face is veiled in places, but where the veil parts she is able to see coherent fountains of power climbing through the turbulence, coming up from the angel's depths, hot cells of fiery matter bigger than entire planets swimming up out of the core of the angel and gliding back down. At the surface itself, again and again, frenzied eruptions leap out across the firmament like daggers of energy stabbing at the cosmos.

And deeper within, behind and beyond all the turmoil of the surface, there seems to be a zone of shining stillness, like a wall separating the flamboyant forces of the angel's face from the calm, imperturbable core of the giant being. Noelle longs to reach that quiet core. But how? How? The roaring all about her numbs her soul. She can barely think in that great tumult.

Angel? Angel, do you hear me? This is Noelle.

Roaring. Hissing. Crackling. Sizzling.

Touch me, angel. But touch me only a little, touch me gently. Gently, please. Because I am so very small and you are such a giant.

A silence, a stillness. Then searing ropes of flame reach up as though to caress her.

Oh. *Oh.*

Around her the whole universe is aflame. The fire—the fire—that burning ocean—those grasping arms of flame—Noelle recoils from them, those writhing fiery strands that are reaching for her—

She pulls back, afraid. Still afraid. It is too much for her; she will be destroyed. She turns. Flees.

Finds a safe place, somewhere. Halts. Draws deep breaths.

Opens her eyes.

All about her is darkness, as usual. There are no flames anywhere near her. Everything is perfectly still. The angel is gone. She is in her own cabin, aboard the *Wotan*. Alone. Trembling. She has failed again.

"I'm going to give it one more shot," she tells the year-captain.

"But if the risk is so great—"

"I don't know that it really is."

"You said—"

"I said, yes. But maybe I was wrong. I'll try one more time, and we'll see."

He is silent for a long while.

"You don't want me to do it," Noelle says eventually, in a completely neutral tone, nothing reproachful about it.

"I do and I don't," the year-captain says. "I've been the one pushing you toward this all along. And pulling you back with the other hand. I'm afraid of losing you, Noelle. We need to see what these things are, yes. But I'm afraid of losing you." And he says, after another almost interminable pause, "You know that I love you, Noelle."

"Yes."

"And if something should happen to you—"

"Nothing will happen to me," she says. "Nothing bad."

This time as she enters the gray Intermundium she pauses before even beginning to search for the angel, and sends a shaft of thought across the light-years to Earth, to Yvonne.

She has had no contact of the kind that she once had enjoyed with Yvonne for months, nothing on the level of message-interchange. But she knows Yvonne is still there and trying to reach her, and in some indefinable way the link between them is still open, however clouded it is by the interference caused by the proximity of the angels. It is that link that Noelle attempts to widen and strengthen now.

Yvonne? Can you hear me? Can you feel me?

There is the hint of a hint of an affirmative reply. Only the hint of a hint, is all, but that is better than nothing.

Ride with me, Yvonne. When I want you to let me lean on you, be there beside me. Let me draw strength from you. I'm going to need you soon.

Does Yvonne hear? Does she know?

I love you, Yvonne. You are me. I am you. We are in this together.

Noelle thinks she feels Yvonne's silent affirmative presence. Hopes she does.

And now. Now. Noelle moves deeper into the void beyond the ship. She can feel the force of the angel now, the vast godlike thing that waits for her out there.

Angel? Listen to me, angel! This is Noelle!

The angel is listening. The angel is waiting.

I am Noelle. I come to you in love, angel. I give myself to you, angel.

This time she holds nothing back. She yields herself completely, permitting herself no fear. Yvonne is with her. Yvonne stands beside her, lending her her strength.

I am yours, Noelle tells the angel.

Contact.

optic chiasma   thalamus
sylvian fissure   hypothalamus
medulla oblongata   limbic system

pons varolii   reticular system
corpus callosum   cingulate sulcus
cuneus   orbital gyri
cingulate gyrus   caudate nucleus

— c e r e b r u m ! —

claustrum   operculum
putamen   fornix
choroid glomus   medial lemniscus

— m e s e n c e p h a l o n ! —

dura mater
dural sinus
arachnoid granulation
subarachnoid space
pia mater

cerebellum
cerebellum
cerebellum

The universe splits open. The whole cosmos is burning. Bursts of wild silver light streak across the shining metal dome of the sky. Walls smolder and burst into flames. Worlds turn to ash. There is contact, yes. A sensory explosion—a dancing solar flare—a stream of liquid fire—a flood tide of brilliant radiance, irresistible, unendurable, running into her, sweeping over her, penetrating her, devouring her. Light everywhere. Fire. A great blaze in the firmament.

Semele.

The angel smiles and she quakes. *Open to me, Noelle,* cries the vast tolling voice, and she opens and the force enters fully, taking possession of every nook and cranny of her brain, sweeping resistlessly through her.

And she and the angel are one. She lies within its bosom, resting, regaining her strength steadily, moment by moment, as its great warmth fills her and revives her.

After a while she is strong enough to rise and move about within the angel. She discovers that she can travel freely and at will, going as she pleases into any sector of the great being. She drops down beyond the zone of outer turbulence, past the huge fiery cells of angel-stuff that come constantly floating up from the interior, and disappears into the tranquillity of the angel's core, the cool hidden place where no firestorms rage and the deepest of wisdom resides. There she remains for a considerable while, feeling a peace that she has never known before, until at last it comes to seem to her that if she does not move along she will stay there forever; and so she moves upward again, toward the surface, entering the realm of fiery turmoil that is the angel's outer semblance. But the fire does not harm her. She is of the angel now; the angel is of Noelle.

Come. Let me show you things.

They drift across the face of the cosmos together. There are angels everywhere, a vast choir of them wherever she looks—great ones, small ones, bright ones, faint ones, some massed in clusters, some burning in solitary splendor. The sound of their voices fills the heavens.

She and her guide halt in a place of deep darkness, and there Noelle sees what she understands to be a new angel coming into being, barely glimmering as it is born. It coalesces swiftly as she watches, out of a cool, dark cloud of dust that is collapsing inward on itself to become a compact ball. As it shrinks and takes on spherical form it begins to turn, slowly and then faster and then much faster yet, and to give off heat, faintly at first, and then with increasing force, until it is glowing red-hot, white-hot. It has begun to spit matter into the void too, feverishly hurling segments of itself in every direction in what seems like a tantrum: a prodigious and prodigal outpouring of energy, ferocious and yet somehow comical.

A playful baby. An infant angel savoring the first throes of life. They watch for a while; and then they leave it in the midst of its sport.

Come along, now. Onward.

Onward, yes. The sky is very bright here, full of angels, and all of them are singing as angels should sing, a wonderful celestial choir whose harmonies fill the void. There is brightness everywhere, a sea of light.

Here Noelle sees a giant angel that burns with so steady and fierce a radiance that she does not understand why it has not already exhausted its own substance. It blazes in the firmament like an angry blue eye, unwearyingly hurling its fires outward to an immense distance. It is more like a god than an angel, this giant, an angry god, pouring itself forth in inexplicable wrath upon the fabric of the universe.

And then here, farther away, in one of the deepest places, are angels all in a cluster, old angels, ancient ones, thousands of them, millions, each pressed up close against its neighbor so that they seem to form one huge shining wall, a single brilliant mass. But Noelle's angel shows her that they are many, not one, and lets her reach toward them so that she can experience their great age, their inordinate wisdom. How old are they? Millions of years? Billions?

We were old before the sky was young, one of them tells her.

And another says—or perhaps it is the same one—*We came out of the All-Engulfing and one day we will return to the All-Engulfing, but we have been here since before the before, and we will remain until after the after.*

And a third tells her, *We precede and we follow, and we exist when there is no existence, and we are love when love no longer is. And we are you and you are us.*

Noelle understands perfectly, or at least thinks she does; and when they give her their blessing, she gives them hers. And moves along, for her guide has other things for her to see in other parts of the cosmos.

And here is a very old angel, an angel that is dying.

That surprises her. She says that she would not have believed that it was possible for angels to die, and her angel tells her calmly that it is, it is not only possible but necessary. If angels can be born, angels must also die. Everything dies, even angels; and everything is born again. The only thing that has neither a beginning nor an end, it says, is the universe itself, which was there at the beginning and before, and will be there at the end and afterward.

Look. Here.

They have reached the dying angel, in a region apart from the others. Its light is very dim, though there still is warmth coming from it, the midday warmth of a winter day, perhaps. There is no brilliance to this angel. Its face is dull and dark, as though it is covered by an ocean of heavy mud, or thick lava, perhaps, sultry in color, a deep purple streaked with occasional widely separated regions of crimson and scarlet. Across the cooling surface of the dying angel there still is some sparse sign of sluggish activity, the slow, difficult movement of lumpy masses of matter sliding forward in the mud, some of them black or gray, some glowing dull red like metal ingots that have fallen from the forge but are not yet cold.

There is no roaring here, no hissing, no crackling, no sizzling. There is only the deep muffled sound of titanic forces grinding to a halt, of colossal energies winding down. Even as Noelle watches, the painful movements of the traveling masses grow even more slow and the bright streaks of crimson and scarlet give up much of the richness of their hue. Everything here will stop, soon. There will be nothing left but cinders and ash. But when she looks up, beyond the place where the dying angel hangs in the firmament, she sees dust already coalescing in the distance, the first glimmers of brightness taking form. This angel is going; a new one will soon be arriving. And so it has been, Noelle understands, since the beginning of time. And before the beginning.

And now see this one, Noelle's angel tells her.

They travel onward, and come to a golden angel, a small one in a region of the void that has very few other angels around it. It pays no heed to them, but goes on turning steadily on its axis like a child amusing itself in a playground.

Noelle understands that this is a young angel, not a newborn one by any means, but not yet mature—an adolescent one, perhaps. They remain in its vicinity for a time, watching its self-absorbed antics. There is something extremely pleasant about being near this charming young angel, Noelle thinks. Watching it, she feels almost as though she has returned to her own childhood. Yvonne seems very near, closer than she has been in a long while. They are girls again together, giggling, running, colliding, giggling again as they tumble down in a heap.

There is more to see. There is so much to see that Noelle is dazzled and dazed by it all, here in this universe of angels, this infinity of godlike beings, beings who were old when the sky was young, beings who have seen the before and will see the after. After a time she can absorb nothing more of it. Her guide seems to comprehend that; for the tour is brought to an end, and Noelle returns to the bosom of her own angel, and glides downward and inward, to that hidden zone of serenity that lies beneath the roiling tongues of fire, and there she rests, there she sleeps.

Sleeps. Sleeps.

How long has she been in the coma now?" the year-captain asks. "Is it a week yet?"

"This is the eighth day," Leon says.

"The eighth day. Do you think she'll come out of it at all?"

Leon shrugs. "How can I say? What do I know? Am I an expert on things of this sort? Is anybody?"

"I understand," says the year-captain softly.

She has been wandering in delirium most of the time since losing consciousness. Troubled, fearful, the year-captain has kept a somber vigil at her bedside, losing track of the time himself as the days slide by and there is no change in her condition.

Sometimes it seems to him that she is rising toward consciousness; intelligible words, even whole sentences, bubble dreamily from her lips. The dreaming Noelle talks of light, of a brilliant unbearable white glow, of arcs of energy, of intense solar eruptions. A star holds me, she mutters. She tells him that she has been conversing with a star.

How poetic, the year-captain thinks: what a lovely metaphor. Conversing with a star.

A metaphor for *what*, though? Where is she, what is happening to her? Has she been speaking with angels, actual holy angels, or are they stars, or has she simply shed the last shred of her sanity during her venture into the gray nothingness beyond the ship? She seems lost in some unknown and unknowable realm. Her face is flushed; her eyes move about rapidly, darting like trapped fish beneath her closed lids. Words continue to come from her from time to time. Mind to mind, Noelle whispers, the star and I. Mind to mind. Sometimes she begins to hum—an edgy whining sound, climbing almost toward inaudibility, a high-frequency keening. It pains him to hear it: it has the force of hard radiation, expressed as sound.

He has never felt so tired before. He has scarcely slept at all since he and Huw pushed open the door of her cabin and found her in the coma.

ROBERT SILVERBERG

She is humming again now, that terrible sound. He clenches his jaws, balls his hands into fists, and forces himself to withstand it. After a while she is silent again.

Then her body goes rigid, pelvis thrusting upward. A convulsion of some sort? No. She's simply stirring, awakening, at last! He sees lightning bolts of perception flashing through her quivering musculature: the galvanized laboratory frog, twitching at the end of its leads. Her eyelids tremble. She makes a little moaning noise. And her eyes are open.

She looks up at him.

The year-captain stares into her eyes. There is something different about them now. Something new. Something astonishing.

Gently he says, "Your eyes are open. I think you can see me now, Noelle." He moves his hand back and forth across her face, and her eyes follow the movement.

"I—can—see you, yes. I can see you."

Her voice is hesitant, faltering, strange for a moment, a foreign voice; but then it becomes more like its usual self as she asks, "How long was I away?"

"Eight ship-days. We were very worried."

"You look exactly as I thought you would look," she says. "Your face is thin and hard. But not a dark face. Not a hostile face. I like your face, year-captain."

"Do you want to talk about where you went, Noelle?"

She smiles. Nods. "I went to visit the . . . angel. I talked with it."

"Angel? Really, an *angel*?"

"Not really, no. That's just a word, 'angel.' It wasn't an angel, I suppose, not the kind people used to pray to. Not a physical being, either, not any kind of intelligent organic lifeform. It was—was—"

He waits. He stares at her in wonder and bewilderment. He is stunned by the beauty of her eyes, now that her eyes are alive and focused on him.

She says, "It was more like the energy creatures that Heinz was talking about. Incorporeal, is what I mean. But bigger than we could have imagined. Bigger than a whole planet, even. Tremendously big. I don't know what it was. Not at all."

"You told me you were talking with a star."

"—with a star!" As though it is a completely new idea to her.

"In your delirium. That's what you said. Talking with a star."

Her eyes blaze with wild excitement. "Of course! A star! Yes! Yes, year-captain! I think that's what it was, yes! I was talking with a star."

Despair engulfs him. She is very far gone in madness, he tells himself.

But he keeps his voice calm. "But how can you talk with a star? What does that mean, talking with a star, Noelle?"

She laughs. "It means talking with a star, year-captain. Nothing more, nothing less. A great ball of fiery gas, year-captain, and it has a mind, it has a consciousness. I think that's what it was. I'm sure now. I'm sure!"

"But how can a—"

The light goes abruptly from her eyes. They have lost focus. Has she reentered the coma? Apparently so. At any rate she is traveling again; she is no longer with him.

He waits beside her bed. An hour, two hours. Rises. Paces. Sits. Waits. Where has she gone? In what bizarre realm is she journeying now? Her breathing is a distant, impersonal drone. So far away from her now, so remote from any place that he is capable of comprehending.

At last her eyelids flicker again. And then they open.

She looks up at him. Her eyes are living eyes, as they were before. Her face seems transfigured. She is in bliss. To the year-captain she seems still to be at least in part in that other world beyond the ship. "Yes," she says. "Not an angel, year-captain. A sun. A living intelligent sun." Her eyes are radiant. "A sun, a star, a sun," she murmurs. The words are crazy, but not the voice. "I touched the consciousness of a sun. Many suns. Do you believe that, year-captain? Can you? I found a network of stars that live, that think, that have minds, that have souls. That communicate. The whole universe is alive."

"A star," he says dully. "You talked with a star. The stars have minds."

"Yes."

"All of them? Our own sun too?"

"All of them. They sit out here and talk to each other. We were moving between them, out here in the middle of the galaxy, and their conversations drowned out my link with Yvonne. That was the interference, year-captain. It was the stars, talking to each other out here. Filling my wavelength, leaving me no room to get through to Yvonne."

This conversation has taken on for him the texture of a dream. Quietly he says, "Why wasn't our sun overriding you and Yvonne while you were still back on Earth?"

She shrugs. "It isn't old enough. I saw it—the angel took me to see it. Our sun. It's like a child, a little child playing a game of hoops in a playground. It takes—I don't know, many billions of years—until they're mature, until they can talk to each other on the main frequency. Our sun just isn't old enough, year-captain. None of the stars close to Earth is old enough. But out here—"

"Are you in contact with it now?"

"Yes. With it and with many others. And with Yvonne."

Madness. Madness.

"Yvonne too?" he asks.

"She's back in the link with me. She's in the circuit." Noelle looks straight into his eyes. "I can bring others into the circuit. I could bring you in, year-captain."

"Me?"

"You. Would you like to touch a star with your mind?"

"What will happen to me? Will it harm me?"

"Did it harm me, year-captain?"

"Will I still be me, afterward?"

"Am I still me, year-captain?"

He is silent for a long time.

Then in a dull, strange voice he says, "I'm afraid, Noelle."

"No. You've never been afraid of anything."

"I'm afraid now. Afraid of this."

"No. No."

"I am."

"Open to me. Try. See what happens."

"And if I don't like it?"

"You will. You will. Have faith, year-captain. You had faith in something when you joined this expedition, didn't you? You must have. Have faith now. Tell me: do you believe any of what I've been saying to you since I awakened?"

He hesitates.

"Do you?"

"Yes," he says, recklessly.

"Then have faith in me. Touch a star, year-captain."

He puts his hand on hers. "Go ahead," he says, and his soul becomes a solarium.

fterward, with the solar pulsations still reverberating in the mirrors of his mind, with blue-white sparks leaping in his synapses, he says, "What about the others?"

"I'll bring them in too."

The year-captain, for all the changes that he has undergone in these last few moments, nevertheless feels a sudden surprising flicker of momentary petty resentment. He does not want to share with all of them the thing that he has attained with Noelle. She is his; he is hers. But in the instant that he conceives his resentment he realizes the absurdity of it, and he abolishes it. Yvonne is here too. He can feel her, Noelle's other half. Earth-sister, star-sister, both together once more, and he is with them. The others should join them also. Yes. Yes. *Let them in.*

"Take my hand," Noelle says.

They reach out together. Their mind moves through the ship and one by one it finds and touches the other voyagers. Sieglinde is the first they encounter, blustery, recalcitrant Sieglinde; and she seems to understand at once, and yields. Then Zena; then Leila; then Elizabeth, with a cry of joy. Heinz. He dives in without hesitation. Paco, after just a moment of uncertainty, gives himself to it in the deepest gladness and relief. Leon. Roy. On and on through the ship. One after another, and the more of them that are in it, the more swiftly the rest accede. The year-captain feels Noelle surging in tandem with him as the union grows, feels Yvonne, feels greater presences, luminous, ancient. All are joined. The whole ship is one. The words of the final verses of the ancient Norse poem that he once knew so well, that dark saga of the Twilight of the Gods, roll through his mind. *Now do I see the earth anew rise all green from the waves again. . . . In wondrous beauty once again shall the golden tables stand 'mid the grass . . .*

He and Noelle step out into the corridor. They are all out there, wandering around in wonder. No one speaks. He sees shining eyes everywhere. The year-captain realizes that he is captain no longer: there is no need for a captain here. And the days of playing *Go* have ended too. They are one person; they are beyond games. *Go* would be impossible now for them to play, for how can one compete against oneself?

. . . then fields unsowed bear ripened fruit. All ills grow better, and Baldur comes back. . . .

"And now," Noelle whispers, "now we reach toward Earth. We put our strength in Yvonne, and Yvonne will—"

Yvonne draws Earth's hundreds of millions of souls into the network in one great gulp, everyone, everyone, and the next phase of human life begins.

The *Wotan* hurtles onward through the nospace tube. Soon they will arrive at Planet C; and they will send down explorers to see if the newest world they have found is a fair and lovely place where the sons and daughters of mankind can thrive. If it is, they will settle there. And if not, they will go on, on toward Planet D, and Planet E, and Planet X and Y and Z. They are confident that eventually they will find a world whose air they can breathe and whose water they can drink and whose land they can farm, and where they can plant the seed of Earth in a new beginning. But it will not matter at all if they never do. All will be well, even so. The ship and its hundreds of millions of passengers will course onward through the universe forever, warmed by the light of the friendly stars.

ROBERT SILVERBERG's many novels include the bestselling Lord Valentine trilogy, the Nebula-winning *A Time of Changes*, the critically acclaimed *Hot Sky at Midnight*, *Kingdoms of the Wall*, and *The Face of the Waters*. He is also the co-author, with Isaac Asimov, of *The Positronic Man*, as well as the co-editor of the new *Universe* series of original short-fiction anthologies. He has won numerous awards for his fiction, including five Nebulas, four Hugo Awards, a Jupiter Award, and the Prix Apollo. He lives near San Francisco with his wife, Karen Haber.